MW00915570

ONCE UPON A BILLIONAIRE

Blue Collar Billionaires, Book 1

JESSICA LEMMON

Lemmon Ink

Copyright © 2020 by Jessica Lemmon

All rights reserved.

Once Upon a Billionaire is a work of fiction. Names, places, and incidents either are products of the author's imagination or are used fictitiously. Any resemblance to actual events, locales, or persons, living or dead, is entirely coincidental.

No part of this book may be reproduced in any form or by any electronic or mechanical means, including information storage and retrieval systems, without written permission from the author, except for the use of brief quotations in a book review.

Published in the United States by Jessica Lemmon.

Cover concept by Jessica Lemmon

Cover design by Passion Creations

Dedication

For romance lovers everywhere.
Read for fun!

ONCE UPON A BILLIONAIRE

Chapter One

Vivian

Vivian Vandemark isn't my real name.

It sounds fancy, though, doesn't it? That alliteration of both Vs is to die for and reminds me of a classy label on clothing. Vandemark could have been the next Gucci. Maybe in another life.

I changed my name because my actual last name has been tainted by the man who gave it to me. My father is a criminal. Was. *Was* a criminal. It's hard to get used to the idea that he's no longer living. One would think since he was in prison for the last several years he'd be easy to forget, but that's only because I haven't told you who he is yet.

Walter Steele.

Yes, *that* Walter Steele.

The man who robbed his investors of millions and millions of dollars to line his own pockets. That man is my father.

Was. Damn. That really is hard to wrap my head around.

The trial was bananas. It lasted one hundred days, and during that time my mother, brother, and I were harassed nonstop by the press. That was six years ago. Since then I've fallen off the radar.

My mother quite literally fell off the radar when she swallowed a lot of pain relievers and chased them with a lot of vodka. That was the day my father was sentenced. By then I was twenty-three and out of the house. My younger brother, Walt, was twenty. He's been trying to finish what booze my mother didn't since then. He'd been an addict most of his young life. I've never enjoyed escapism as a hobby.

Until now, I suppose.

Chicago is a far cry from Clear Ridge, Ohio. Clear Ridge has an unassuming Midwest vibe. The town is mostly shopping malls and chain restaurants, tall maple trees, and fences surrounding green, grassy yards. The live-work site currently being built is unique to this area. It's impressive, even if the company building it is the bane of my boss's existence.

I'm employed in a government office in this aspiring city. The building I walk into each day is half the size of my father's former summer home. *Half.*

I used to be a high-powered executive. All my faith, trust, time, and savings were wrapped up in our family's company. And then it all turned out to be a sham. On my watch, everything fell apart. Steele Investments toppled like a house of cards, taking my position with it. My father went down with the ship, the rest of my family "spared," if you could say that.

I've never felt more powerless. Watching my life crumble reminded me of TV footage of the World Trade Center vanishing in a plume of smoke on 9/11. When I left that life behind, I swore *never again.*

I'll never again stand by, unwittingly, while someone steals (steal/Steele—how about that for irony?) people's life savings and retirement funds. I thought I was living the good life, but it was blood money.

Now, I buy my clothes at department stores or Target—they have some really nice clothes, by the way. I also cook at home a lot —not well, but I'm learning. And I endure the office coffee even though I pass a drool-worthy Starbucks each and every morning on my way to work.

I'm paying penance for a life I never chose. *Thanks, Dad.*

The second I set foot in the office, I'm met with raised voices. The loudest of the two is Gary, an otherwise mild-mannered inspector at our bureau. I don't think I've ever heard him raise his voice. My boss, Daniel, however, has a well-known temper. His blood pressure often runs high—you can tell by his reddened face.

Gary and Daniel are in Daniel's office, and while I can't make out what they're saying, it's obvious they're having a disagreement.

"Amber." I lean into my coworker's cubicle. "What's going on?"

She looks over her shoulder and gives me a smile that is half amused, half surprised. "Gary is fit to be tied."

"Yeah, I hear that. What's it about?"

"Who do you think?" She raises one prim, blond eyebrow.

"Nathaniel Owen," I answer. The billionaire in charge of the live-work project has been mentioned about a *billion* times since I started working here, and never favorably.

"The one and only." Amber, still smiling, stands and leans a shoulder on the cubicle wall. We're both facing Daniel's closed door where the "conversation" is going strong. Nathaniel Owen's name is used like a curse word in this place. I've never interacted with him personally, but I'm familiar with the type.

Rich. Entitled. The kind of man who believes he's above the law.

The door swings open and Gary steps out, his mouth a firm line of disapproval. He huffs past Amber's cubicle and we brace ourselves for Daniel's wrath when he looks at us. No, wait.

Looks at *me*.

"Vandemark. Get in here." He vanishes into his office.

Daniel is in charge of my paycheck, a paycheck I need very badly, since I refuse to touch the money in an account I set up after Dad's trial. That money is for my brother's rehabilitation.

Those places aren't cheap, and I'll drain every dime out of it if it makes him better. I failed him once—I won't fail him again. He's the only family I have left.

Anyway, my paycheck. It's all that stands between me and homelessness, so I tend to be more gracious to my boss than he deserves.

Amber whispers "good luck" as I leave her side and enter the lion's den, aka Daniel's office.

"Good morning." I try to sound breezy.

"Not even close." He's pacing the floor, hands on his hips, frown marring his receding hairline. "Nathaniel Owen is a burr in my ass."

That should be the motto of the Clear Ridge Bureau of Inspection.

"I need you to go to the Grand Marin site," he tells me. "Owen's crew is there today, and I have it on good authority he has a meeting with the mayor which means he'll likely be onsite. I don't care if the mayor is in Owen's pocket. We are not. At least we aren't any longer." He mutters that last part while looking out the window facing the alley.

"Not Gary?" I can't imagine a scenario where Gary would do anything short of aboveboard.

"Owen paid off Gary. He had to have." Daniel's face turns beet red. "That electrical inspection paperwork flew in here on wings for my approval. It was way too fast. Gary was bribed. Mark my words."

I'm not a conspiracy theorist, but in this case Daniel makes a great point. Nothing happens fast in our little government bureau, and it's particularly suspicious that Owen seems to make things happen at lightning speed compared to everyone else.

"Did Gary quit?"

"I fired him." Daniel puffs up his chest, proud.

"Seriously?"

"No one at CRBI accepts bribes and remains on my payroll."

He ices me with a glare. "You'll do well to remember that since you're heading over there."

My blood heats. I'd never accept a bribe. Especially one from a stubborn billionaire.

"We have a narrow window to teach Owen a lesson. You're just the woman to do it."

"I hope you understand that I will not falsify paperwork in order to shut him down, either. I respect your mission, Daniel, but I'm not going to stoop to Owen's level."

My boss's grin is a tad creepy, but approving. "I know you won't. All you have to do is ask Owen for proof of a passed electrical inspection. He won't be able to show you one because he doesn't *have* one—not legally, anyway. I never signed off on it. Therefore, you can shut him down."

"Wouldn't you be a better candidate?" I don't do site visits. In my six months as chief desk jockey, I haven't been to a single construction site. It's part of my plan to lay low. If I'm not in charge of anything I can't fuck it up. Not to mention I'd have no idea what to do once I got there. "We both know how much you'd enjoy nailing his ass to the wall."

"More than you can imagine, but my schedule is full. Since Gary was fired, the next inspector in line handles their shit-show. Our other inspectors are busy, and frankly, I don't want to wait another second. So, you get a raise. Congratulations. This project is a nightmare."

Did he say raise? My ears perk. Despite wanting to lay low, an increase in my income would be nice. Given that I refuse to touch my brother's and my nest egg, I have to keep the lights on at home somehow.

"If Owen isn't there when you get there, let the site manager know you mean business."

Nathaniel Owen has a reputation for completing projects on time, which is a rare and coveted quality in a builder. He also sidesteps rules and does things his way rather than follow the letter of the law. The city of Clear Ridge doesn't take kindly to rule-benders, and Daniel hates them. Look at that, my boss and I have something in common.

"No problem," I assure Daniel.

Maybe delivering justice will be cathartic. I can't go back in time and keep my father in line, or recoup the money of the people who trusted him, but I can prevent Nathaniel Owen from lining his pockets with even more money. The Owen name is stamped on nearly every new build within a thousand miles. How much more can the guy possibly need?

That's the thing about greed. It knows no bounds.

"I have a meeting in five minutes and they'll probably keep me for the afternoon." Daniel swipes his sweaty brow. He's a good seventy pounds overweight and even on his tall frame, it's too much girth. "Can I count on you not to fuck this up?"

I force a smile. His wasn't the most wholehearted vote of confidence, but I'll take it. "Of course."

"He's cocky, strong-willed and needs a knot tied in his tail," Daniel says, not quite finished with his tirade. "You're strong. Smart. The perfect candidate to take him on, Viv." His voice gentles, and I feel an odd catch in my chest at the compliment.

The last man who praised me was my father. When I learned I couldn't trust him at the end, I wondered if every ounce of praise he gave me before was a lie. There are two versions of him in my head. The man who encouraged me to believe in myself and never give up, and the man who told me those things while stealing money from innocent people.

Disgusting.

"Shut him down," my boss repeats. "Let's teach him a lesson."

I draw my chin up at those words. Owen needs taught that you can't do what you want and give the rules the finger.

"Grab a hardhat from the back. Don't want you busting that pretty noggin of yours and then suing me."

Aaaand…moment over.

"Sure thing," I reply blithely.

I grab a hardhat from the back and walk outside to my 2014

Hyundai the car salesman assured me was "reliable." I don't even miss the sleek black Audi RS I used to own. Okay, I do *a little*. But a car is a car. This gem will deliver me to Grand Marin just as well as that Audi.

Grand Marin is a soon-to-be massive live-work community. An open-air style shopping, dining, and retail area interspersed with offices for professionals as well as apartments for young, vibrant tenants who want to live in the middle of—or above—the action.

Live-works have been growing in popularity, and whenever there's a trend, I've noticed the Owen family has their mitts all over it. I've never had any personal dealings with Owen, but I know rich people. They're not that great.

As a former rich person, I speak from experience.

I also know that Gary, the city's former mild-mannered inspector, came into the office with his bottom lip dragging the ground each and every time he had to deal with this site. Gary was a softie, and we all liked him. He was rocking a five-foot-three frame and had a shy way of watching his shoes when he talked. Then he blows up at Daniel? I wouldn't have guessed he'd raised his voice a day in his life before today.

People can surprise you, though, and for me that should come as no surprise.

Gary's despondence, and the possibility that he took a bribe, proves what a bulldog this Owen guy can be.

Bring it on, buddy. I've already been through the wringer.

Daniel's grumping about the mayor isn't totally inaccurate. Rumor has it the Owens grease palms. Mayor Dick Dolans might well be their pet.

I come to a stop the moment I merge onto the highway. So much for taking a shortcut. I-70 is a parking lot, and the heat index on the car's thermometer reads 97° F.

Worse, I'm wearing a synthetic-but-made-to-look-like-real-silk shirt and it's sticking to me like a second skin. Waves of heat waft off the road as if the cars are in the process of being melted down into one big metal glob. The month of June is going out like it has a score to settle.

Again: *relate.*

I crank the A/C down and rest a hand on the steering wheel. I refuse to panic. I'll get to Grand Marin when I get there. I wish I would have dug up some much-needed intel about the site before Daniel rushed me out of there. I know next to nothing about it.

At least I'm wearing my nicest, most slimming pencil skirt and high heels. Not the best getup for tromping around a construction site, but it's a good look when wanting to bust some billionaire balls. I smile to myself, straightening my shoulders.

I'm out for a win for the good guys. A win for justice. I picture myself as Wonder Woman and lift my chin. If she did it in a bustier and panties, I can do it in a pencil skirt and knockoff silk.

Ready or not, Nathaniel Owen, here I come.

Chapter Two

Vivian

The Grand Marin site is further along than I imagined.

The brick buildings are standing, windows and doors installed—manufacturers' stickers on most of them. Dirt roads in every direction cut through the buildings and around them. When paved, those roads will lead through an open-air shopping center with a small-town feel.

Perfect for the city of Clear Ridge.

Huge construction equipment and trucks stand sentinel, none of them in operation at the moment.

I climb from the car, wilted from the A/C and sun beating the windshield during my drive. I was stuck in traffic for forty-eight minutes, and when I was moving again completed the twenty-minute trek to Grand Marin.

Bright side, the traffic jam gave me an opportunity to call Amber for an assist. She did a thorough digging and found out *many* exceptions were made for this property. It's been humming along even with Owen's special requests. That they didn't gum up the system boggles the mind.

One of the city ordinances requires high wattage on streetlights, but Nathaniel Owen requested lower in order to preserve stargazing. Another ordinance requires sod, and Owen quibbled about that too, insisting forest flooring is better. Yet another states in this area of Ohio, the buildings must adhere to a specific style guide, but Owen insisted on using his own.

Our resident billionaire builder either delights in being a pain in the city's rear end and uses workarounds as a way to save money, or he enjoys watching city officials jump through hoops.

I'm not in a jumping mood.

I pull the white hardhat over my hair and carry a storage clipboard with my cell phone tucked inside. I'm going for aesthetics. I'm not an inspector, but I can look like one.

The guys onsite seem to be in a light, airy mood, and there are a lot of them. Most holding Starbucks cups and leaning on either buildings or shovels. I must have stopped by at break time.

Heads turn as I approach. Their conversations and laughter ebb. All I hear is the crunch of gravel under my high-heeled shoes. I look left and then right, noting more hardhats and tool belts, before my eyes land on a man in a suit.

Owen.

It has to be him. I'd bet my tiny, budget-busting apartment on it.

His charcoal-gray suit is well-made and expensive and too hot for the day, hinting that he spent most of his day in A/C. His suit jacket is tossed over one arm and a pressed white shirt stretches over his broad back. Sweat darkens the material between his shoulder blades.

One hand is raised to shield his eyes as he studies the uppermost floor of one of the buildings. I approach, curious and disgusted in equal measure.

Rich people. *Yuck.*

I stand next to him and crane my head as well. I'm not sure what I'm looking at, so I study the pitch of the roof while waiting to be acknowledged. He doesn't flinch.

"Mr. Owen, I presume?" I finally say.

I feel the turn of his head, the weight of his gaze like a hawk that's spied his dinner.

"Who wants to know?" His voice is low and rough. Despite the day's heat, the tiny hairs at the back of my neck stand on end.

It's the kind of reply I would expect from a guy who doesn't do things by the book. The kind of reply that might've come from my father.

"Do you have drywall in these units, Mr. Owen?" I turn to meet him face to face. The second we lock eyes, heat flames my cheeks and my heart rate soars.

As much as I want to blame summer or anxiety on my physical reaction, I can't dismiss the man's attractiveness. Of their own volition, my eyes drink in the sight of him. The men I've encountered since I started working for the city are never this good-looking. Rarely are they *average* looking.

Whenever Daniel or Gary mentioned Nathaniel Owen, I pictured a cantankerous old codger, not a guy in his thirties. A fan of lines surrounds Owen's eyes. *Late thirties,* I mentally correct. He's probably a few years older than me.

His brawn doesn't belong in a tailored suit but he wears it well. Like it's bending to his will, not the other way around. Let's blame my reaction on surprise. Owen is fifteen years younger and *fifty* times more attractive than I imagined. That would throw anyone for a loop.

"Now, why would you ask me something like that?" He offers the barest tip of his lips.

I size him up, taking inventory. His blue eyes sparkle from behind long eyelashes. His nose has a crooked bend like it's been broken more than once. That's not surprising. He has a knack for pissing people off.

A breeze kicks his dark-blond hair. It's thick, wavy on top. Every inch of him, from his wide shoulders to his confident stance, the stubble on his cheeks and jaw in need of a shave, is disturbingly male. The most disturbing part is that I haven't stopped staring at his stupidly handsome face.

"Miss…" He trails off and waits for me to fill in the blank.

"Vandemark." I offer a hand. "Vivian Vandemark."

"Nathaniel Owen." He takes my hand and pumps twice, long enough for me to notice the calluses on his palm. A little shiver runs through me.

Interesting.

This is one billionaire that is full of contradictions. He stinks of wealth, with that suit and his stature, but there is a hefty dose of rough and tumble beneath his smooth exterior.

"Why do you ask about the drywall?" The bemused tick of his mouth is distracting. The way he takes a step closer to me, insulting. Is he trying to intimidate me? I straighten my spine and stand at every inch of my five-six frame.

"It's a waste of resources to install drywall without an electrical inspection, Mr. Owen. You're also breaking the law. If you proceed, you'll have to tear it out for us to reassess. That could cause a huge delay."

His smile disappears, a hard glint shadowing his ocean-blue eyes. There he is: the cold-hearted billionaire. So much for the brief glimpse of charm.

"You're looking for Gary Williams, Ms. Vandemark. He completed the inspection three days ago. Thanks for stopping by." He turns and dismisses me.

I don't think so.

"If you can't provide proof of a passed electrical inspection today," I gleefully inform my opponent, "I'll be shutting you down." I smile, but his expression grows more intense. His lip isn't quite curling, but damn close.

Oh, yes. I was right. This *does* feel good. Wealth can buy a lot of things—prestige, a good reputation, and sometimes, friends. But not everyone is bribable.

Owen turns on the heel of one shiny leather shoe and stalks away from me. I blow out a disbelieving laugh. He's running away? Really?

That's a sure sign of guilt.

I follow, my mind rewinding to the day my father was arrested. He came home and began frantically packing suitcases. He'd slipped out of his office building when the FBI entered. They found him at home, half his closet emptied into too many bags for him to carry.

My mother was helping him pack.

"Mr. Owen!" I pump my arms to catch up to his long strides. I'm a little winded as I can't afford a gym membership. I have to settle for walks around the block rather than hire a trainer to come to my home gym three times a week like I used to.

I know, I know. Don't say it.

"Running away won't solve your problems," I tell his back as a trickle of sweat rolls down mine.

"You can peddle your threats and your prissy skirt off my property, Ms. Vandemark." He turns in a plume of sexism and rage. "Talk to Gary."

"This isn't Gary's property," I snap. "It's yours." He starts walking again so I march after him over the uneven dirt-and-rock terrain, my heels not exactly cooperating. "The burden of proof lies with you, not a former employee of the city."

"Former." He stops so suddenly I nearly smack into him. I'm still teetering when he whirls around. "Did he quit?"

"Did you bribe him?" I lift my chin not only to take in his height, but also to let him know I'm not backing down.

There. Now *that's* a curled lip.

"I'm the one in charge around here, Ms. Vandemark." He pokes a blunt finger against his own chest. "I say when we proceed with this job, not you. You think prancing in here to slap my wrist is going to scare me? It won't. You are succeeding at pissing me off, though."

The firm, full set of his mouth is bizarrely attractive, even as he attempts to intimidate me. He doesn't merely stand over me, he *surrounds* me.

Poor Gary and his five-foot-three-ness.

"You can't intimidate me, Mr. Owen." I keep my voice even, a feat since chasing him left me gulping for breath. His legs are a lot longer than mine. For every step he took, I had to take two and a half.

"Afternoon, Mr. Owen," one of his guys greets as he walks by.

"Nate," Owen corrects, clapping the man's dirty shoulder with one big palm. He then explains to me, "New guy," before an amiable expression makes a brief appearance.

"Nate—"

"You can call me Mr. Owen. You don't work for me."

Like I said, a brief appearance.

I've had it. Had it with Owen and his rich-guy no-one-can-touch-me attitude. My father thought that way too. And he was wrong. Just as "Nate" is wrong. I don't have to chase after him. I hold the cards in this situation.

"I'm shutting your site down until further notice," I call out. "Until you can provide proof. *Nate.*"

Well, well. Look who's giving me his full attention.

"Proof." He sweeps back to me so quickly I'm engulfed by the fragrance of his cologne. Either he smells of crisp ocean air, or those blue, blue eyes are triggering my senses. "You want proof?"

"No." I make a show of hugging my clipboard to my chest. "I demand proof. I have the support of the city, Mr. Owen. No matter what deal you struck with the mayor, I have the authority to shut you down."

I'm not sure my threat holds water. Daniel barely has any power, and I'm Daniel's lackey. Owen's fists ball at his sides all the same. Either he believes I have that power, or he simply hates being inconvenienced. His expression is Angry's older, meaner brother—meant as a warning for me to back off. He wants me to regret crossing him. I feel the opposite. I'm quite enjoying myself.

He thrusts his suit jacket against my arms. Instinctually, my hand wraps around the expensive material. I carry it rather than let it hit the dirt. He's on the move again and this time calling over his shoulder, "I have your proof, Ms. Vandemark."

I exhale impatiently, the sun's heat mocking me. What is he up to?

Owen snaps his fingers at a bearded guy leaning on the handle of a sledgehammer. "I need to borrow that, Nick. Glasses too."

Owen unbuttons his cuffs and shoves the shirtsleeves over thick forearms dusted with golden brown hair. I spot an expensive watch and black beaded bracelet on one wrist.

My heart hits my throat as he takes the tool. He's not only wearing half an Armani suit, but his bulky arms are flexing while wielding a huge hammer in his grip.

He's Wall Street Thor, an image as out of place as the scent of his cologne. Meanwhile, my feminist tendencies are letting me down. My lizard brain begs for a taste of unapologetically masculine Nathaniel Owen.

No, Vivian.

"Thanks, Nick," Owen says and then slips the safety glasses onto his crooked-with-plenty-of-character nose.

I stare dumbly, his jacket is draped over the clipboard in the crook of my arm. A smile makes Owen appear downright approachable. Without it, he reminds me more of a UFC fighter in a cage.

"Right this way, Ms. Vandemark." He beckons.

A few snickers echo behind me. The battle of feminism will be fought at construction sites. Mark my words.

"Beck, door," Owen tells a craggy-faced man. Beck obeys and opens the door to one of the buildings. I follow Nate inside and find a partially completed unit. The drywall is up, and an unpainted door stands between the entry and a makeshift office equipped with a desk and laptop. There's a ladder in one corner.

Shiny spackle hides the seams on the wall. An industrial-strength fan is aimed at it and blowing on high. This wall is brand-spanking new.

"This is one of one hundred and forty units," Owen tells me, his voice raised to be heard over the fan. "The drywall is complete in all of them. I'm not breaking the law, Ms. Vandemark. We passed our electrical inspection. Gary gave me every assurance."

I narrow my eyes, trying to decide if he is lying or not. I can't put my finger on it, but I'm becoming suspicious of the "innocent" inspector who was just shit-canned. "Daniel doesn't sign falsified paperwork."

"Falsified?" A smirk crosses his lips. "I'm not tearing down one hundred and forty units' worth of drywall because your boss won't do his job."

I'll die before I admit it, but I agree that tearing perfectly good walls out is a waste of resources and energy.

But. I work for Daniel. My job isn't to reason.

"Rules are rules, Mr. Owen." I toss his suit coat over a rung on the ladder. "The good people who move their homes and businesses into this unit, and the one hundred forty like it, deserve peace of mind. Faulty wiring could cause a fire and your precious live-work would be reduced to ash. Rules save lives. And money," I add, assuming him losing millions would take precedence.

His jaw ticks, his eyes never leaving mine.

"A great way to pull a back muscle and land yourself on worker's comp is swinging this baby wrong." He grips the sledgehammer with both hands. I don't have much (any) experience with sledgehammers, but I'm guessing it weighs more than he's making it look. He's handling it as if it's a bamboo fishing pole. His voice dips into an almost seductive husk. "The trick, Ms. Vandemark, is to let her do all the work."

The seduction leaves his voice in a snap when he gruffly adds, "Here's your fucking proof, lady."

He swings, aiming for the center of a panel of fresh drywall. A chunk of it hits the floor, dust exploding overhead like a magician's trick. He swings again as I back away from the destruction. His form is fluid, the next blow as smooth as warm butter. Each hard hit widens the jagged hole. He doesn't stop until he's exposed every stud and the bundles of neatly affixed wires attached to some of them.

I'm impressed and horrified. Delighted and flummoxed. I'm not sure how to react to his display. Is he throwing a tantrum? Does he have a mean streak a mile wide? Or is he caught in a lie and trying to cover for it?

The commotion draws attention. Faces appear in the windows and the open door. A few low laughs and swearwords of praise trickle into the office as the dust literally settles. Settles into Nate's hair, making it appear a lighter shade of blond. Settles onto my shirt and the metal clipboard I'm cradling. It's blown into a pattern like desert sand by the fan whirring away in the corner.

Owen swipes his brow with one forearm, watching me closely. A blip of concern puckers his brow, like he's worried he might've frightened me.

Sorry, buddy. I'm schooled in keeping my expression neutral.

"I'm not certified," I inform him calmly.

His face pinches. "What?"

I gesture to the gaping hole in the formerly pristine wall. "I'm not certified to approve the wiring. I don't know what any of those are for. That could be a gleaming example of the finest electrical wiring on the planet, or a fire hazard of the worst degree. Again, I reiterate, you went forward without a permit. I'll have to shut you down."

His face droops in suspended disbelief.

"Excuse me." I push my way through the onlookers and leave the building. My shaking arms betray my calm, cool exterior. I felt a rush when he took out that wall… Not fear. I'm not afraid.

What I feel is more potent, and far more dangerous. Unadulterated excitement with more than a rush of attraction.

Damn. That's inconvenient.

Chapter Three

Nate

Once I knocked a guy unconscious with a single blow. I can bench press 360 pounds on a light day. And before I was adopted by the Owens, I thought all women were liars.

My birth mother was often in tears thanks to her husband. Dear old Dad was an addict. Tears were as commonplace as air in my childhood home. They were cheap, and, I later learned, devices of manipulation. My mom loved my dad's habit more than she loved me.

Vivian Vandemark isn't anything like my mother. I wasn't trying to enact some sort of twisted revenge scenario by taking out fresh drywall. Now that I'm standing here with dust on my new suit, my arms tingling from the effort it took to swing this hammer repeatedly, I feel sort of stupid about it.

She's not an inspector? Is she shitting me?

She's also not crying, which I respect. Not that I was trying to make her cry, but I wouldn't have been surprised if she had. I can't be manipulated by tears, but I suspect Ms. Vandemark isn't one to use them for sympathy. She's made of tougher stuff than my mother, that's for sure.

A different breed, this woman.

I push past my brethren, aka employees, and tell them to get to work. Vivian is coolly and calmly crossing my construction site. No, she's nothing like my mother. She is class from the top of her sleek blown-out, dark-just-shy-of-black hair to the tips of her cheap shoes.

I frown. Cheap shoes?

I'm good at reading people. Call it survival instinct. At first glance, I pegged Vivian Vandemark as a wealthy woman. She carries herself like she's used to having her way—and having things done for her. Like she's used to being served. My adoptive mother, Lainey, has that same air about her.

When I first looked into Vivian's warm, brown eyes, I didn't assume she was a government employee. She was far more beautiful than I expected, which stalled my brain for a hot second. When she threatened to shut me down, my brain stopped functioning entirely.

I have one unbreakable rule: Finish the job early.

The adage about "on time" being late and "late" being unacceptable is one I take to heart. No one slows me down, especially a city inspector. There are ways around, over, or under every strip of red tape. Anyone who says differently is lazy or inept.

So, now that I've calmed down and thought it through, her cheap shoes make sense. The government isn't exactly known for its extravagant wages.

When she blew in here and spoke in a whiskey-smooth voice, I assumed she had both power and money. I thought for a split second Vivian was a woman who'd come to strike a bargain.

If you know what I mean.

That happened to me before, though it's been a while. Deborah was older than my current guest, but no less curt. She demanded I halt construction on her ex-husband's project. I told her there was no way in hell. She didn't cry, either. She laughed. And then she made me an offer I fell for, right before I fell for her.

I ended up in bed with her and losing the job after falling woefully behind on the project. Her ex-husband fired me, but Deborah and I stayed together for a few months after that. She became one of my biggest supporters, even after the affair met its imminent demise.

I follow Vivian and consider I wouldn't mind indulging a similar offer to Deborah's in exchange for a clean bill of health on my site.

Off the record, I don't know if *all* 140 units have drywall installed. Probably more like half. But I'm not going to kneel at the throne of the fucking Clear Ridge Bureau of Inspection. Since when has bureaucratic bullshit made the world a better place?

Never, that's when.

I should let her walk her tight ass out of here. I can have Beck redo his drywall job I destroyed and take this up with Daniel—the putz. I would, except Vivian cracked open my curiosity like the Fabergé egg I knocked off Lainey Owen's shelf when I first went to live with my new foster parents.

Lainey, my new and improved mother, smiled and cleaned up the mess. Her comment of "it's just stuff" froze me into a solid block of shock. After living with parents who sold off everything not nailed down so my father could have "one more hit," I couldn't understand how Lainey and Will Owen could let me live in their house for another second.

Now that I have enough of everything, though, I understand. I went from working on construction sites to running them. I manage part of Owen Construction, the company established by my new parents and parceled off to their three boys.

Another foreign concept I came to understand while living with the Owens is that all women aren't liars. I learned that first from Lainey, next from Deborah. Deb wasn't free of sin, but at least she never lied to me.

So why, while I chase Vivian Vandemark, am I suspicious of

everything about her? Her fanciful name, at odds with her cheap shoes, the air of superiority that absolutely doesn't belong on someone who works in a government office…

I recognize down on one's luck. I am familiar with hard knocks. This woman isn't either of those things. Even though she's dressed like she wants me to believe she might be.

Paranoid, much, Nate?

Not sure I ever recovered from my youth. I'm suspicious of everyone at first. Maybe my first impression of Vivian was right and she's a fox in sheep's clothing. Maybe she's lying after all.

Time will tell. It always does.

"Ms. Vandemark." I catch her easily. She isn't navigating construction debris in those shoes quickly. My dressy leathers aren't doing me any favors, either, but I move faster than she does. If it weren't for a meeting with the mayor soon, I'd be dressed a hell of a lot more comfortably. I check my watch and swear under my breath. I'm going to be late thanks to this fiasco. Fantastic.

She picks up speed as best she can, grumbling something I can't discern. So, okay, I might've overreacted. I'm not a big fan of the word "no," which is why I favor forgiveness over permission when it comes to decisions I make about my job sites. Gary also lied to me. And after I gave him a sizeable "gift" to hurry things along. So disappointing.

Vivian hit a hot button when she threatened to shut me down. Hell or high water, I will finish this job on time. Her stomping in here all pomp and sass and threatening a shutdown puts me up Shit Creek, sans paddle. She pummeled one of my sorest spots.

Still. I didn't have to act like a horse's ass.

"Viv."

"You had your chance, Owen." She stops walking and faces me. "You used our valuable time by sledgehammering a wall. Why don't you take down the rest of them while you're at it? I'll send over an inspector to check your wiring and we'll take care of the pesky paperwork issue you're having." She gives me a disingenuous smile. "You can expect a penalty fee and a lengthy delay, but I'm sure your bank account will bounce back."

I have to fight not to react. She knows, somehow, that I hate being delayed. It's her arrogance that makes her more than what she seems. Mild-mannered city workers don't breeze in like they own the place. Even Daniel can't look me in the eye when he's angry about something. And Gary? Incentivizing him to speed up the paperwork process wasn't remotely difficult.

It took me years to establish Vivian's confidence in business situations. I used to be an asshole, but, very recent sledgehammer incident notwithstanding, I've learned some finesse.

I try that next.

Smiling, I spread my arms and try to look affable. Not easy for a guy of my size but sometimes it works. "Come on. You don't want to shut us down. How can we fix this issue succinctly? Quietly."

She chokes on a laugh. "Does that smooth-as-a-fox move work on most inspectors? Is that how you wooed Gary into falsifying your paperwork?"

"It wasn't falsified." I grit my teeth.

She shrugs as she flips a few strands of silky, dark hair sticking out from under her hardhat.

What a beautiful, stubborn pain in my ass.

"You can't shut us down. I have friends in high places, Ms. Vandemark." My smile vanishes. I'm not fucking around here, and she needs to know that. Gary was a pushover. Most men are when you meet their price, and they all have one. I didn't want to deal directly with Vivian's boss on a trivial matter, but she's not giving me much choice.

"Watch me," she says breezily and then marches away from me again. What happens next happens so fast, I don't have time to think. I just react.

The chunk of rock she steps on tips, her right high heel snapping. Off balance, she flails, arms out, heading straight for the dumpster. I bolt into action and close the gap between us in record time, catching her in my arms. I slam my shoulder into the metal bin in the process—where her forehead would have hit if I hadn't been there.

Chest heaving, she's looking up at me like I'm a sorcerer, her eyes the same whiskey essence as her voice. She blinks long lashes as I take inventory of her face. Fine cheekbones, the barest dusting of pale freckles, and a parted mouth that tempts me to bend in for a taste.

Her hands are clawing my forearm and as slowly as it takes for her cheeks to tinge rose with embarrassment, the pain in my shoulder intensifies.

"Are you okay?" I ask instead of what I'm thinking, which is something to the effect of, *Motherfucker, that hurt!*

I have an old rotator cuff injury, and as much as I'm loath to admit it, it's easy to re-injure. Once it's back, I'm reduced to a whiny, unmanly specimen who can't point across the room without a whimper emitting from my throat.

Very unsexy.

"I'm fine." She jerks her gaze away as I help her to her feet. She straightens the hardhat, still perched on her head. I can tell she's embarrassed. I can also tell she doesn't know how to handle being embarrassed.

"Stupid goddamned shoes." She removes the broken one, tenderly setting her foot on the rubble. When she arcs one arm toward the dumpster I catch her wrist.

"Don't. You walk to your car barefoot, you're going to need a tetanus shot."

She considers my grip, and then her shoe, and for half a second I wonder if she'll stomp to her car barefoot to spite me. Maybe.

In the end, she slides the broken not-high-any-longer heel on and limps to her car.

I watch her go.

Her gait is uneven from the varying height of her shoes. She should look silly, but I can't take my eyes off her. And not only because her ass is wiggling in an enticing way. The long hair spilling down her back is rich and dark against her lighter colored shirt. I recall that smattering of freckles on the bridge of her nose. Those clear, brown eyes.

I couldn't be more intrigued by her if I tried. My shoulder throbs in sync with my heartbeat.

Before she shuts herself into her car—an older Hyundai with a dented fender—she tosses both shoes onto my construction site. "Throw those out for me, will you?"

I smile. I can't fucking help it.

"Viv!" I shout, and her head pops over the roof of her car. "Call Gary!"

Her lips form a thin line of consideration. "Call him yourself!"

Okay, so that wasn't consideration.

She shuts herself into her car and drives off, pulling into traffic and blending in with the rest of the cars on the road. My forehead is itchy; I'm guessing because there's drywall dust in my hair.

When I turn around my crew is watching me, some smiling, some not. I ignore them and retrieve Vivian's discarded shoes, taking note of the size before I chuck them into the trash.

We'll see if she can be bribed yet.

Chapter Four

Vivian

Daniel came into the office whistling, which seemed like a bad omen. I didn't acknowledge it just to be safe. One can never trust a good mood on that man. A few hours later, I realize my paranoia was spot-on.

"Vandemark," he growls from the opening of my cubicle.

"Yes?" I don't turn around, focused on the email I'm typing.

"Nathaniel Owen is here to see you."

"Me?" I spin in my chair and find my boss's expression as rough as his voice.

"Yeah. You."

"I suspect my raise is forthcoming," I say with a smile. "I nailed his ass to the wall yesterday *and* left him speechless. It was pretty awesome."

Aside from my windmilling arms and the breaking of my shoe, that is. Both ruined my exit. However, that graceless tumble gave me a chance to be close to Owen, which wouldn't have happened otherwise. So, it sort of evened itself out.

I stand and smooth the skirt of my black dress. I bought it at a thrift store, but it used to be expensive. The hem was torn. I mended it with my passable sewing skills. Given I left my best shoes at Grand Marin, I had to resort to a pair of flats. They're my only other black dress shoes.

"It's been worked out," Daniel says. He's no longer happy, but he's not unhappy. His neutral reaction is as rare as a winged unicorn. "I'll send him back."

"Did he say Nathaniel Owen?" Amber asks from her cube. I peek past my wall to find her leaning out of her own cubicle.

"Yep."

"Did you really nail his ass to the wall?" Her eyes widen, impressed.

"Not quite," answers a low voice. I clock the moment Amber sees him for the first time, somewhat justified she hasn't shut her mouth all the way yet.

Apparently, I'm not the only one gobsmacked by Owen's looks.

"Nate, good to see you again." I purposely toss out his shortened name since he corrected me on it yesterday. I do so enjoy irritating him. "Step into my office."

I welcome him into the gray square I call home. He indulges me and steps inside. There's a petite plastic chair in the corner for guests. My desk is a wraparound with my office chair under it. His bulk and his ocean-scented cologne engulf me when he enters the tiny space.

I clear my throat and lean on the edge of my desktop, trying for casual as I cross my arms over my chest. "What brings you here, Mr. Owen?"

I find it hard to address him as Nate when he's standing over me with those piercing blue eyes and attractive bumped nose. He's authority personified. He's also disarmingly masculine, and I can't afford to be disarmed. I haven't been very, erm, *active* with the opposite sex in the years since my father's sentencing. Dating is too awkward, and casual sex unfulfilling. Besides, I can take care of my own needs. There are no strings attached to my vibrator.

"I have something for you." He hands me a shoebox.

I regard it as if it contains a live rattlesnake, blinking in shock when I recognize the script on the box's lid. *Christian Louboutin.* I should have known he was up to something.

I school my reaction, hopefully before he notices. "What's this?"

"Shoes," he answers. "To replace the pair you broke."

Louboutins are not merely *shoes*. They represent status and wealth. Just being in such close proximity to this box reminds me of my former closet in Chicago. My reaction is borderline Pavlovian.

Drool.

"We started on the wrong foot, so to speak," he tells me with a half smile. "This is my attempt to make up for it."

I hum, suspicious. "Where was your charm yesterday?"

"This isn't charm. It's a peace offering. I was unprofessional."

"We're all wrong sometimes, Mr. Owen. There was no need to buy me a gift."

"Oh, I wasn't wrong." He holds up the box. "Please."

Much as I want to argue how wrong he was, I instead take the box and remove the lid. Before I mean to, the words *"Pigalle Follies"* fall from my lips.

I had a pair of these. I felt beautiful whenever I slipped into them. Crafted in black *veau velours* with those iconic red soles, this particular pair boasts four-inch spiked heels. They're *divine.*

"You know your shoes," he comments arrogantly.

"So do you. This is a fine pair." They retail for about half a month's rent. My mom bought me my first pair of Louboutins. I didn't keep any when I downsized, telling myself I didn't need them. Holding this pair makes me miss her. "I can't accept them. Obviously."

"Of course you can." He fishes a paper tucked behind one of the shoes and unfolds it. I thought it was a receipt, but no, it's an electrical inspection signed by none other than my surly boss.

"Wait...how..."

"Like I told you, we passed. Daniel and I had a little chat and he realized he was mistaken in assuming that Gary lied."

Daniel walks by, his face an unreadable mask. Owen turns to look over his shoulder before his eyes once again land on mine.

"Did one of your henchmen pay Daniel a visit with a sledgehammer?" I ask.

This elicits a sharp, brief laugh from Nate. His grin is equally brief, as well as my reaction. Full head-to-toe goosebumps. My nipples tighten. I lean in his direction the slightest bit.

I'm not typically attracted to assholes, I swear. Either I'm having an off day or Nate Owen is emitting hallucinogenic pheromones.

"Our inspection passed because we are compliant, not dishonest. Daniel assumed the opposite. He had a change of heart this morning, which worked out nicely for my schedule on the site. We're back on track now. Isn't that great?"

"Fantastic." I offer him a wan smile.

"And I don't have henchmen, by the way. I do my own dirty work."

The word *dirty* sends my mind into a freefall. Then, I imagine Nate in the mob and threatening Daniel's life. That stops my visceral reaction to him in its tracks.

I thrust the shoebox against his torso.

"Unlike everyone else you come in contact with, I *don't* accept bribes."

"It's not a bribe. I have what I need. This visit to your"—he studies our surroundings—"*office*...was for show."

"You put on a good one yesterday." I nudge his middle with the shoebox he's refusing to take. It's like pushing against a brick wall. The corner of the box crumples on impact.

"How do you know a damn thing about Christian Louboutins?" His tone is more curious than accusing.

"I'm a woman. How the hell do you know about them?"

"The shoes you tossed out yesterday cost thirty dollars at a discount shoe warehouse. I looked them up."

The way he's talking, like a cop who has information on me, is making me nervous.

"Maybe I'm a fashion junkie who can't afford the finer things." My voice is smaller than I'd like it to be.

He considers my outfit. Slowly.

"Did you used to be a shoe salesman, or do you have a foot fetish?" I snap, hoping to knock him off course and gain the upper hand.

"Neither. I'm observant. I've been in the presence of a lot of very wealthy women, and I know how they carry themselves. How they behave in certain situations. They can smell a knockoff from an authentic name brand fifty yards away. Even so, I haven't yet met a woman who uttered the words *'Pigalle Follies.'*"

"Maybe you should choose your company more carefully."

"Maybe you should," he counters.

We stay in limbo for a moment before I blow out a gusty laugh.

"You caught me." I hold my free hand up like I'm confessing. "I fence stolen shoes as my side hustle."

"No, you don't. You'd have worn a more expensive pair today if that were true." His eyes rake over me and I resist the urge to squirm under his blue inspection. "You're not trying to pretend to be rich. You're out of place in middle class, aren't you? You belong in the upper echelons, yet you're hiding in the suburbs."

His assessment is scarily accurate. I cover with a laugh, but it doesn't sound convincing. "Very funny. Much as I'd like to indulge your fantasy—"

"Would you?" he cuts me off to ask. The blood rushes to my face. Now I'm thinking about what his fantasy could be. A rogue, sinful wave of heat rolls through me. It's not as unwelcome as it should be. He's taking up half my cubicle, his eyes boring into mine. "You don't belong here."

"Pardon?"

"You heard me."

My heart mule-kicks my chest. *What does he know?*

Maybe he figured out my real name is Vivian Steele. Maybe he spotted old courtroom footage or stumbled across a snippet of press from years ago. Despite my darker hair color and six years of maturity since, he could have recognized me. Damn me for running my mouth at the site yesterday. I should have laid low at the office.

I'm not ready to start over so soon. I want peace, and if a billionaire like Owen knows my real name and needs me in his pocket, this gemstone of information is the perfect bit of intelligence to keep me in line.

But I don't kowtow to rich folk. Not any longer.

"I… I don't know what you mean," I stall. It took a lot of effort to reach this mediocre point of existence. A name change, legally, is a series of frustrating hoops and a lot of waiting. I don't want to change my identification. I don't want to move. Find a new apartment, a new job. A new friend, if Amber can be considered a friend. Fudge the truth about my patchy, and mostly fabricated, work record. Leave my life behind. *Again.*

My father took my life from me once. I'm not starting over.

"I think you do." He takes the box, extracts one of the shoes and bends on one knee. While my mind reels, he gingerly lifts my foot, his calloused palms smoothing along my calf.

Unbidden, visions of the fantasy he alluded to burble to life. One where those palms touch more than my leg.

"I have an offer for you, Ms. Vandemark."

Did he overemphasize my last name or am I paranoid? He removes one of my flats and slips on a Louboutin in its place. It's as different as climbing into a shiny new Porsche when you're used to driving a Camry. Or a rickshaw.

He takes the other shoe from the box and makes the swap as well.

"A perfect fit." He presses his hands to his thick thighs and stands. He's closer than before. We're not quite chest to chest, but it wouldn't take much to bring him there. God, he smells good. "That's the shoe you belong in, Vivian."

He tips my chin with his knuckle and I have the crazed thought he might kiss me. Which is insane. I don't want him to kiss me. I decide I'll drive my four-inch spiked heel into his toe if he kisses me.

"I have reservations for tomorrow night at seven thirty at Villa Moneta. Join me."

I'm tempted to refuse, but I'm not sure what he knows, or what he might tell Daniel about me. I suspect Nate Owen could make my life hard if he wanted to. I came to Clear Ridge for an attempt at normal. Have I failed?

"Tomorrow it is," I reply coolly, my mind a hectic scramble.

"I'll send a car."

"I'll meet you there," I argue.

"Very well. And, Vivian"—he pats my cubicle wall before he leaves—"wear the shoes."

Chapter Five

Vivian

I arrive home to find an urn on my doorstep.

At first I thought a florist paid me a visit and the neighbor's cat dragged off the greenery, but at a second and then third take, I recognize the container for what it is. It's resting on top of a tiny-font, graphic designer's nightmare of a menu from the local Chinese restaurant. They deliver. Which is super convenient if you want to eat a lot of deep-fried food covered in syrupy orange sauce while lounging on your sofa.

I stoop to pick up the menu and flip it over, recognizing my brother's tall, thin cursive when I do.

Dad belongs with you.

I take a step back from the urn as if my father might rise out of it like Marley's ghost and warn that I'll be visited by three specters tonight.

"Hi, Vivian!"

I nearly leap out of my thrift-store dress at the sound of Mrs. McAffey's voice behind me. I turn to my left and find her juggling two bags of groceries awkwardly while trying to insert her key in the door.

"Would you mind, dear?" She smiles, but her smile vanishes when she notices what's at my feet.

"No problem." I stuff my brother's note into my purse and take a bag of groceries from her, positioning myself in between my neighbor and my dead dad.

"Is that…?" She points with her key. "What I think it is?"

"Yes," I say solemnly. "My cat."

Ms. McAffey frowns. "You had a cat?"

"My family's cat. My brother dropped him off. He doesn't want to keep him in the house. He says he's having nightmares."

Before my elderly neighbor can accuse me of having had a really *big* cat, her expression melts into grandmotherly concern. "I'm so sorry, sweetheart."

She smashes me into a bosomy hug with her free arm and I pat her while trying not to squish the bag of bread sticking out of the top of the paper grocery sack. "Thank you," I say, my voice muffled.

"I used to have the sweetest boy," she says, finally opening her door. I follow her into the kitchen. "His name was Dapper and he was jet black with a little white diamond on his forehead. Prettiest cat you ever saw. What'd your baby look like?"

"Oh, uh…" I glance around the room for inspiration, which doesn't help. Floral patterns as far as the eye can see. "He was a, um, a gray cat. We found him. In an alley." There, that's generic.

"And his name?" She sets down her bag and takes the one from me.

"Steele," I blurt.

"An appropriate name for a gray cat. I'm sorry for your loss, Vivian."

"Thank you. I should—"

"Yes, go! I wouldn't dream of keeping you from your grieving. If you ever want to swap cat stories, you let me know."

"Uh-huh." I'm out of there in a flash and picking up my father's remains. Inside my apartment, I pace the urn from living room to kitchen and back again, indecisive. I have no idea where to put him. Or it. I don't even know what to call this.

Also, I'm going to choke my brother when I find him. You might think this is a sure sign he's using again but this stunt reeks of sobriety. Of responsibility, which isn't something he's known for.

When news came that my father passed away, I sure as hell didn't claim the body. Evidently my brother did.

I place what's left of Walter, Senior on the counter next to the coffee pot and chew on my lip while I think. I grab my phone and video-call a friend from my former life. One of the only people, except for my brother, obviously, who knows I changed my name and ran away from my last life.

Marnie Lockwood picks up on the second ring.

"Vivvie!" Her face fills the screen and I'm happy just seeing her. I haven't kept in touch like I should, but she's one of those friends you can fall back in with no matter how much time has passed. "I miss you, doll!"

"I miss you too." She also makes me miss parts of the world I told myself I was glad to leave behind. I minimalized when I left the world of the wealthy. How much stuff does a person need, anyway? "Your skin looks incredible."

"Pierre," she explains, touching her cheek. Pierre is her esthetician. He's a miracle worker. If I had two-hundo for a facial, I'd totally get one. "You look…well, I love you, but you look not good."

She doesn't mean my skin, though I should exfoliate more.

"I'm not." I flip my phone around and show her the urn. She gasps.

"Is that…"

"In the flesh." I scrunch my nose. "Or not. You know what I mean."

"Where? How?"

"Walt dropped it by my house."

"I thought your brother was in Atlanta." Marnie smooths one

caramel-colored eyebrow with a manicured fingernail. I miss mani/pedi day too.

"Well, evidently he's in Clear Ridge." I look out my front window like he might leap out of the bushes. "I'm surprised he didn't dump the urn into a trashcan somewhere." I admire the decorative chalice holding my late father. It's nice. If urns can be nice. "Or sell it for drug money."

"He must be clean," Marnie says, arriving at the same conclusion I had.

For now, I think but don't say. It's too sad to say aloud.

"What are you going to do with it? Or should I say 'him'?"

I shake my head at my friend. "No idea." On either count.

"I have something else to show you." I tilt one Louboutin and point the phone at my feet.

Marnie gasps. Again. She knows I don't wear anything showy in my new life. "Where did you get *those*?"

"From a billionaire." I smile at my friend's shocked expression. "I went to shut down his construction site and broke a heel. He showed up at my office with these."

She tucks her chin and lifts her eyebrows. "Who is he? Anyone we know?"

"Like all billionaires know each other?"

"They all knew your dad," she quips.

I sigh. "That's what I'm worried about. This guy told me I belong in these shoes. That I don't fit into the middle class."

"Was he complimenting or threatening you?"

"I don't know." And I don't, not for sure. "I can cause him trouble on this project if he doesn't follow the rules. He has a reputation for finishing projects on time and cutting corners to do it. He wasn't happy when I showed up with a roll of red tape."

"Money can make that go away, Viv."

"That's not what the nest egg is for," I say. "It's for emergencies."

"And you being threatened isn't an emergency?"

"It's for Walt-themed emergencies," I mumble.

"You have to stop punishing yourself, Viv. Your father's sins aren't yours to absolve. He died for them, you know."

That part makes me sad. He had the chance to help people but instead he robbed them. I change the subject. "I have a date tomorrow night."

"Wow, I don't hear from you for six months and then you call with all the news. Congrats." Marnie lifts a glass of bubbly and I know it's our favorite brand of champagne without seeing the bottle. We shared many a glass over brunch, or at girls' nights, or on random Tuesdays.

"What are you celebrating?" I ask, nodding at the glass.

"Nothing big." She turns her head and rests her left hand on her cheek really obviously. The size of the diamond solitaire on her ring finger could signal an aircraft.

"He asked." I smile, happy for her but slightly hurt she didn't call to tell me. We're growing apart, no big surprise there. I feel like I live on a different planet than I used to. Aaron and Marnie have been dating for seven years. She and I had many conversations revolving around whether or not he would ask. "I can't believe it."

"Me neither. My last name's going to be White." She rolls her chestnut-colored eyes and then we both laugh.

"It's about time something good happened to you, Marn," I say, meaning it.

She sobers quickly and holds the phone close so that her face takes up the screen. "You too, Viv. You too. We should talk more."

"Yeah," I agree. "We should."

Chapter Six

Nate

I've been plagued by thoughts of Vivian since I walked out of her cubicle, the soft vanilla scent of her perfume tickling my nostrils. It wasn't cloying or sweet. It was musky. When I sank to my knees to put those shoes on her feet, the scent intensified like she'd slathered fragranced lotion onto her long, smooth legs.

Damn.

She makes me inexplicably curious, and explicably horny. Which doesn't make a lot of sense. I don't "need" her—the paperwork Daniel signed was legit, by the way. I greased Gary's palm for speed reasons *only*. I didn't need him to lie for me. My men do quality work. I have a perfect record for finishing the job on the day I say I will finish it and I refuse to allow a power-tripping jackass who works for the city to set me back to zero.

I do what I have to do to maintain my reputation—to maintain the Owen reputation. They took me in and gave me their name—I don't take that lightly. My reputation is practically inherited. God knows I didn't do anything noteworthy in my former life.

Anyway, while I may not do everything "by the book," I don't mess around when it comes to safety. You can't cut corners and have a reputation as a decent builder, and I'm in this for the long haul. The Grand Marin project is humming along smoothly, which is always the goal.

Why invite her to dinner, I hear you ask.

Honestly, I don't know. I lied about the reservation when I arrived to Cinderella those shoes onto her feet. I didn't have one. I had no plans to see her beyond the delivery of the shoes. I was merely satisfying my curiosity about her.

The inkling that she was a ritzy wolf in shabby sheep's clothing was reinforced when I slipped those shoes onto her feet. She *belongs* in expensive shoes. Her back straightened and she held her chin a little higher after I put them on her. Whenever I wear a suit, I feel like an overstuffed suitcase. No matter how well-tailored, it never seems to fit. Much like I feel in high society. I'll never fit in as seamlessly as my parents or my brothers.

Speaking of, I arrive at the Owen house, cake in hand. It's our mother Lainey's birthday today. The entire event will be fancy and catered, and there are probably three cakes in there to choose from. But I know she loves the buttercream frosting at Caketopia, so I ordered her a chocolate-with-buttercream masterpiece in the shape of a Fabergé egg. Genius, right?

The massive front door swings aside and I'm saved from cradling the cake box under one arm to open the door myself.

I'm greeted by one of my brothers.

Archer Owen is the "real" Owen. Born and bred. It's Benji, Benjamin if you're looking at his business card, and me who are from much, much humbler beginnings.

"Welcome, Slumlord," Archer greets with a sharky smile.

"Fuck off." I grin.

Arch likes to give me crap for building live-works because he'd die before he touched any property resembling residential. He prefers commercial clubs, bars, and restaurants. They're not my style. I enhance lives. I give people a place to live. I want them to have a taste of the good life, as good as they can get. Not all of us can be adopted by billionaires, after all.

I was lucky. Well, me and Little Orphan Benji.

"Has it started yet?" I ask, taking in Archer's champagne glass. He'll switch to bourbon after dinner. We all will. Paired with a cigar with our father, William…if Lainey allows him to smoke one tonight.

"There he is! Only one to go." Lainey sweeps into the foyer in a slimming black dress and her own pair of Christian Louboutins. If you were wondering how I knew about ladies' shoes, now you know. She's opened more than one pair on Christmas morning.

The house is a monstrosity. A big, beautiful, tall, posh, comfortable, warm place. Just like my adoptive mother. Minus the monstrosity part. Lainey's pretty. And even if she wasn't, her kindness would make her so.

"Happy birthday, Ma." Chicago leaks out of me sometimes since that's where I grew up. This is one of those times.

"Caketopia. You're my favorite son, Nate." She kisses my cheek and hugs me.

Archer swipes a hand over his neatly trimmed beard and affects a dramatic eye roll. I hold Lainey closer and soak it in, and not only to rub it in Archer's face that I'm her favorite. When you have a crappy mom and then the perfect one, you hold on to hugs like these for dear life.

I vowed when I started working for Owen Construction that I would make her and Will proud. She's told me a hundred times she's proud of me, and Will at least half a dozen, but my debt to them is so great, I'm still working on it. Probably will be for the rest of my life.

The door opens behind us.

"Finally!" Archer says dramatically.

"Fuck off," Benji tells him, echoing my greeting. "The hood of Nate's car is still warm. I haven't missed anything. Happy birthday, Mom."

Golden brown Benji takes Lainey into his arms and gives her a squeeze. He's Israeli, second generation. He was raised in Idaho. William Owen's sister, Aunt Judy, worked at the hospital with Benji's late parents and was dating Benji's then neighbor when his parents died. That's how the Owens received word that Benji was a parentless kid chock out of family one cold, snowy December evening.

"I'm her favorite," I tell Benji as I show him the cake.

"I love my boys equally," Lainey says, betraying me. She pats my cheek, her version of condolences.

Benji was adopted a year before me, when Archer was thirteen years old. I was the latecomer at age fifteen. By then Benji was eleven and Archer was fourteen and I was the shithead foster kid who wouldn't follow the rules. These two have been my brothers in every sense of the word since the day I was given my own room in a house so nice I couldn't believe I was allowed to live there.

Regardless of what you've witnessed tonight, I'd take a bullet for any of them. I never met a family who cared about each other until the Owens. My parents were less "all for one and one for all" and more "look out for number one." Had I been raised to completion by Jewel and Jarod Weeks, I would be a blight on society like they were.

I'm wearing a dark suit, sans jacket, for the festivities. Predictably, Benji chose the stylish combo of slacks, a checkered shirt, and a pair of Salvatore Ferragamo shoes. He inherited Mom's penchant for fancy footwear. Archer is in a sleek gray suit that costs twice as much as mine. The prick. One-upmanship is his pastime.

The front door swings open again and in scuttles Cristin Gilbert, Benji's "life assistant coach." At least that's how he refers to her. The rest of us know Cristin as his best friend-slash-woman who is madly in love with him.

"Hi, guys!" Cris chirps. She's adorable. Big, doll-like gray eyes, chin-length dark blond curls. She used to work for the Owens, before Benji claimed her for himself. She's comfortable in this dynamic. The Owens are like her second family.

"I didn't know you were coming," Lainey tells Cris with a smile. "I'm so glad to see another woman. Not as if any of my boys would bring a date." Our mother *harrumphs*. Cristin sends a look of pure longing over at Benji, who cluelessly doesn't pick up on it. Mom drags her into the next room.

"How are things with the life coach?" Archer asks, sipping his champagne.

"Life *assistant* coach. You should consider one. You'd never forget a haircut again." Benji smirks at Archer's disheveled locks.

"Exactly what I don't want in my life," he growls. "Someone telling me what to do."

Control is Archer's thing. Can you tell?

"She is the reason I sit at the big-boy table with the grownups and you two scurry around job sites trying to make the bills," Benji replies smugly. He runs the finance department for Owen Construction. He's a math wizard. In other words, he's really fucking nerdy.

"But you miss all the fun," I tell him. "Nearly got shut down yesterday. A woman in a pencil skirt and heels was sent to reprimand me for not having the appropriate paperwork."

"I do love a pencil skirt." Benji's interest is palpable.

"You love to be reprimanded," Archer says, chuckling at his own joke.

I can't help laughing. That was a good one. I'll hand it to Benji, though. He has a mystical way with women that Archer and I never quite grasped. I tend to fumble. Archer is as malleable as forged iron. Vivian had it wrong when she accused me of being charming. Benji has the market cornered.

"Nate, when are you going to learn to stop sleeping with the inspectors?" Archer grouses. "It's unprofessional."

"She's not an inspector," I say, instead of admitting I didn't seal the deal. There's always dinner tomorrow. I'm not sure if there's anything to uncover when it comes to Vivian Vandemark, or if my assumptions are off. I doubt it. My gut rarely steers me wrong. Something tells me she's hiding. Normally, I'd let it go. I have what I need, my site is up and running. But I didn't miss the flare of heat in her eyes while I was sliding those shoes onto her feet. She tried to pretend she wasn't interested in me. I know better.

And, yeah, sex is not off the table. If I'm really lucky, we'll have it *on the table* after we eat. I can clear Villa Moneta with a wave of my American Express card.

After dinner, I'm admiring the expansive backyard with my adoptive father. William Owen is the OG blue-collar billionaire. He didn't inherit his wealth, he created it. He started with cleaning companies—you heard me—franchised them and, after fifteen years of solid growth, sold the company for a mint. He'd been in touch with many large businesses by then, so he branched into new-builds—mostly office buildings. Once my brothers and I came along, we were groomed to run our own sectors of Owen Construction based on our talents and skills. Will never missed an opportunity to teach us to get dirty, either. We may have wealth, but hard work is the backbone of this company.

Arch and Benji took to it better than I did. I never lost my rough and tumble. I don't exactly fit in at corporate meetings, and whenever I visit our headquarters, I'm sure everyone can tell. Will, on the other hand, has learned to blend. He can attend a charity function or an investor's meeting without standing out like my thrice broken nose. I've never had the reputation for being easygoing. I don't suspect I'll have one soon.

"How's Grand Marin?" he asks. It's time to talk business since we aren't allowed to talk business at the dinner table. That's Will's rule. He wants to keep Lainey happy and she's happiest when we talk about our personal lives at dinner instead of the goings-on of the company.

"On schedule. Ahead, actually," I say proudly. "We start filling units next month."

He raises one bushy eyebrow. He's shaven, but a dark five

o'clock shadow presses his jaw. Like his son, Will could easily grow a full beard. If Lainey let him. "I hear you took out a wall with a sledgehammer."

"Shoddy craftsmanship doesn't stand with me."

He offers a half smile of disbelief. He knows I don't mean it. I'd never berate or belittle the men and women I employ. I know the struggles they face. I understand they have bills to pay and families to support. I relate to them, and that's what makes me aces on site.

"You shouldn't cause problems where there aren't any," he warns.

I suck on my cigar and crane my head to take in the stars. The Owen property sits on several acres. Without light pollution, I can see the Pleiades. Which is why I fought those restrictions for lower-wattage bulbs at Grand Marin. Everyone should be able to see the stars, not just rich folk. I don't know that I ever looked up when I lived in Chicago. There was too much going on in front of me I had to keep both eyes on.

"I keep my enemies close," I say, the cigar between my teeth.

And I keep my *would-be* inspectors closer, especially when they look like Vivian. Which, by the way, they never do.

"Not every relationship can be exploited, Nate," Will explains. I'd be insulted, except he's not wrong. I've used my reach and money to woo people over to my way of thinking. When you're a hustler, you hustle. In lieu of business brains, I lean on my street smarts.

That electrical permit stood between me and a C.O., better known as a Certificate of Occupation. If I don't have my permits in order, I can kiss retail and residential contracts *adios*. A little money in Gary's palm sped up the process and a little more in Daniel's persuaded him to sign in a timely manner. I think he still hates me, but the feeling is mutual. Vivian in the middle was a kink I hadn't seen coming. She's hellbent on following the rules for some reason.

She fascinates the hell out of me.

"The big picture is what's important," I tell Will. "These live-works are going to employ and house a lot of people. People who will have date nights and attend book signings and celebrate grandma's eightieth birthday. They need what I'm building. If I have to smooth rough roads along the way, so be it."

Will puts his cigar in his mouth, answering with silence. For good reason. He inquires about my arm of Owen Construction on occasion, but he lets me run it. He understands the value of mistakes. I've made plenty. The more mistakes I made, the more I learned. And the more cautious I am not to make them in the future.

I think of Vivian and wonder if her caution is born of her desire to stick to the straight and narrow or make up for her past mistakes. Maybe both. I admire the stars and blow smoke rings over my head.

Guess I'll find out if she shows up for dinner tomorrow night.

Chapter Seven

Vivian

Villa Moneta reminds me of an Italian place I used to frequent in Chicago. It's dark and moody, the tables set with fine, white, crease-free linens. A single flickering candle in a glass votive holder sits at the center of each table. The restaurant's palette is classic black, white, and gold. Luxury.

Clear Ridge proper doesn't have restaurants quite this fancy, so coming here required some traveling. It was worth the forty-minute commute to satisfy my curiosity.

"Ms. Vandemark," the host greets. I eye him with suspicion. How the hell does he know who I am? "Mr. Owen left word you'd be arriving soon."

Did he, now. I wonder how *Mr. Owen* described me. Dark hair, sort of tall, resembles infamous thief Walter Steele… I hope he hasn't figured that part out. I've had people sniffing around my past enough to last two lifetimes.

I dug into the back of my closet for my nicest little black dress. It's one of the few items of clothing I kept from my former life. Thank goodness it still fits. Slipping into Dolce & Gabbana followed by a sleek pair of Louboutins for my date was a lot like slipping into my old identity. I remember dressing up with my mom before she made a habit of day and night drinking. We would stand shoulder to shoulder in front of her big bathroom mirror and share makeup.

That thought makes me miss her again. An ache carves into my chest and I shake it off and confirm to the host that, yes, I'm Ms. Vandemark.

I checked Villa Moneta's website before I drove here tonight. Proper upbringing kept me from wearing a thrift store dress. And…fine, I'll admit it. Part of me wants to wow Nathaniel Owen. He might think he has my number, but he has no idea what he's up against. I am skilled at pretending I have no idea anything is amiss.

I haven't had this much excitement in a long, long time. Six years ago I decided I was done with excitement. I sought, and attained, an ordinary, plain, blend-in-with-the-woodwork life. Entanglements with men were rare, and I kept things light. I haven't been on a date since I moved here, so that could explain my sudden curiosity for the scenic route.

I have to be careful. If he's figured out I'm the daughter of Walter Steele, he could threaten to share that information with Daniel. If he strips my identity to the studs, and forces me to start over with a new job and a new name in a new town…well, he'd better be prepared to offer up some secrets of his own. I won't go down without a fight.

My date stands to his full height as I approach. The host pulls my chair out and I sit, setting my clutch on the edge of the table. Our table is tucked into a corner and the vibe is almost romantic. Nate smooths his tie and nods his head to the host in a secret signal before retaking his seat. Candlelight dances on the imperfect lines and angles of his handsome face.

When I dated in my former life I stuck to country club guys. Bankers. Lawyers and, once, a software developer. Pretty boys, all of them. Nate isn't pretty. He's… I don't know the word. I react to him on a carnal level, though. Way down deep. Almost dangerously deep. I can't be deep with anyone. Especially a billionaire.

"You wore the shoes," he says. Arrogantly.

I cluck my tongue as I unfurl my napkin. "You had a chance to compliment me, but instead complimented yourself. Poor form."

He watches me, not taking his eyes from mine as a sommelier pours wine into our glasses. Nate waves off the offer for a taste test.

"It's perfect," he says. "Trust me."

"I'm not sure I do." I raise my glass and await his toast.

"Touché." He touches his glass to mine. After holding the red wine in my mouth a moment, I determine he's right. The wine is perfect.

"Have you been to Villa Moneta?" He tries to come off as innocent, but fails. He should know better. A man like him could never pass for innocent.

"No. I haven't lived in the area long."

"Where are you from?" he asks casually, like he's not sniffing around for answers.

"The city," I answer cryptically. "What about you?"

"Chicago."

I stare at him. That's where I'm from.

"You have that air about you," I say to cover for the staring.

"Now who's noticing details? Was it the accent? I've tried to tone it down."

"Chicago is rough and relatable. Like you. And yes, I noticed a hint of an accent." I lift my wineglass to my lips again. I'll have to take it easy since I'm driving. I could easily settle into this seat and sip on a fine red while taking in a candlelit Nate for a good, long while. I remind myself to keep my guard up. "Why'd you invite me here?"

"I wanted you to put those shoes to good use. They're wasted in a government building." He dips his chin. "As are you."

"I'm good at my job." Sort of. "I've only been there a handful of months."

"Do you enjoy it?"

"Other than the site visit I made to Grand Marin, yes." We smile at each other. The waiter returns and Nate orders in Italian.

"Did you just order for me?" I ask.

"The chef's menu is eight courses. It was either that or the basic tasting menu. You don't strike me as basic, Ms. Vandemark."

"Why did you invite me out tonight, Mr. Owen?" I sort of repeat.

"Nate."

"I'm allowed to call you Nate now?"

"I was being an ass."

"You don't say."

He smirks, his cobalt blue eyes glittering in the subdued light. "I could use a friend at CRBI."

"I thought the mayor was your friend."

"He's okay." He sips his wine, watching me over the rim of the glass.

"What about Daniel?"

"We're not friends." His voice is almost a growl.

I hum, not committing to a response.

We're polite during the first two courses. Nate observes me as I choose the proper forks. Watches me down an oyster without flinching. I wonder if that's why he brought me here. To suss out his suspicions. Not that I expected him to point at me and shout, *"I know who you really are!"* dramatic-courtroom-TV style, but you never know.

Maybe he's telling the truth about needing a friend at CRBI. He wants something from me or I wouldn't be sitting here.

By the time the main course arrives, I'm warm from the wine and, surprisingly, enjoying his company. "You're better on a date than you are on a job site," I quip.

"Is this a date?" He watches me carefully and I realize I walked into a trap.

"Meeting, then?"

His turn to hum. The sound reverberates low in his throat as he cuts into his dinner and forks a bite of veal into his mouth. I follow suit and try not to look like I'm waiting on his answer. I am. On tenterhooks.

"This is more intimate than a meeting. I want something from you, Vivian."

A flare of desire blooms in my belly. "Is it my loyalty?"

"You came to my site and threatened the one thing in this world I hold precious. My work. I can't allow you to do that again."

"Follow the rules and you won't have to worry about it." I slice another bite of veal and tear my eyes off his attractive mug. I don't have to look at him to know he didn't like my answer.

"I can't allow timeline delays. There are too many people counting on me."

"And here I thought you and your ego were the only two involved." I send him a sly smile.

"I play well with others, Vivian. You caught me on a bad day. This is my attempt to make it up to you." He spreads his hands to gesture at our dinner while his forearms rest on the edge of the table. "Aren't you impressed?"

I swallow a smile before it pushes my lips to one side. "I've been treated to nice dinners before, Mr. Owen."

"In gifted shoes?"

"Pretty impressed with yourself, aren't you?"

"Generally. So are you. Admit it." He holds my gaze for a good, long while. "I noticed your shoes. Found out your shoe size. Bought you a pair that suited you. Slipped them onto your feet. You liked every moment of it. You're the kind of woman who appreciates a man who appreciates details."

"I appreciate men who tell me the truth about what they really want from me."

He shakes his head slowly. "No, you want to be chased. Not presented with an offer."

I suck in a breath and take another bite of my food. He's right but I'll die before I admit it. I'm beginning to think he doesn't know who I am after all. Which makes tonight a different kind of game. One where I can be Vivian Vandemark and let this "chase" play out a bit longer. I can't remember a time I've been more tempted.

"Owen Construction is a large company. Tell me about it."

He cocks his head at this somewhat tepid turn of topic, but allows me to take us there.

"It's a family affair," he says, and then mentions that he and his two brothers were at his parents' house for his mother's birthday party last night. He doesn't seem embittered while talking about family like I do. I'm filled with an unfamiliar emotion: jealousy. And a more recent one: loneliness.

"The Owens are incredible people," he goes on. "They are generous. Kind. Open and loving. I couldn't have been luckier." He makes the emotional admission casually. I can tell he cares about them, deeply. His career revolves around honoring the family's reputation. That's important to him.

Our dessert plates arrive. At the offer of a cappuccino, coffee, or other after-dinner spirit, I can't resist. "Cappuccino, please."

Nate holds up his hand as a "no, thank you."

"So you're adopted," I say after the waiter leaves.

"You didn't do your research on the Owens before you visited Grand Marin?"

"I wasn't given much time, seeing as how Gary was thrown out on his ass minutes prior to my assignment."

"What about after I saved your life and you returned to the office? You didn't research us then?"

I try to hold in a laugh and in the process emit a quiet snort. His eyebrows lift in amusement. He wants to know if I was curious about him. I was, but I didn't satisfy my curiosity. Dig deep enough on anyone wealthy and you'll find one common denominator. *Lies*.

But. I've been in his company for a good hour and I'm no longer sure I'd find lies. He doesn't seem to be driven by power the way the men in my past were. I don't know what to make of him. He's rough, charming, attractive, surprising, superior, and kind. It's an odd cocktail of attributes.

My father was secretive, efficient, self-serving. He supported Walt and me out of a sense of duty more than from the goodness of his heart. The optics on the Steele name and all that. A name I ran from.

I answer his question with one of my own. "Are your brothers adopted too?"

"Benji, yes. Archer, no. He's authentic. A born-and-bred billionaire. I entered the family as a punk kid with a chip on my shoulder."

"So, you feel less than authentic?"

"Sometimes." He shrugs big shoulders. The suit is delicious on him. There's no other word for it. All his brawn outlined in fine fabrics. *Yum.* I wonder if it took him a while to feel comfortable wearing one. As if proving my point, he tucks his finger into his collar and scratches underneath where his tie is knotted.

"What about you, Viv? Any family struggles?"

I hesitate a moment before saying, "No family. I'm an orphan." I decided when I changed my name that'd be my story if anyone asked.

"No foster family?"

I shake my head. "I was an adult when I lost them."

Thankfully, he doesn't press for details.

"What do your brothers do for Owen Construction?" I ask, curious about everyone's roles. Are they as saintly as Nate implied, or yet another family of billionaires hiding a secret that will eventually put some, or all, of them in jail?

"Benji crunches the numbers. Archer builds bars and clubs."

"And you gravitated to live-work communities?"

Nate pulls his shoulders back. Just when I think he's going to brush off the question, he answers so sincerely it takes my breath away. "Home is important. It provides a sense of belonging and love. At home you should be able to relax and feel safe. Something I wasn't able to do during the years before I met Lainey and Will Owen."

I never expected a testimony to come out of my date's—er, Nate's—mouth. He's either buttering me up or telling the truth.

"Why do you do what you do?"

"Are you asking if I'm passionate about working at the bureau?" I lift my cappuccino to my lips, nervous he knows the truth. As a woman who came from a high-powered corporate environment, I'm grossly overqualified for the position at CRBI.

"You seemed plenty passionate when you came to my site."

"You broke a rule."

"Bent," he corrects. "There are a lot of ethical gray areas in life."

"And you operate from several of them."

"The sooner the site is complete, the sooner wide-eyed, *passionate* entrepreneurs can move in." He sounds slightly defensive. "I provide a place where they can thrive. That's worthy. More worthy than words printed on papers that haven't been looked at closely in decades. Bureaucracy has its shortcomings."

"So does seeing oneself as a saint."

His firm mouth shifts to one side, a ghost of smile playing on his lips. "You were hell-bent on shutting me down. Why?"

"That's my job." I shrug.

He shakes his head, not accepting my answer. "That was Gary's job. That *is* Daniel's job. You wanted to shut me down for another reason entirely."

"I don't like cheaters," I mutter before I can stop myself.

"Thanks to an old boyfriend?" he guesses wrong.

He's fishing but using the wrong bait. "Sure."

The check arrives and we lock eyes for a good, long while. He pays while I finish my cappuccino.

"You weren't going to halt construction at Grand Marin no matter what I said or did, were you, Mr. Owen?" I ask. But I know the answer.

He shakes his head, content to be honest. "There's always a

way to smooth out rough patches during construction, Ms. Vandemark. This isn't my first rodeo. I have an important job to do. A reputation to uphold."

"A reputation for finishing early, I heard." I grin.

"Maybe someday you'll find out." His answering grin is honey-smooth. "As you now know," he says, serious, "my reputation involves more than me. It's the Owens I protect and serve."

I consider his loyalty and feel the pang of jealousy again. He has a family. A good one.

"Is Daniel worth fighting for?" he asks of my boss.

"What's right is worth fighting for," I hedge. "You can't do whatever you want just because of your family's last name." A lesson I have learned over and over again.

"Is this your own rotten-grapes experience speaking or are you envious of the haves?"

The waiter returns and Nate signs the receipt with a flourish. When he tucks the slip into the black book, he sits back in his seat and waits for my answer.

I don't give him one. "Dinner was lovely. Thank you."

"I wanted you to see how the other side lives. We're not so bad after all, are we?"

We have a mini standoff. He had to have noticed the chilled veal wasn't a new experience for me. Noticed how I viewed the braised winter chicories, duck confit and tartare with parsley root as commonplace a meal as they come.

"It's what I expected," I say. "A lot of show for a little food. Expensive wine and cheap table linens." The truth is the food was exquisite, the company enthralling, and the table linens not cheap at all.

"Not impressed then?" he asks, but he's smiling like he knows I'm lying.

"Were you trying to impress me?" I'm unable to keep from bantering with him further.

His smile gives nothing away. We're embattled in some sort of warped foreplay that I can't allow to wind up in the bedroom.

Pity.

"I'll walk you to your car." He stands. When I turn, a broad, warm hand touches the small of my back.

I give my ticket to the valet who scampers off to retrieve my car.

"Until next time." Nate lifts my hand and kisses a space between the knuckles of my index and middle fingers. It's unexpectedly erotic. Before I accuse him of acting debonair to work an angle, he floors me with more of his signature eye contact.

He's close, his head angled. Electric awareness zaps between us. I want to kiss him. Push to my toes and taste his firm, full mouth. Smash my nose against his crooked one and rub up against him.

I shouldn't want that. I can't afford to be close to anyone. Not after my entire life fell apart. My car arrives and I take a step away from him, the moment lost. Nate rounds my Hyundai and opens the driver's side door. Is that disappointment in his eyes? Or challenge?

"See you around," he says before he closes the door.

I pull away from the curb and smile.

Definitely challenge.

Chapter Eight

Vivian

I'm having lunch with Amber at a sidewalk cafe downtown. The homemade croissants on the chicken salad sandwiches could give Villa Moneta's fancy-pants menu a run for its money. I finish half and debate the other buttery half before diving in, carbs be damned.

Amber has been chattering nonstop since we sat down. I don't mind. Changing my name made me a good listener. When I speak I have to be vague, so she's saving me the trouble.

"Enough about me and my life-woes," she says suddenly. Her woes are adorable. I don't mean that disrespectfully. I complained about my mom and dad too, before Steele-Gate. Back when we were a normal family who wasn't under investigation by the FBI. "Did you go to dinner with Nathaniel Owen yet?"

So she did hear him ask.

"You've kept quiet about that until now," I tease as I reach for my iced tea.

"You're not the kind of woman who appreciates a prying friend."

I wince. Amber's and my relationship is surface, and she just pointed a finger at that obvious fact. Marnie and I have no boundaries. There's no need for them since she knows the truth.

"I went to dinner with him last week," I tell Amber. No reason not to tell her about it. Nothing happened. I feel a smidge of disappointment as I consider that fact.

"He's incredibly good-looking. How did I not know that?"

"It wasn't like Daniel and Gary came into the office swooning over how hot Nate is."

"Nate, huh?" Her eyebrows jump. I throw her a bone.

"At first I took Daniel at his word and assumed Owen was another powerful rich guy trying to take more of what he doesn't deserve. I suspect our dinner was mostly about Nate staying in my good graces, but I have to admit, I think he actually believes in what he's doing."

He sounded passionate about his construction project, and almost humble when it came to the Owens.

"Those shoes seemed more like he was trying to wedge his way into your skirt, not your good graces."

She's usually not this frank. It's refreshing. Am I intimidating? I smile sadly. Maybe I overcorrected when I tried to be aloof.

"I'm not interested in Nate." More like I refuse to be interested in him.

"Really?" Her frown is genuine. "Not to be presumptuous, but you don't think he'd be fun?"

I laugh instead of envisioning how *fun* sleeping with him would be. If our banter over dinner, the gentle way he slipped my shoes onto my feet, and the combustible energy between us when he didn't kiss me was anything to go by, we'd bring down the house if we slept together. I shiver at the thought and adjust myself in my seat to cover for it.

"Men like him are more work than they are fun, Am," I say pragmatically, trying to convince both of us.

She smiles warmly when I use the shortened form of her name. Definitely, I need to loosen up. "I'm glad we did this. You eat at your desk so often I wasn't sure you'd accept a lunch invitation."

"I appreciate you asking." I mean it. It's nice having a friend. "We'll do this more."

"Good. Actually..." Her pausing gives me pause. "I was going to ask you for a favor."

Ah. I remember why I was keeping to myself now.

My smile is plastic. "Oh?"

"Daniel asked me to attend a function on Saturday but my sister is having a baby shower. I know, a baby shower on a Saturday night? It's inhumane."

I agree.

"Anyway"—she waves a hand—"It's at the art institute. Daniel needs someone who's good at mingling to be the 'face of our division.'"

I bet. Daniel and "mingling" go together like foie gras and peanut butter. "You were going to be his date?"

"I'm trying to eat." She holds two fingers to her lips and pretends to be nauseous, which is pretty funny. "Would you mind going in my place? It's a paid gig, and I'd feel better telling him I can't do it if I could offer you up as my replacement."

"You mean human sacrifice?"

She chuckles. "To be clear, Daniel won't be your date either."

"Good. I'd hate to be sick on this lovely croissant."

"But he'll want you to stay close so you can bail him out of any uncomfortable conversations."

I could do that. Mingling at functions used to be second nature to me. I could use the extra pay. Plus, and this is what ultimately tips me, a *boujie* gathering will attract a lot of fancy folk. The Owens might be in attendance.

"What's the actual date?" Not that I have plans on *any* Saturday night.

After she tells me, I hear myself accept with, "I could use the overtime."

"Thanks, Vivian!" She brightens. "If I can return the favor, let me know."

My heart races at the possibility of seeing Nate again. How disturbing. I frown.

"The dress code is black and white," she tells me before returning to her own sandwich. "I'm sure Daniel will wear that horrible suit that makes him look like an undertaker."

I know just the one she means.

"And, hey, the Owens might even be there." She waggles her eyebrows.

"I guess anything's possible," I say as if I hadn't thought of it yet.

I smile before taking another bite of my sandwich. I'll have to wear a dress Nate hasn't seen yet.

Just in case.

Nate

"An evening under the stars," Benji reads from the invitation sitting on my desk. He stopped by Grand Marin to take me to lunch but I've yet to finish returning emails. "So original."

"Those events are all the same," I say distractedly before closing my laptop.

"When are you going to hire a new assistant?" My brother sounds peeved. He has no problem handing over his to-do list. Archer and I tend to hold ours close. Archer because he's a control freak and me…for sort of the same reason. It's hard to trust someone else with my baby, aka whatever site I'm currently building. I wasn't kidding when I told Vivian I do my own dirty work.

"That last email I fired off was in response to a new virtual assistant," I inform Benji. "Happy?"

"Ecstatic," he answers, deadpan. "Took you long enough."

I have a shit-ton of work to do. I'm fooling myself trying to handle it on my own. My last virtual assistant, Sylvia, quit after she became pregnant. "I've been busy."

"You like doing everything yourself. Admit it."

"It's the hustler in me." I pocket my keys and lock my temporary office. The drywall I demolished has been replaced. Beck wasn't happy about having to redo the job, but he did it anyway. Benji hasn't let me live it down.

He knocks on the wall as he walks by. "Did you see her again?"

"Beyond dinner?" I ask. No use pretending I don't know who he's talking about. "No."

"Really." As he holds the door open for me, I blank my expression for clues that I give a fuck. I do, so I'm careful not to bat an eyelid.

I walk toward my Tesla, sweat already beading my brow. It's a scorcher today. I'm anticipating settling into its perfectly cooled interior. Gotta love technology.

"You're interested, though," he observes. "I can tell."

"I'm interested in Vivian Vandemark because I like to keep bureaus close." That and the warm vanilla scent on her skin drives me wild. After dinner, when I was standing at the valet station with her, I saw the exact moment her eyes darkened. She wanted me to kiss her. Her lips parted and she tilted her head ever so slightly. She was silently begging, and I'll bet you a thousand dollars she had no idea she was doing it.

I didn't give in, which I've regretted more than once. I can't decide if I was testing her or testing myself.

"Well, then, I suggest you RSVP yes to the Stargazer event Saturday on behalf of Owen Construction." My brother plunges his hands into his pants pockets.

"Why? Because you'd rather not?"

"I'll go with you if you want." He shrugs.

"And do what, pencil pusher?" A joke. He's great in a group of stiffs and, unlike me, everyone likes him instantly. It's the big-ass grin that makes him approachable, or it could be his perfectly straight nose. My large frame and crooked facial features tend to spook the locals. But not Vivian, I think with a smug curve of my lips.

"A representative of CRBI will probably be there, you know."

I hadn't considered Vivian might be in attendance. My interest spikes. I try to hide it with a blasé, "And?"

"Like you don't want to see the woman consuming your every thought."

Every other thought, maybe, but not *every*.

"Haven't seen you this distracted in a while. Not since Deb—"

"That was a long time ago, Benji." Eons. And the only way she ever "consumed" me was praying-mantis style. "I don't fraternize anymore. A dinner here or a professional function there is acceptable. A full-on affair?" I shake my head but it's hard to do when my entire body is screaming YES. An affair with Vivian is too tame a term for what would happen if we wound up in bed together. We'd incinerate the sheets to ash. Cinders would burn for days…

"Sure, Nate. Whatever you say."

"Don't push me," I warn, pointing at the car for him to get in. "Unless you'd like me to start asking a bunch of questions about Cristin."

"Ask away," he says easily as he slides into the car. "She's a family friend, and arguably my closest ally."

"Ally. Could you be more of a robot?" I reverse out of Grand Marin, vowing to take my car in for a bath today. Have to clean her up since I'll be visiting the art institute on Saturday.

"I'm exercising the control you evidently can't," Benji says. "Keeping my business and my private life sequestered. Cris is a close friend and a professional. If I came on to her, she'd—"

"Faint dead away," I finish for him.

"No. She'd—"

"Orgasm instantly."

"Jesus, Nate." He sounds perturbed, but not because of my lewd comment. If you ask him, he'll say he doesn't like to think of

Cris that way. If you ask me, I think it's because he *very much* likes to think of Cris that way. It's a shame he won't let himself have nice things.

What Benji lost as a kid was unwarranted, unexpected. Devastating. His parents were professionals—his mom was a nurse and his dad was a doctor. Talk about two people who should live as long as possible.

Meanwhile my parents were destroying themselves and the people around them. How long were a junkie and his codependent wife meant to live? Who were they helping? Not long, and no one are the answers. Anyway, Benji has a wound and it keeps him from letting himself be too comfortable.

"Vivian's an orphan," I say before I mean to. "She mentioned she was parentless at dinner, but she was an adult when it happened." Whatever "it" was. I didn't ask. I haven't shaken the idea she's hiding something from me, but why does it matter? Like Benji, I should keep my personal life and business life sequestered.

Unfortunately, I like amalgamation.

"A woman who works at CRBI is destined for a frumpy husband who sells insurance."

I make a face like I ate an olive—I hate olives.

"If you saw her, you'd never say that," I grumble. I don't like the idea of Vivian with a frumpy *anything*. Including her wardrobe. She dusted off her finest frock for our dinner together. I noticed, but didn't mention it. She wanted me to notice, but not mention it. I was merely obeying her wishes.

"I took her to Villa Moneta," I tell my brother as I drive.

"Villa Moneta." Benji whistles. "Fancy place if all you were trying to do is keep her in your pocket."

"I wanted to observe her in that environment."

"Harsh, Nate. If you wanted to make her uncomfortable, why not invite her to the Owen house for dinner?"

"That's just it," I say, my mind on her behavior at dinner. "She wasn't uncomfortable. She wasn't impressed. She didn't ask what a single item was on her plate. She casually mentioned the wine. The label was in French and the name of it rolled off her tongue."

Sexiest words I've ever heard in my life.

"So city employees can't be sophisticated?"

"When have you known me to be a snob?"

"Never." He shakes his head.

"That's right. Never. As a guy who came from nothing, I recall vividly how difficult it was to learn the ropes of high society. She was comfortable. An eight-course meal didn't ruffle a single one of her fine feathers."

"Cris didn't grow up in wealth either, and she's comfortable in those sorts of circumstances. Maybe Vivian used to work with a wealthy family."

"Maybe." But the idea of something bigger and more secretive won't leave me alone. I want to know more about her. I have since the moment she stomped onto my work site. I know I should leave it alone, but when it comes to her I can't seem to help myself.

"I was upper middle class, you were dirt poor, and we do fine blending in with these people."

"Benji, we *are* these people." I pull to a stop in front of Club Nine. We're picking up Archer for an Owen brother powwow before his club's grand opening. "Speaking of, a cigar has had our name on it since you skipped having one on Lainey's birthday."

"No can do. Cris doesn't like to smell cigar on me when I go back to the office."

I keep my pot/kettle comment to myself.

Chapter Nine

Vivian

The Stargazer function began at seven. I arrived at six o'clock with Daniel, feeling awkward for several reasons. Firstly, we looked like we arrived together as a couple even though I drove separately, and secondly, this crowd is a blast from my past.

My father dragged our family to who-knows-how-many business functions to celebrate his accomplishments. Whether it was a dinner or there was a podium or it was an excuse to get hammered like this one, they were basically the same. Rich folk like to see and be seen. They like other people to know who they are. I was one of them before my father went down in a blaze of shame. There's a thought.

I sweep my hand down my dress and consider I'd fit in better if it had six more inches of length and fewer sequins. I stand out, but not because my dress is gaudy. Because it's *fun*. No one here is dressed for fun.

It took two hours and a lot of sifting through racks before I found a dress that wouldn't break the bank. The top is sleeveless, black sequins leading down to a skirt cut high in some places, low in others. It reminds me of the dress my salsa instructor wore when I was into that sort of thing. It's a bit over the top for this event, but I couldn't help buying it after I tried it on. It moves with me when I walk, the layers of skirt floating behind me. Pretty, if a little showy.

I didn't pair it with the Louboutins. In the event Nate shows up tonight, I don't want to appear overeager. I popped into a Lowz Shoe Depot and bought a gold pair of high-heeled sandals that loop at the ankle. They're killing my feet, not gonna lie.

My hair is down and wavy, and my lips are muted pink. I'm approachable and friendly. Daniel meanders away from me, off to the side, and busies himself checking his cell phone every thirty seconds. He really is bad at this.

An hour into the event, I wish I would've worn the butter-soft Louboutins over the cheap, plastic-but-made-to-look-like-leather pair. This is the price of pride, people.

There are no chairs or tables, so guests mill around, drinks in hand and small-talk. I've been mingling for an hour. I'm bored, but not particularly pained by it. Evidently it's like riding a bike.

"What was your name again?" Bob Londers asks me. He owns the golf course that's been a Clear Ridge staple for over sixty years. He's opened several courses in Florida. He once played Augusta. I nodded politely through each of his stories. I secretly wonder if he ever played on one of my dad's golf courses. Walter Steele built several with his stolen money. Bob is trying to impress me.

"Vivian," I answer. "I'm in the process of being certified as an inspector for the city, but I've been with the bureau for a while."

"Well, you belong somewhere more regal if you ask me." He smiles and a similar frisson of panic laces through me as when Nate said something similar. Am I so obvious? But then he continues and I realize he's not calling me out. He's hitting on me.

"I'm attending Jazzfest here in two weeks." Bob's eyes dip to my cleavage. "Will you be there, dear?"

"Ah, sorry. Jazz isn't my thing." I signal Daniel to save me but his eyes are on his cell phone.

"If I wasn't married." Bob shakes his head, his beady eyes traveling down my body. A pity date from a seventy-something golf course owner. Go me.

"I appreciate the offer." I smile and hope it looks sincere. Told you this schmoozing stuff is like riding a bike.

I make a quick, polite escape and walk back to Daniel.

"Thanks for the assist with Bob over there," I growl. "He asked me out."

"Bob's married." Daniel tears his eyes from his phone and frowns at me. "Plus, what did you expect me to do? Rush over and say you were mine?"

"Ew, no." I offer an apologetic half smile. I wasn't supposed to say that out loud. "I *expected* you to mingle. Isn't that what we're supposed to be doing here?" I'm growing increasingly uncomfortable the longer I'm here. Not only because of Bob, but that didn't help. I'm suddenly itching to escape. Yes, small talk is second nature, but it's also chipping away at my energy. I'm tired in my bones.

"I'm only here because my boss made me come," Daniel says.

"Funny, me too."

"All of these people"—he gestures around the room—"build things. They come to us for permits. Without us, they couldn't succeed. Which means we come to these little circle jerks—"

"Gross."

"—and kiss ass for a few hours."

"How much longer should we stay?" I check the room again, just a casual sweep. No sign of Nate. I wonder if one of his brothers or someone else from the company came in his stead. Disappointment sinks into the pit of my stomach.

"Are you looking for Owen?"

I snap my head around and face Daniel who looks less accusatory than curious. "You two seem to have a connection."

I prop my hand on my hip, defensive since he's right. "No, *you two* seem to have a connection. By the way, is that a new watch?"

"*No.*" Daniel's frown returns. "Is that a new dress?"

I strike a pose. "Clearance rack. Fifty-nine, ninety-nine."

"Money well spent," I hear behind me.

My heart jumps. I'd know that voice anywhere. I spin around and face Nate Owen, who seems to have a penchant for sneaky entrances. He's mouthwatering in a dark suit and a black tie with a subtle pattern. It could be the same Armani he wore the day I met him, or perhaps it's a different one. I imagine his billionaire's closet holds a slew of expensive suits.

"Owen," Daniel says, his back straightening.

Nate dips his head in silent acknowledgement.

Daniel's eyes shift from Nate to me. "I'm going to grab a drink and say my goodbyes. Vivian, feel free to leave whenever you're done here." He pauses before walking away. "But since it's time and a half, no longer than another hour."

He hustles off, moving his arms like they're propelling him.

"Guess you're stuck with me, then," Nate says.

"Are you still here?" I swallow the last of my sparkling water and place the empty on a tray of discarded glassware. My heart races, the attraction between us ratcheting up now that he's standing next to me. I remind myself entanglements with anyone are a bad idea, and with Nate, possibly the worst idea of all, but I make no effort to move away from him.

His mouth pulls into an entirely too attractive half smile. "Let's find you a real drink. This crowd can take care of itself."

He offers an arm. I hesitate momentarily before I slip my hand over his jacket sleeve.

"How much did you pay Daniel to sign off on your permit, again?" I ask, desperate to steer us back to choppier waters.

"I didn't bribe him," he says, sticking to the same story. "Owen Construction made a generous donation to a cause he cares about."

"Daniel cares about something?"

"Every man has their price."

We walk along the fancy parquet flooring, overhead lighting reflecting on the shiny surface. The cream and black and gold pattern is 3D and almost dizzying if I watch my feet. I avert my attention to the art on the wall. Paintings of men and angels and naked women and dragons line these halls.

At the bar, Nate orders a bourbon, neat. "Vivian?"

"Dirty martini, vodka." I don't miss the subtle cringe from Nate. "What's wrong?"

"Olives." His big shoulders shudder, and I can't help laughing.

"I promise not to kiss you later." I don't know why I said it, but when he gives me his undivided attention, I'm glad I did.

I'm not the only woman in the room who's noticed him. Tall, fit, well-dressed. He stands out. The backdrop of sullen paintings and rich folks falls away. There is only Nate. Only me.

This is why I looked forward to seeing him. It's been a long time since being under someone's attentive gaze has felt this welcome. We have this… Is connection the wrong word?

The bartender hands over our drinks and Nate tucks a large bill into the tip jar. My glass is so full I have to take a sip to avoid spilling it on my toes.

"I was hoping you'd be here," Nate tells me, proving he's more comfortable with transparency than I am. We stop in front of a painting and pretend to study it. Or, well, I'm pretending. Maybe he's contemplating the meaning behind the woman standing on her porch looking out at a desolate field.

"Didn't have your fill of me at dinner?" I like flirting with him. I tell myself it's harmless.

"No."

That one word carves a path of longing into my chest. I've felt unwanted for a while. Or wanted for the wrong reasons. For a magazine interview. For a ghost-written autobiography. For a consultation on the movie based on Walter Steele they're peddling around Hollywood right about now.

Suddenly warm, I take a gulp from my glass and change the subject. "How can you not like olives? They're so…briny."

"You said it." He makes a face that makes him look a lot younger. Like, thirteen.

"When's the last time you had one?" I challenge.

He lips pull into a grim line like he's figured out what I'm about to request and he's already unhappy about it.

"If it's been longer than seven years, you should try one. Your taste buds can change, you know."

His dark expression remains. I happily offer my glass.

He sighs and it sounds like it comes from the depths. For a moment I think he'll refuse. To my delight he takes the plastic skewer from my glass and eyes the bulging, dripping olives with disdain. I watch as he licks his lips and his throat moves reluctantly. Then he takes an olive with his teeth, rolls it on his tongue, and bites into it.

Convincing him to do what he doesn't want to do is oddly erotic. I imagine him doing what he wants will be even more erotic. He chews, his expression carefully neutral. An involuntary shift of his shoulders betrays him.

He takes a long sip of bourbon to wash down the olive. He coughs and clears his throat. "God, Vivian. How can you put something like that in your mouth?"

I lift the skewer and pluck an olive with my teeth before chewing merrily. "I've had worse."

Heat engulfs the space between us. Yes, the attraction hasn't gone anywhere since our shared dinner—hell, since I first met him. He's the last person I should entertain any kind of relationship with, but my body isn't interested in heeding my brain's warnings.

Somehow I know sex with him would be an unbelievably satisfying experience.

We move to the next painting. A dragon is being stabbed in the heart. The mournful look on the creature's face makes me feel sorry for it. It's cornered, unfairly, so the knight can have his fifteen minutes of fame.

Definitely, I relate to the dragon.

"What do you think it means?" Nate asks.

I blink out of my musings. "I'm not an art critic."

He steps closer to me, but his eyes are on the painting. "You don't have to be an art critic to appreciate art."

"No, I suppose not." I take a breath and sift through my thoughts. "The dragon lives a peaceful life in a cave but there are men who hunt it. They want the beast unearthed, exposed. They believe the dragon to be evil when its only desire is peace." I feel Nate's eyes on me. When I look up at him he's wincing.

"That's dark."

"Death is dark."

He nods and then says something I didn't expect. "At dinner, you mentioned you were orphaned as an adult. Was it long ago?"

When I'm silent for a beat, he shrugs. "Just curious."

"Mom passed about six years ago and Dad died last year," I answer. Just the facts.

"Were you close to them?"

I shake my head automatically. "Not in the end. Not like your family. What about your birth parents? Were you young when they died?"

He nods. "And in juvie."

"Why?"

"Stealing from a convenience store a handful of times. My parents didn't exactly keep the cupboards stocked." He watches his shoes, his thoughts elsewhere. "They weren't good people."

"Are you?" I tilt my chin to take him in. Even with his bulky features and UFC body, he seems like good people. And the speech he gave at the restaurant suggests his work is about more than money.

"I'm trying to be," he says. "But there's a lot of ground to cover."

"I know what you mean." I look back at the dragon, frozen in time mere moments from death.

"We're all lonely sometimes, Viv." His voice is low and kind. When I face him his expression is raw with sincerity. My instincts tell me he's more than a cardboard-cutout billionaire. Is he lonely too?

"I want to show you something." He tips his glass and finishes his bourbon, gesturing for me to finish my drink as well. Never one to shy from a challenge, and because I have no idea how to respond to his sincerity, I gulp mine down, enjoying the last olive for dessert.

I walk with him through the crowd of well-dressed people in my on-sale dress and uncomfortable shoes. Unsurprisingly, heads turn. We garner male and female attention alike. The women fiddle with their necklaces and watch him with longing before sending me decidedly less favorable glances. I have the idea many of them wouldn't mind a moment on his arm.

Or in his bed.

I can't blame them. He's tall, handsome, and powerful. He's not wrong about loneliness. I've been there. Since I met him, though, that shadowed corner has seen some light. What I crave is attention, and yes, *connection*. I didn't expect to find it in Nathaniel Owen.

Navigating through this gallery and that, I ignore the throb of my toes in these shoes. *Never again.* Nate nods to the guards. I have a momentary fantasy in which I'm Rene Russo to his Pierce Brosnan in *The Thomas Crown Affair*, which only adds to the surreal-ness of this moment.

We arrive at a pair of double glass-paned doors and Nate pulls a key from his pocket. "Lainey Owen—my mother—donated the roses."

He slips the key into the antique doorknob and opens the doors, gesturing for me to walk ahead of him. The courtyard is lit by iron lampposts shining softly overhead. I admire the night sky and wonder if he stipulated low wattage bulbs to allow for stargazing here as well.

Rose bushes tower on my left and on my right. A stone path cuts through the garden and wraps around. I follow it, admiring the various-colored roses at every turn. They choke the air with their sweet, unique fragrance.

"Beautiful." I touch a pale peach bud.

"Yes, very." I turn to tell him to keep his cheesy lines to himself, but the words lock in my throat. He's watching me, intent, his eyes blazing. He cups my hip with one hand, then lifts the other to my jaw. Then. He kisses me.

His mouth is firm, surrounded by a rough five o'clock shadow practically invisible given its light color. I feel it, though. My eyes close when his tongue slides into my mouth. I don't resist.

I grip the lapel of his suit jacket with one hand and tug him against me. Heat surrounds me, infiltrates me, assaults me. His tongue tastes of bourbon and the faintest tinge of brine from the olive he ate.

When his lips leave mine, his chest expands to take a breath. "That martini tastes better on you."

As lines go it's a good one. I don't hide my grin of appreciation.

"You've stepped outside your comfort zone tonight," he observes. I have. I drew attention to myself the moment I rested my palm on his forearm. All eyes were on us when I let him lead me away from the event. "Care to take it further?" His palm still warming my hip and my jaw, he dips his chin in the direction of the lit exit sign. "I'll cover for you with Daniel. Tell him you stayed the whole hour. He'll believe me."

"Hmm. You two seem chummy lately."

Nate's grin makes that comment worth it. "Vivian Vandemark. You really do believe the worst of me, don't you?"

I lift and drop one bare shoulder. His blue eyes take in the move. He wants me. The feeling is mutual. And after that kiss, more like sixty-forty.

"Stop denying yourself," he murmurs with a cocksure tip of his lips. He pulls me closer, teasing with his mouth hovering over mine. We're practically chest to chest but he doesn't kiss me again.

I've been denying myself for years. Truth is, I'm damn sick of it. My craving for him is visceral. He's potent and he was also right. I'm lonely. We can take advantage of each other in the most delightful way…

I don't need a formal invitation but he offers one, mistaking my silence for hesitation.

"Come home with me."

I shed my guard like a second skin, pressing my breasts to his suit and whispering my answer against his mouth. "Okay."

Chapter Ten

Nate

I convinced Vivian to ride with me, promising to have her back to her car at the art institute by morning. She told me I was presumptuous, I admitted I was, and then she gave me a foxy little smile before sliding into the passenger seat of my Tesla.

On the way to my place, we don't talk much. The moment I confessed to her that we're all lonely sometimes wasn't a scripted attempt to draw her from her shell, or point out my own weakness. It was the truth. And whenever Vivian's around, I find myself being more honest than I need to be. I'm glad I made the admission, though. Without it, I doubt she would have let me kiss her. Or agreed to come home with me.

She's given up resisting me. For the moment.

Me? I have no interest in resisting her. She may be the flame to my hapless moth, but I have a feeling the burn will be worth it.

The car ride is torture. Her legs are distracting, especially in a peekaboo skirt cut at different lengths. One moment she's covered, the next she moves her leg and the material slips and gives me a view of one supple thigh.

I weld my teeth together and force my attention on the road. I absolutely cannot wait to have her naked.

Presumptuous or not, she's coming to bed with me tonight. Not because I'm an arrogant prick accustomed to having his way —though, arguably, I am—but because Vivian takes what she wants. I respect the hell out of that approach. It's one I use often.

Inside, I hang my keys on a silver hook by the door. Hands in my pockets, I follow behind her, trying to see what she's seeing for the first time.

The foyer opens to the living room, the tall ceiling extending all the way up to the second floor. The living room and staircase are divided by huge panes of glass framed in black and complemented by glass coffee and side tables. The flooring is textured brown wood, which "lends the space warmth," according to my decorator. A modern cream-colored sofa with bold navy blue decorative pillows invites anyone to sit, the shag rug beneath it begging you to slip off your shoes and wiggle your toes.

Vivian does that next, after sinking onto a couch cushion and unstrapping her shoes. "These are the worst."

Her forehead pinches as she reaches for her foot. She didn't wear the shoes I bought her. I suspect that was intentional. She's built her guard sky-high, and she wouldn't want to flatter me too much. On the plus side, she anticipated seeing me tonight. Maybe even when picking out her dress. I like that I was on her mind.

I sit next to her and take the opportunity to touch her. She has one leg crossed over the other and I slide my hand around her foot. When she doesn't stop me, I dig my thumb into her arch. She moans.

"Lie back," I say. "You won't be sorry."

Her narrowed eyes hint she's going to challenge me, but her smile disagrees. Adjusting her skirt, and giving me another glimpse of her mouthwatering thighs, she props herself on a fat down pillow. I make myself comfortable too, and lift her feet to my lap. I start with her right one and begin to rub. Thumb to arch, then up to the wide part beneath her toes.

Her eyelids shut and she sighs. She actually seems relaxed. A rare look on her. Have I ever seen her not on the move? At dinner, she sat, but she was ducking and dodging constantly. Not now.

"As foreplay goes, this won't get you far." A smile plays at the corners of her lush mouth. She's putting me through my paces.

The kiss earlier was too brief. I'm already nostalgic for her flavor. Martini be damned, her taste was more like rich, velvety white chocolate. Or maybe I'm thinking of the heady vanilla scent of her perfume.

"I'll fall asleep on you and then where will you be?" she murmurs sleepily.

"In that case, I'll carry you upstairs," I answer.

Her dark eyes open. She studies me carefully. "To tuck me in?"

Was that longing I heard in her voice? Does she crave connection as much as I do? Is she using me to feel less lonely? Do I mind being used?

Hell, no.

"Of course," I answer.

"You'd let me sleep in your bed all by my lonesome?" I can't tell if she's sincerely asking or flirting with me some more.

"Sorry." I dip my voice as I massage her foot. "Women don't go to my bed without me."

"How noble."

Her mouth is good for more than kissing. She's sass and class. Wrapped up in a reduced-price department-store dress and shoes that hurt her feet. I want to clothe her in the finest satin and lavish her with gifts. If you haven't picked up on it, I'm a family guy who likes to take care of people. That said, I'm not usually this taken by a woman. This one already has me in knots.

"You can't bribe me, you know."

This again? "I haven't."

"You bribed me with shoes."

"I *gifted* you with shoes. They weren't a bribe."

She puts her feet on the rug and sits up. Her dark, almost black, hair ruffles around her shoulders, having lost some of its bounce. It doesn't take away from how beautiful she is. She let her guard down for a moment, but now it's up again. As if she's back on the clock. As if she's trained herself to look and behave a certain way. I don't like her buttoned-up. I want her *wild*.

"Shoes you should have worn instead of those," I tell her as she flexes her toes in the deep-pile rug.

"I didn't want you to know how much I liked them." She turns her head to regard me over her shoulder. I can't resist her delicate expression or the unexpected honesty that arrived with it.

"Admitting how much you like me seems equally difficult."

"What makes you think I like you?" she purrs. Her eyes grow darker as she tilts her head.

"Hell, I don't care if you do," I lie. I like people to like me. It helps me sleep at night. "But I won't deny wanting another taste of your lips." I lift her hand and tug. She comes closer, and before I know it her lips land on mine.

That wasn't difficult to orchestrate.

She allows me to take her other hand, but before I have a chance to pick my next move, she's leaning against me, her breasts on my chest.

Clothing has never been more inconvenient.

"Sleeping with me won't give you an inch at the bureau," she informs me while unknotting my tie.

"Ironically, sleeping with me will give you more inches than you can handle." I grin when she laughs. She has a nice laugh.

"Oh, I can handle your inches." She undoes my shirt buttons, her attention on her work. "I don't see the point in resisting you."

"I know just what you mean." The silken strands of her hair run over my fingers like water. When her lips hit my bare chest, I suck in a breath and shove my other hand into her hair. I'm holding her head while she licks a trail down my chest. The wet heat from her kisses sending me on an erotic roller coaster ride.

Tempting as this is, no way is she blowing me before I have her naked.

I unzip the back of her dress, and her face lifts to meet mine.

This time when I kiss her, I pull the bodice of the dress down and cup her generous breasts. Her black lace bra costs more than her dress and shoes combined, I'd bet my bank account on it. I've purchased this brand for women before—it's luxury. I know how to treat a woman and how to give a gift that will land me in her good graces…and between my bedsheets.

I unclasp the bra and slip the straps off her shoulders, then slide them from her arms. When her breasts are released to my capable hands, I suck in a breath of pure need.

They're *gorgeous*. Heavy C-cups with nipples the color of the peach rosebud she was touching in the garden tonight. I touch them with the same reverence, watching her cheeks stain pink and her lips part. When I tug those tender buds and pinch lightly, her breathing takes on a hectic pattern.

Her fingers busy themselves undoing my belt as I continue my leisurely play. When she puts her hand into my pants and cups my erection through my boxer briefs, I let out a hiss.

"Well, well," she says. "Big everywhere."

"I promised you inches."

"So you did."

She stands, robbing me of her touch and her breasts, and drops her dress on the floor. Her lace panties are part of a matching set. I cradle her ass and place my mouth over the cotton panel covering her pussy, inhale the intoxicating vanilla musk scent clinging to her skin. Massaging her butt cheeks, I bite the material before clutching it with both hands and yanking it down.

She's bared before me. A beautiful sight. I slide my tongue between her folds to taste the heart of her. Craning my head I look up to find her pink cheeks brightening, her peach-colored nipples tightening. Her hands are in my hair, pulling hard, so I do my job and I do it well.

When I find her clit, I zero in on the spot. I hold her hips steady but bring her as close as I can to my seeking tongue. Boldly, she lifts one leg and rests her foot on the couch while riding my face. I was right. She needs this.

I slow my ministrations to test her reaction. She tugs my hair harder.

"Tell me," I murmur, her dampness on my lips.

"I'm close," she pants. "Please don't stop."

"Not a chance." I squeeze her ass. "You want faster?"

"Yes. And flatten your tongue."

"Yes, ma'am." She likes having control. So do I. But in her case I'll make an exception. Her orgasm is a trophy, and I intend to take first place.

I experiment with cupping her ass before moving my hand along her seam. I slip one finger inside, gentling her open. The sounds she makes are heavenly. A high-pitched gasp here. A fast exhalation there. Followed by a series of machine-gun-rapid *yes-yes-yes*es.

Sliding my finger in and out, I watch for her *O* face. She's not there yet, but she's watching me with lust-blown pupils.

"I want you to come," I instruct. "I want to taste you."

She offers a jerky nod as sexy little pants of excitement escape her still-open mouth. I return to my work in earnest, lapping at her clit while she swivels her hips and pulls my hair.

I feel her release before I taste her; a full body jolt that weakens her knees. A shake works its way up her legs and along her torso. I drink her in as she tips her head back, letting out a gusty exhalation followed by a reverent, "Oh, God."

Call me egomaniacal, but there is no better praise for my hard work than an *"oh, God."*

She loosens her hold on my hair and right when I expect her to fall bonelessly onto my sofa, she surprises me again.

"Take off your pants." She doesn't wait, but drops to her knees and tugs at my trousers. I kick off my shoes and peel off my socks while she yanks the material to my knees. Before I can take off my pants too, my cock is being sucked.

She wraps me in her hot mouth, suckling the tip gently before running her tongue along the ridge. I grunt in shock, my mind blanking of anything but the sensation of her wet heat on me.

Fingers in her hair, I don't pull and tug the way she did. Instead, I sweep the length of it away from her striking face. I watch her mouth work me—a heady sight.

She takes me deep before releasing me, her wet lips sliding along the shaft. A hiss of excitement streams through my teeth as my hips pivot on their own. I have the idea she's trying to even the score—reclaim some of the control she lost.

I'm not going to miss the opportunity to be inside her by finishing in her mouth. Cupping her chin, I ease her off my cock, memorizing the vision of the glistening length leaving her plump lips.

"I have to be inside you," I tell her, my voice a dry rasp.

She raises an eyebrow in challenge. "Hmm. What do you saaaay?"

My nostrils flare in frustration. The fight for control continues.

"Please," I growl.

She's satisfied by that bit of groveling, but not as satisfied as she's about to be. I roughly yank off my pants and fish a condom from my wallet—a condom I put there in case I happened upon one Vivian Vandemark tonight and successfully wooed her in my family's rose garden.

Score.

She snatches the condom and tears the packet open with her teeth. I watch, rapt, as she rolls it on me, her fingers working quickly while my balls draw up in heady anticipation.

When she moves her leg to climb over me, I don't let her. Instead, I lay her back to the couch and I'm on top of her before she knows what hit her. She blinks up at me, the heat in her eyes prevalent. I put that heat there. *Me.*

"What do *you* say?" I ask, nuzzling her nose with mine.

Her breathing is erratic but she presses her lips together, refusing to give in. I tease her opening with the head of my dick as her breaths grow choppy. She wants me, but is too stubborn to beg. Pride, she'll find, is a fool's game.

"Vivian." I give her a gentle nuzzle and smile. "Give us what we need."

Her expression softens and she whispers, "Please."

Finally.

I tilt my hips and slide past her slick folds. Deeper, deeper, as her neck arches. I'm seated to the hilt, her tight channel gripping me. Her breasts brush my chest, her fingernails dig into my shoulders.

"Please, please," she says now, compliant. Her eyelids squeeze shut as pain-pleasure pleats etch into her forehead.

The *oh, God* was great, but the multiple *please*s might be better. I'm high on the fact she surrendered her control while my own erodes. I was intent on bringing her to the pinnacle but even under me she's taking me for a ride as well.

Before I regain some much-needed control, she's squeezing me from within, writhing beneath me while I rut her into the pillows. One falls and hits the floor, another squishes behind her head and into the corner. I slam into her when she demands, "Harder, harder."

Right when I'm about to pass out from oxygen deprivation, she shouts my name. One wheezy, weakened, breathy *Nate.* It's fucking amazing.

Her orgasm hits her a millisecond before my release splits me at the core, rattling my teeth and igniting my spine. I drop my head to her shoulder and catch my breath, my steamy exhalations on her neck.

Her hands go to my hair again, but she doesn't pull. She delivers a few loving, gentle strokes. Then she makes a request as unexpected as this entire encounter.

"Give me your weight." She kisses my ear. "I like it."

I obey without a moment's hesitation, lowering my arms and smashing her into the couch. She hums, pleased, and continues to stroke my hair.

Chapter Eleven

Vivian

Dire need. That was my state when I arrived here.

Sated bliss. That's my current state.

I blame sleeping with him on my being alone for a good, long while. I've been as chaste and well-behaved as I could over the last several years, but this year in particular I stepped it up. I've been an angel. It just so happens even angels have their limits.

Then again, no other man has been able to bring out my wild side. Nate is charming and attentive. So good-looking it's criminal. So undeniably male, each and every cell of my body leans toward him when he's near. I wanted what his kiss promised in the rose garden. And, damn, it was better than I imagined.

The sex was *so* good I wanted to savor it—make it last the night. I could have ridden out a dozen of those orgasms if I was in fighting condition. My bout of celibacy didn't do me any favors. I gave it all and left no room for more. As they say, all good things must come to an end.

And he is very, *very* good.

He excuses himself to the bathroom. I lie here, too tired to turn and admire the staircase or his naked ass, which I imagine is flexing with each heavy step. I hear him walk upstairs, the sound of water running, and then he comes back down. When he returns, soft cotton pools on my naked, chilled skin. I reach for the garment and hold it up.

A white T-shirt. *His* T-shirt.

I pull it over my head, his ocean scent engulfing me. It's hot outside but chilly in here, especially after our sweaty workout and the A/C kicking on.

He's wearing black boxer briefs and nothing else. It's a good look for him. His chest is wide and fit. A dusting of light hair encircles flat male nipples and dances over the bumps of his ab muscles.

Thick, muscular legs aren't usually my preferred male attribute, but he wears those as well as the boxers. He sits next to me in a half lean, touching my body with his arm. His hand rests on my belly over the T-shirt, and he kisses my nipple, leaving an impression on the material.

"I can't stay." He didn't ask, but I figure he will.

He flattens his hand on my stomach and kisses my shoulder next. "Okay."

That was easy. Not that I expected him to be clingy. What we have is visceral and physical and has nothing to do with staying the night or cuddling. What we have is about us taking what we need from a convenient source.

I've learned to act on instinct and prioritize survival since I left my name behind. The rest of the fluff that comes along with "making love" is more suited for a rom-com movie than real life.

"This isn't the only time," he says.

I laugh at his arrogance. "Is that so?"

"That's so." He rests his chin on my shoulder and I steal a kiss. I can't help myself. He smells good and looks better.

I figure he's right. It's futile to pretend I wouldn't do this with him again. It was...what's the word I'm looking for? Superb? Delectable?

Dire.

That word again. I needed him. He needed me. There's no denying it.

"You've only seen the living room," he states.

"You're a shitty host."

He grins. He has the most oddly handsome face. Long lashes shadow blue, blue eyes. Wavy dark blond hair cut short but long enough to grab. His crooked nose and easy, contagious smile. I notice a scar on his eyebrow and run my finger over it. So imperfectly perfect.

"Stitches?" I ask, giving in to my curiosity.

"Twelve of them."

I wince.

"I wrecked my bike." He gives me a cocky grin before adding, "Into someone."

I finger the black beaded bracelet on his wrist and wonder about it. It's out of place next to the luxury watch.

"You're not like any billionaire I've met." It's out of my mouth before I mean to say it. His eyes spark.

"Met a lot of us, have you?"

Shit. My guard is down and causing me to blurt out things I normally wouldn't. Not good. Time to say good night.

I move to stand but he presses me deeper into the sofa with his big body.

"La Perla isn't cheap," he points out. He's referring to my lingerie. Another special purchase I couldn't bear parting with when I fled my old life.

"It was a gift from an old boyfriend," I lie.

Nate hums.

"I should go."

"You're not going anywhere without me. I promised to deliver you safely to your car, after all."

"I could call a car to take me back to the art institute," I inform him.

"You could. But don't." His sincere request stops me cold.

"Okay," I agree. I should be reeling. Sleeping with him was careless. I gave in to my needs and took what I wanted. I haven't allowed myself to do that in a long, long time. I'm out of practice. I can't make myself regret it. Us having sex was as inevitable as the tide rolling out after it's rolled in. And the possibility of seeing him was exactly why I wore my finest lingerie.

God, that was great sex.

Memories of what we did together run over me like silk. It's been a while since I've been laid, a longer while since I've been laid so thoroughly. His mouth on me, bringing me to orgasm with his tongue, was decadent.

I could stand more of that in the near future.

He tasted good too. I haven't gone down on anyone since… wow, an even longer time than the sex. That typically doesn't appeal, but I was compelled to bring him to his knees after he weakened mine.

Don't think I didn't notice he wouldn't let me be on top. I've never had more fun battling for control.

"Let's play a game." He sits up.

"Thought we just did."

"I want to know more about you. You don't want to tell me. Why?"

"Because it's none of your business," I inform him with a breezy laugh. "Access to my body doesn't give you free run of my being, *Nathaniel*."

"I'll answer your questions if you answer mine."

"No deal. I don't find you very interesting."

His grin is wolfish. "You lie well, Viv."

I like when he calls me Viv. It's like he knows me, and there's a part of me lurking beneath the surface who wants to be *known*. Keeping up my guard is even more tiring than small talk.

"I'll give you one pass if I ask something too sensitive. Maximum three questions for each of us."

"Are you this curious?" I ask, more flattered than alarmed.

"Yes."

I'm sliding through my life on half-truths. He's so honest it's flooring. The risk of answering his questions is at once exciting and frightening.

"But first..." He rises and walks to a small bar cart with glass shelves matching the tables and the wall behind us. His house is a shrine to gleaming glass and expressive woods. His handsome face and broad chest are reflected in a round starburst silver mirror over the bar cart. He winks at me when he notices I'm watching.

He has good taste. His style is masculine and clean. Add a few more throw pillows and a coffee table book about France, and this could've been my old apartment in Chicago.

He turns with two shot glasses of clear liquid. "Truth serum."

"Vodka?"

"Tequila."

I'm already shaking my head, but a smile sneaks onto my lips anyway.

"Come on, Viv. Live a little. I'll go easy on you."

"I don't believe you." I accept the shot glass. "But I enjoy living dangerously."

Nate

Two shots later, Vivian is snuggled into the corner of my sofa giggling. She was a little wobbly on her last trip to the bathroom, which means she's not going to need her car tonight. She *will* need a deluxe hangover breakfast tomorrow if she's not careful.

I'm not a snuggler after sex, but I like conversation. What started out as an excuse to keep her here a while longer has turned into genuine curiosity. She's curious about me as well, which is fun. She's been aloof and cool until tonight. Peeling back her first layer and then a second has only made me want to peel back more.

She chucks back a third shot—a small one since I'm a gentleman—and waves the empty glass at me. "You told the truth. You've been taking it easy on me."

I have. I asked her where she lived. Drysdale Avenue in Clear Ridge. I asked her where she worked before she worked at the CRBI and gave me a *blah* answer of "I worked in management at a financial firm."

I didn't press, somewhat satisfied I was right assuming she's overqualified for her position at CRBI.

"You're in need of a meal," I tell her. "The chef left dinner in the fridge. I never ate it. Veal parmesan and spring mix salad if memory serves."

She throws herself into my arms and I accept a tequila-flavored kiss. "Your mouth makes a nice snack."

I give in and kiss her again, making out long and slow to the music in the background. I selected a playlist earlier. The chill atmosphere leads to thoughts I don't intend to have. Thoughts of her here on the regular, in my arms, relaxed and cozy. Me bringing her a martini after a hard day's work—with olives. A fire in the fireplace in the winter. A lit Christmas tree in the corner.

I'm not one for homey fantasies. They're mildly alarming.

"Question three," she purrs up at me, her eyes half-open. "Who broke your nose?" She untangles one arm from my neck to tap my nose with her finger. Her first two questions were about my family. How old was I when I was adopted, and when did I make my first million. I was honest. Fifteen and twenty-two, respectively. Well, twenty-two was the age when I made the first million *on my own*. William Owen gave me seed money when I turned twenty-one. Which came with many, many lessons from him on how not to blow it.

"Which time?" I kiss her palm. "You know you're staying tonight, right? I can't let you drive like this. You're a mess."

"Thanks a lot."

"You know what I mean."

"I know I'm staying." Her tone is haughty, like she'd planned to stay all along. Hell, maybe she did. Maybe she's controlling my mind and I'm powerless to resist. I admit, there are worse ways to go. "How many times has it been broken?"

I look to the ceiling in thought. "Three and a half."

"Okay, tell me the story of the last time and a half."

"Both courtesy of my druggie father," I answer.

Her smile vanishes.

"He was trying to take our rent money from me. I was thirteen. If I'd given it to him, Mom and I would have been out on the street. January's cold in Chicago."

"I know," she whispers, running her finger down the bridge of my nose tenderly, tracing the bump. Her "I know" was less a confirmation and more of an *"I remember."*

"Chicago girl," I say. "I wondered."

Her eyes widen slightly. I'm right.

"I have one more question."

"That was number three." Abruptly, she sits up. Since my hand is on her back, I apply a bit of pressure. She doesn't get far.

"That was a statement. I didn't ask a question. And you didn't answer one."

She settles against me again, her body more rigid than before. She appears to instantly sober even though that's impossible given the number of tequila shots she's had.

"Who are you, really?" I didn't think she could stiffen more until her arms go as rigid as rebar. Maybe I shouldn't have asked, but that question has been niggling at me since meeting her that first time. I continue my observations despite her resemblance to a startled doe. "You're familiar with this life. Money doesn't impress you. You own expensive lingerie, at least one designer dress and you walk in the shoes I bought you like you were made to. You don't fit in middle class. You aren't intimidated by being plunked in the middle of a crowd of rich folks. You're confident. You're poised. You're an enigma, Vivian Vandemark."

Her throat works as she swallows. Her eyes go to my bare chest and she smooths her palm over my pecs while she considers what, I have no idea. Then I figure it out. She thinks I have something on her. Something *over* her. My mind flashes to our dinner at Villa Moneta. How she kept dodging my questions. How her guard was sky-high. Cagey, this one.

My former life was filled with secrets and danger. Now my life is under my control. I sense I'll never be able to truly know Vivian, and that in itself is a reason to pull away. But I want to know her more than I want to avoid the fallout *from* knowing her. Maybe it's my white-knight syndrome. Or pure sexual attraction. Too soon to tell.

"I'm a woman who used to have more than I have now," she admits, finally meeting my eyes. "I lost my wealth."

"How?"

"You're out of questions," she informs me.

I stay silent and hope for more. She gives it to me.

"A man took it from me. A man I trusted. A man I loved. He wasn't who I thought he was and when he left I was…bereft."

Bereft. Another word I'm painfully familiar with. I cup her jaw tenderly, filled with the need to pound whoever made her feel *bereft* into the dirt. "Who is he?"

Tears shimmer along the edges of her eyelids. Rage roars through me like fire. I want to slay dragons for her. I want to right every wrong done to her.

"You mean so you can have break number four?" She touches my nose again.

"It'd be worth it."

"He's dead. No need to defend my honor."

"And now you hate rich guys," I guess.

"They're not my favorite."

"Yet here you are." I grasp her hand in mine.

She laces our fingers together.

"This was inevitable." She kisses me on the mouth, releases my hand and then falls back onto the couch with a yawn. "Bring me a blanket, will you?"

"You're not sleeping on the couch."

But she's already dozing off. "Yes, I am."

I stand and tuck my arms beneath her, intending to lift her and carry her upstairs. She shoves my chest.

"Blanket. I mean it," are her final words before she conks out.

Chapter Twelve

Vivian

Usually I wake up with the sunlight streaming in through the window, but the next morning that isn't the case. I open my eyelids a crack and remember I fell asleep at Nate's house. My head pounds like a mid-song drum solo. I didn't mean to stay, or to indulge. It's too easy to laugh and drink with him.

Way to play it cool, Viv.

I push myself up. I'm not on the couch, and neither is Nate next to me. Unless he pristinely made the other side of the bed, I slept alone last night.

Copious light brightens the hallway. Not so in here. Black blinds are drawn over the windows, blocking the sun. I have no idea what time it is—my cell phone is nowhere to be found.

I make a pit stop to the attached master bathroom, taking advantage of a bottle of mouthwash stashed beneath the sink. I send a longing glance at the stone tiles and shower mounted directly overhead. No time for that. I need to go home.

With my face washed and my hair in a ponytail, I walk downstairs in Nate's T-shirt and come across him in the living room. He's wearing cotton drawstring pants and nothing else. With mussed bedhead and a sleepy smile, he couldn't look better.

"Morning," he greets, cup of coffee in hand.

"That smells good."

"Want one?"

"Yes."

"Cream? Sugar?"

"Cream."

"Odessa, coffee with cream for my guest," he calls over his shoulder. A woman's voice responds.

Instinctively I tug his shirt lower over my thighs. He bends to kiss my forehead.

"Where are my clothes?" I whisper.

"Hanging in the laundry room. I slept on the couch in case you were wondering."

"What happened to 'women don't go to my bed without me'?"

"I don't sound like that." He chuckles, a warm sound, as he hugs me against him. "Passed out women *do* go to bed without me."

"I didn't pass out," I say, my voice small.

"Okay." Another kiss lands on my forehead as a petite blond woman, probably in her early fifties, breezes into the room with a mug of coffee in hand. She hands it to me, her smile nonjudgmental. As if she's accustomed to finding half-naked women in Nate's house in the morning.

"Can I fetch you anything else, Mr. Owen?" she asks.

"No, we're good."

"Very well. Your breakfast is on the table, Ms. Vandemark. Have a good day." With that, Odessa leaves via the front door.

"What time is it?" I sip my coffee. Heavenly.

"Eleven."

"Eleven! Ow." I put my hand on my throbbing head. Maybe I did pass out last night. "I have to go."

"It's Slow Sunday, Viv."

"Is that a holiday or something?" I ask, massaging my temple.

"In my house it is. Stay and eat. I'll have you back to your car by this afternoon."

I shake my head, irked at myself for sleeping in. He picks up on my hesitation, takes my hand and walks me to the kitchen.

"You have to be somewhere?" He pulls a chair out from under a modern white kitchen table. The plate of scrambled eggs, roasted tomatoes and kale, and crisp potatoes looks and smells delicious.

"Apparently not." I set my coffee mug down and take my seat.

He plows his fork into his breakfast while I sip my coffee. It's so much better than the bargain brand I buy.

"Odessa seems accustomed to female guests," I say. Not out of jealousy, but observation.

"She's very professional."

At that non-answer, I grouse. His response was unsatisfying. Okay, I'm a *tad* jealous.

He takes a bite out of a slice of toast and watches me. Shirtless. Over breakfast. No wonder I slept with him. His potency is grotesque. I'm sort of mad at him about it.

"What's next week look like for you?" he asks.

"Oh, you know. The usual forty hours at CRBI." I take a bite of scrambled eggs. They're delicious, and topped with sliced fresh chives.

"Have lunch with me on Friday. I'll show you the progress at Grand Marin."

"Why?"

His eyebrows crawl up his forehead.

"Why?" He laughs, amused. "Why not?"

"I already slept with you. I don't require further dates." I stab a few potatoes with my fork. They are equally delicious.

"Afraid I'll penetrate the protective wall you built around yourself if we continue hanging out?"

Well. Doesn't that hint he already has? I sift through my

memories of last night. I didn't reveal my real last name or my parentage. I remember that much. But he is very, very curious. And protective. When I mentioned the man who left me in the poorhouse, Nate was ready to rumble.

"That's my past. Now's what matters."

The slide of his fork against his teeth sends a shiver down my spine. "Fair enough."

After I eat half my breakfast and am sipping a second cup of coffee, there's a knock at the door. Slow Sunday, my ass. This place is humming with activity and it's not even noon.

A young brunette woman enters through the foyer, dragging a rack of clothing with her. Women's clothing.

And here I am in my panties and Nate's T-shirt, peeking around the kitchen doorway.

"I hope this is sufficient." The brunette is younger than Odessa. She might be younger than me. She's pretty and rail-thin, dressed in black with a flexible tape measure draped around her neck.

"Viv," Nate calls. "Come see what Brandy has for you."

"Um. I'm not dressed," I call back, peeved.

"That's Brandy's job." He takes my hand and pulls me into the living room. To Brandy, he says, "Did you bring shoes as well?"

"Yes! Almost forgot. I'll grab them." She disappears and I take in the rack of designer jeans and summery dresses and shorts.

"What is going on?"

"You're not returning to your car in last night's clothes," he says.

"Ashamed of me?"

"No, but you might be ashamed of me." He smiles, almost sheepishly. I find it sort of irresistible. What is he doing to me?

"That's not necessary."

"I know." He kisses me as Brandy comes back inside with two large bags that, I assume, contain shoes.

It takes less than an hour for us to settle on my walk-of-shame outfit. She brought three sizes, including mine. No tape measure needed.

Nate palms her cash and helps her to her car by carrying the large shoe bags for her. She picked out shorts and a tee, high wedge sandals and jewelry. Nate insisted on sunglasses. He returns with a dress.

"This is for lunch on Friday," he informs me. "Brandy said it was perfect for you."

The safari-green wrap dress *is* perfect for me. It has pockets and pairs well with the wedge sandals.

"Nate, I can't accept—"

"You're welcome, Vivian. Come on. Let's shower."

I allow him to lead the way upstairs to his incredible bathroom I admired a few hours ago. Then he's stripping himself and me and throwing us both under the spray. Any insisting he doesn't have to buy me clothes, or attempts to pay him back, is met with kisses meant to shut me up.

And since his kisses are very good, we stay in the shower longer than necessary to wash ourselves…and each other.

"WHOA, THAT IS A GORGEOUS DRESS." Amber is out of her seat in an instant as I pass by her cubicle Friday morning. Today is the day of the lunch date. Despite the strong urge to be contrary and wear something from my closet, I wear the dress he bought me.

After years of not being treated, being treated feels nice, but it's about more than being spoiled. Nate and I were close last Saturday and I liked the closeness. Wearing a gift from him feels like he's close now. Is that completely corny?

"Thanks," I tell my coworker.

"It's very you."

She's spot-on. It is *very* me. I wonder if she also recognizes I don't fit in at CRBI. I wonder if Daniel noticed how comfortable I was at the event last weekend.

"What's the occasion?" Amber folds her arms over her chest.

"I'm having lunch with Nathaniel Owen."

"For professional reasons?" Her smile says she suspects not.

"Not exactly."

"You're seeing Owen today?" Daniel barks, interrupting our conversation. "In that case, I have something for you to give him. Come to my office."

I roll my eyes at Amber who makes an unsavory face. Then I follow Daniel and pick up an envelope of what he calls "boring forms" for Nate. As my hand grips the envelope, Daniel tugs it toward him. "Be careful. Men like Owen want one thing, Vivian."

"Sex?" I guess.

"Power," he answers, his face turning red. "Don't get caught up with him like some people do."

"Like you did?" He can't look me in the eye. The truth hurts. I get it. "I can take care of myself. You don't have to worry about me, *Dad*."

I turn and walk away. It's been a long time since I called anyone "Dad" and though I was being facetious, the word embeds itself into my skin like a stubborn splinter.

Halfway back to my cubicle, my cell phone rings on my desk. Walt's name lights the screen. It's a video call. I debate going outside, decide that's the best plan, and duck out the front door as I answer.

I'm on the sidewalk between the pizza place and a coffee shop when my brother's gaunt face fills the screen. It's not a new look for him. Walt's never held a lot of weight. Since rehab his color's better, but his slimness remains.

"Hey, sis."

"Everything okay?" It's my first question whenever he calls. He's usually in trouble. I don't see cop car lights or a police station in the background though, so maybe we're okay.

"Thirty days today," he tells me with a grin.

"Really?" He means thirty days sober. Hope blooms to life in my chest. And here I believed that hope had died with Mom.

"Yeah." He lifts a cigarette to his mouth, then holds the butt up to the screen. "My last vice. How's Dad?"

"Trapped in an urn." I take a perfunctory look around even though no one could possibly know Walt and I are talking about the one and only Walter Steele.

"Serves him right." My brother takes another drag. "I'm in the area."

"Oh?"

"Yeah. Pretty close, actually." His voice takes on a tinny, echo-y quality a moment before I notice a man on the crosswalk who looks a lot like my brother. Identical, in fact.

He stomps out his cigarette underfoot and I bounce over to him, heedless of who's watching. He catches me in a bony hug and I hold on to him for a long, long while.

"You ass!" I let go and swat him in the arm. He laughs, and the sound is heavenly. I missed him like crazy. Since he's rarely sober and himself, I've missed him for a long time. I hold on to moments like this one with both hands. "You look well."

He releases me and reaches into his pocket, dropping a bronze coin into my hand a moment later. I turn the coin over, running my thumb over the words "To Thine Own Self Be True."

"Whoa. Heavy."

"In every sense of the word," he assures me. "Are you doing anything right now? I thought we'd grab lunch. Or late breakfast. Or coffee. I'm not picky."

"Well…" His eyes go over my head to my place of employment. The Clear Ridge Bureau of Inspection. "I have a lunch break but otherwise I'm chained to my desk."

"Oh, how the mighty have fallen." He tucks my hair behind my ear and gives me a sad smile. I'm not sure if he's talking about him or me.

"Wait, shoot." I just remembered I have lunch with Nate today.

"What is it?"

"You know what? Nothing. It's nothing. How about there?" I point at the pizza place. "They have amazing calzones."

"That works. What time are you free?"

"Noon." I mentally make a note to call Nate and break our date.

After all, a thirty-day-sober Walt is a rare artifact.

Chapter Thirteen

Nate

I'm at Grand Marin, scowling while Beck updates me on the final touches for the units on Mulberry Street. Our live-work community is filled with fruity, herby street names. Mulberry, Juniper, Persimmon. The grassy area where there are sprinklers for the kids in the summer is Strawberry Fields.

"Are we on time?" I interrupt, distractedly squinting into the distance. I'm standing in front of the unit I'm using as an office while watching the cars on the road.

"We're on time," he tells me. He knows my values. Being late is unacceptable. William Owen taught me that. If your project is late, then your client is pissed. If your client is pissed, then you might not be rehired. If you're not rehired, then it's back to doing the hard part, which is convincing the client to take you on in the first place.

I took to excellence like a fish to water. Back when I was a kid, everything was acceptable. Lateness, stealing from my piggy bank, not having food in the cabinets… Chaos. I don't like chaos.

Vivian is late for our lunch appointment.

Very late.

I told myself I wasn't waiting for her, wasn't watching for her, but then both happened simultaneously. Not that *she's* chaos, but these circumstances tend to lead to it. I can't decide if my pride's been stepped on or if this is a premonition of Things to Come.

"You okay, Nate?"

"No. Someone was supposed to meet me here a while ago." I check my watch even though I don't need to. I've been checking the time every three minutes for the last forty-five of them. No, wait. Forty-*six*.

Beck whistles long and low. He knows I don't like to be late or stood up. I wonder which one my "date" has done. Time to pay Vivian a visit.

Across the street from CRBI, I park and feed a meter. At the crosswalk, I freeze when I spot her embracing some guy.

My fists ball at my sides as a flicker of the old rage I used to feel daily sparks to life. It's unhealthy, that rage. I need to move the needle from rage to disappointment if I have any hope of not losing my temper.

Is he the guy who ripped her off? She told me he was dead, but people say lots of things to escape or cover for their past. I know someone, intimately, who encouraged their own mother to sign over her parental rights to the Owen family. And then told everyone she died.

We do what we have to do, is what I'm saying.

The light changes and I do a neat jog to cross the street. When she sees me, her eyes widen with alarm and she drops the man's hand.

I stalk toward her, upset and borderline betrayed. The guy she's with is tall, rangy, no match for me. Especially when I'm this pissed off. If he hurt her, so help me, God, I'll—

"Nate." Her voice holds more than one note of surprise. Did she think I'd let her stand me up and not check on her? Did this guy do the same to her in the past?

"Who the hell are you?" I ask him. No sense in wasting my anger on her.

He smiles, zero caution in his eyes. Zero fear too. He strikes me as someone who's accustomed to being on the wrong end of situations. I immediately reassess when he offers his hand.

"Walt St—"

"My brother, Walt," Vivian interrupts. Unlike her brother's, her smile is a touch disingenuous. "Walt, this is Nathaniel Owen, he's a builder in the area. We do a lot of work with the Owens at CRBI."

I shake her brother's hand and he nods. "That's cool. Good to meet you, Nathaniel. I'll let you get back to it, V."

"There's a pan of lasagna in the fridge," she calls as he crosses the street the way I just came. Her worry is palpable as she watches her brother walk away. Reminds me of the way I used to watch my parents and wish they'd get better. Dangerous, that hope. It comforts you when it shouldn't and leaves you damaged when the balloon finally pops. And most of the time, it pops.

"I didn't know you have a brother."

"He lives in Atlanta." She turns guarded eyes on me. "He's visiting."

"You could have called to cancel lunch."

"I meant to. I had a busy day and then Walt stopped in and… He has a way of taking all my attention."

I want to forgive her. Family can be stressful. And hers is a doozy.

"Are you safe?" My savior complex emerges again.

"From Walt? Yes, of course."

Anger. I recognize the emotion as if I transferred it to her. She's pulling away, building her wall again. "I have to go back to my desk. I already stayed out fifteen minutes longer than I should have."

She turns, but I catch her hand. She lets me keep her there, and in that brief wordless exchange I sense she wants me to hold her and tell her it's going to be okay.

"Dinner tonight," I tell her. "My place."

"But my brother—"

"Is a grown man. He can reheat lasagna by himself."

"I'm not sure how long he's staying, Nate."

Part of me wants to insist. But I know better than most that family pulls rank.

"I'll check in on him and maybe come over after, okay?"

"Okay," I agree, even though that "maybe" was in there and she stood me up once already. But I'm hanging on to it because she owes me. Not only a meal, but also an explanation. Specifically, about why her brother is the infamous Walter Steele's namesake.

Now I know exactly what Vivian "Vandemark" has been hiding.

Vivian

Nate was wrong about my brother. Yes, Walt is *physically* a grown man, but he's not capable of caring for himself. He's been under the care of nannies, drivers, house managers, and rehabilitation centers for most of his life. So was I, but I also ran a chunk of our father's company.

That ghost haunts me. I was co-captain yet completely in the dark. I don't know what irks me more, that I didn't notice the discrepancies or that my father didn't trust me enough to confide in me.

I open my front door and call out. No answer. I check the rest of the rooms for my brother even though the cavernous feel of the place tells me no one's there. I look in the fridge and find the three portions of lasagna I'd separated into glass containers this morning. If he was here, he didn't eat.

I call his phone.

No answer.

I stare numbly at my father's urn before lifting the lid on the canister next to it. It reads "tea," of which it holds a lot. Beneath the netted bags I have two hundred dollars in cash.

After a brief check, I see I'm incorrect.

Had. I had two hundred dollars in cash.

"Dammit, Walt." I try my brother's phone again. A recording informs me his voicemail box isn't set up. I text him next.

Don't use. Whatever you do. I'll give you all the money you need.

It's a desperate plea, but I type in, *You're thirty days sober. I love you.*

I scrape my keys off the counter and rush for the door, nearly bowling over the man in the doorway.

Walt.

I blink at him dumbly.

He's holding four large reusable grocery bags, barely. "Hey. Heard the phone but my hands were full." He passes me to set the bags down on the kitchen counter while I stare at him like he's back from the dead. He might as well be. When I noticed cash missing, I pictured him facedown in an alley or holed up in some meth house in a seedy, falling-down neighborhood.

I peek into one of the bags and find a lot of fruit. I never buy this much fresh fruit.

"You didn't have a juicer," he tells me. "Now you do."

"That's why you took the money from the canister?" I ask as he pulls a large box from one of the grocery sacks. "To buy a juicer?"

"Yeah." His face falls as he absorbs my expression. "Jesus, Viv. Did you think I stole it from you?"

"Well, technically you did." I fold my arms. Disappointment isn't a foreign emotion in my life and I've been disappointed plenty by Walt. I know he's sick and he can't help it, but the effect is the same on me.

"I know." He looks at his shoes. "I thought I'd get a job here. Stay close. Not with you. Not for long, anyway. Maybe you could float me a deposit for first month's rent—"

"That money is earmarked for rehab. But you can stay with me for a little while. And if you're ready, until you find a job." I guard our nest egg like a mama eagle. The "egg" is the last of our wealth and if I have to spend every dime of it to keep him alive, I will. That doesn't include apartment deposits. I want to believe he's conquered his addiction. That fairy tales come true. That love wins. But it's so damn hard after what we've been through.

"I'm ready." He kisses my forehead. Then he starts unboxing the juicer. "Do you want one?"

"I, uh, I have a date." Sort of.

"Let me guess. Nathaniel Owen."

"Perceptive."

"He looked at me like he wanted to pound me into a greasy spot on the sidewalk," he says. "I have to admit, I like that he's looking out for you."

"I can look after myself."

My brother, a handful of packing plastic in one hand, squeezes my arm with the other. "So can I, sis. I won't stay long. I swear. Just long enough to make myself a respectable citizen."

"That could take *years,*" I tease. It feels good to tease him. It's a sign things aren't in a downward spiral for once.

A bubble of hope rises to the surface. And, oh, it feels good. And weird. And terrifying. Who knew one feeling could be so many things?

"You're moving to Clear Ridge? What about Atlanta?" I ask.

"I left a lot of old friends in Atlanta." Junkies like him, he means. He pulls the shiny juicer from its home. "I stashed my clothes in the room you're using as an office. I'll sleep on the couch."

"That's fine." I let out a breath of relief. For right now he's okay, talking about sleeping on the couch and preparing to juice himself a healthy drink. It's hard to trust things are okay after they weren't for so long, but I'm getting there.

"If you're sure you're okay without me..." I mutter, unable to let go all the way.

"You have cable?"

"Netflix."

"Even better." He whistles while he rinses off the many parts of the juicer. I consider his cheery state and weigh it against my own unexpected desire to see Nate. "I'm fine, Viv. *Go.*"

"If you're sure," I repeat.

"Get out of here."

I decide to trust him, scraping my keys off the table and grabbing my purse.

Chapter Fourteen

Vivian

I knock on Nate's door, expecting him to answer.

Odessa answers instead. "Right on time, Ms. Vandemark. Don't worry, I'll be out of your way in a flash." She's wiping her hands on a kitchen towel. We had a house staff when I lived with my parents. Muriel made the best enchiladas in the whole wide world. Dad stole her entire savings and retirement funds. He convinced her to invest with him and promised to 10X her money. The last time I saw her she was in court shooting daggers at me from her eyes. When a good woman like Muriel turns on you, there's a decent chance God's not your biggest fan, either.

"It smells wonderful in here," I tell Odessa.

"It should. I've been cooking all afternoon." She waves the towel to invite me to follow. She's not formal, which suits Nate's style. "Prime rib, garlic mashed potatoes and French-style green beans await you."

I set my purse on a chair in the living room. Tilting my chin, I take in the tall, open ceilings, the black-framed glass separating this room from the staircase that leads to the bedrooms. I smile at the memory of what Nate and I did in this room, and upstairs in the shower. Odessa slips back into the kitchen. She's humming.

I'm still wearing the green dress and wedge sandals. I considered changing, but this outfit was meant to be worn on our lunch date and I figured wearing it to dinner was the least I could do to make up for leaving him hanging.

"Decide to show up after all?" Nate comes downstairs in jeans and a snug T-shirt molding his firm chest. I've never seen him in jeans before and the look is, well…it's fantastic. Worn denim and sneakers suit him. His upper body was built for gray cotton. His hair is damp and combed against his head like he's freshly showered.

"Are you upset with me?" I ask, a little nervous he might be.

"You worried?" He comes closer, and I don't answer, running my hand over his chest instead. He embraces me and we stand there, soaking each other in. He's not supposed to feel this comforting and I'm not supposed to be this needy. I can't help it. Today my brother stopped *and* restarted my heart.

"I'll take my leave." Odessa clears her throat from the foyer. "I trust you can handle serving dinner."

"I can. Thank you." He watches her go and I watch him. His eyes crinkle in the corners, sexy. Comforting. His mouth loses its smile when he looks at me.

"I'm sorry for not canceling lunch," I blurt out. I owe him that.

"I understand."

Funnily enough he sounds like he understands. He doesn't seem angry that I didn't join him for lunch, even though I'd have deserved it.

"Wine?" He releases me and walks to the bar.

"I'd love a glass."

He pours us each one. I take a sip and let out a low hum of approval. It's a fruity red. "This is very good."

"It better be after what I paid for it."

The men I used to date liked to brag about what they paid for wine. They'd die before admitting it was overpriced. "You don't talk like a billionaire."

"You do."

I cradle my glass against my chest, my heart thudding against my breastbone. His was a loaded statement, and paired with an unerring stare feels borderline accusatory. "Do I?"

"You're Walter Steele's daughter."

My face goes cold and I literally take a step away from him. I don't know why. It isn't like I'm going to make a run for it. I'm not a felon. He's not a cop with a warrant for my arrest. The urge to flee is there all the same.

"I recognized your brother when you interrupted his introduction. I remember him from when the press was covering your father's court case. There wasn't as much focus on you." He sets his glass aside and plunges his hands into his front pockets. So casual.

Meanwhile, my heart is racing, my palms sweating. I haven't been confronted since I changed my name. I thought I'd escaped my past. But here it is, ironically arriving with Walt.

"You were the good kid," Nate continues. "Walt made for a better story. Drug addict. Alcoholic. In and out of several rehab joints since he was a teen."

"You've done your research," I say carefully.

"When I saw him across the street I thought he was the guy who originally hurt you. That you'd lied to me about him being dead. I had to make sure you were safe."

"That's not your job," I snap. Habit. I'm actually flattered by Nate's concern.

"You're right. You're not my job," he agrees, sounding perturbed. "You're not my anything."

I hold my breath and nod slowly, trying not to feel the sting of those words. Part of me has known all along I'm alone. Why should I expect Nate to be different?

I set my wineglass on the bar next to his. "What now? Are you going to try and bribe me or are you going to be a decent human being and keep my identity to yourself? I don't have a lot of pull at the bureau, so I'm not sure I can help you. Daniel's petty. He'll watch me like a hawk once he knows I'm lying, if he doesn't fire me first."

"You changed your name legally. You're not lying."

That's true, technically.

"You didn't lie to me, either. The man who hurt you is dead. You were talking about your father." He takes a breath. "I'm not interested in using this information against you, Vivian. I want you to know you're safe with me. If anyone understands taking on a new identity and living a life a world away from where he came from, it's me."

Reassurance is a strange sensation. I haven't been able to count on anyone for a long time.

"I lied to you though." He spills a bit more wine into his glass. "My mother is alive. After my dad OD'd, my mom started using. I was fifteen and in juvie at the time. One of the counselors there had a brother who owned a shopping plaza built by the Owens. That counselor saw an opportunity for me to win the foster-kid lottery. I could have a new life with the Owens, who were looking to adopt a teenage boy. We're the hardest kids to home."

I stare at him, envisioning an angry fifteen-year-old Nate, and my heart squeezes. He's suddenly a whole person, not only the object of my infatuation. The shift is jarring. I wanted what we had to stay on the surface, to be a release valve for the pressure building inside me like a dormant volcano for years. He's just proven he's more than that. I'm not prepared.

"I went to my mom and asked her to give up her parental rights. It wasn't hard to convince her, especially after she was offered a hefty sum of money." He looks away as he mumbles, "Hell, I guess she's still alive. She was three years ago. I stopped checking on her. It hurt too much."

His pain echoes in the caverns of my soul. I can relate to feeling rejected. To feeling like you don't matter.

My thoughts circle to the sum of money he mentioned. I don't have to wonder where that came from. The Owens. Obviously. Rich people pay to have their way, or to weasel out of any predicament that doesn't serve them. I know all too well.

"How very lucky for you." My voice is hard. Nate's one of them and he knows the truth about me. I have to maintain my guard, for my own safety. Why else would he tell me what he knew if he didn't want something from me? I doubt he's merely commiserating.

"You're running from yourself," he says. "I recognize the tactic. Thing is, you can't escape yourself. Wherever you go, there you are. I'm still a street kid from Chicago who's had his nose broken three and a half times. You're still a wealthy woman from the same city who believes she has to suffer for the sins of her father."

"My father stole from good people."

"Yes, but you didn't."

"I worked for him."

There's a pause while he soaks this in. "Did he share his plans with you? Did he tell you what he was doing?"

I shake my head. "No, but I didn't notice, either."

"You were twenty-three years old."

Same thing my therapist told me. I sensed disdain in her voice. I don't think Marissa blamed me, but she had a hard time looking me in the eye knowing what my dad did.

"You deserve a life not defined by Walter Steele, Senior. Making thirty thou a year in a city building isn't going to right the scales."

"What about you building live-works to house and employ others when you couldn't keep a roof over your own family's head? I'm not the only one attempting to right my family's wrongs."

He drinks his wine instead of commenting.

I gesture around at the house I'm standing in. "How is this you being true to your roots?"

"My *having* has nothing to do with others not having. I'm not your father. I didn't steal to gain. I earned my wealth. I worked for it. I'm hustling my ass off, and in case you haven't noticed, I work for the good guys."

"The Owens, who paid your mother to go away? Are they 'good guys'?" I'm lashing out, and a ping in the center of my chest warns I'm being unfair. I don't think I care. Anger feels better than fear.

His eyes darken. Pointing at the floor to make his point, he steps closer to me. "The Owens paid my mother's rent for a year, stocked her up with groceries. She took it like a severance package and had no problem saying goodbye to her son." Pain ekes into his voice. "There *are* good guys in this world."

The Owens sound like good guys. I've never known a rich person not out to build his own portfolio. Which says a lot about the people my parents consorted with.

"I care about you." Nate's proclamation is simple. He doesn't wait for me to respond or act like he's expecting one. "You can trust me. No matter what happens. I wanted you to know."

The finality of his statement hints the ball is in my court. I can stay, basking in the company of one of the few people in my life who knows the truth and doesn't hate me for it, or I can walk away and leave the most exciting, intriguing man I've ever met.

Funny, both sound like arguments to stay.

Nate

Vivian talks between bites during dinner. Once I blew up the dam, she had a lot to say about the Steeles. About the trial. About her position at the company that eventually folded under a mountain of falsified financials.

I listen, rapt, while eating the finest piece of beef I've had in a long time. Could be the quality of the meat, could be the company. This woman is under my skin, and I can't say I don't like it.

And yes, I hear you accusing me of saving Vivian for my own selfish needs. That my savior complex is a beast and it needs regularly fed. Proving there is good in the world is my mission as much as housing people. I refuse to believe the world is shit. I like to think the people who selfishly take and take until they die in prison are the exception, not the rule.

I want Vivian to know there are good people. That I am one. Hell, maybe that *is* my savior complex talking. But is it bad if we both stand to gain from it? Insight. Sex. Connection.

"I held a few jobs as Vivian Steele," she's saying, "but inevitably my character came into question when my coworkers and higher-ups figured out whose daughter I was and stopped trusting me instantly. I didn't have a choice but to start over."

"Why here?"

"It isn't Chicago, where everyone knows the Steele name. And Clear Ridge isn't so small that everyone gossips." She chews a bite of steak and swallows, her delicate throat working. "Why do you live here?"

I set down my fork and reach for my wine. "The Owens are here. I always wanted a real family."

"So did I."

We share a tender moment. The walls hiding her have fallen, briefly. Like me, she was once a scared kid who wanted to be loved. Instead she was disregarded. Used. Slotted as a cog in the machine fueled by her parents' betrayal.

Also like me. Just in a totally different income bracket. Interesting how the tables have turned.

Walt, her brother, was a cog too, but he's not as strong as Vivian. He cracked under the pressure while his sister achieved her way through a rebirth.

"What now?" I ask.

"You mean now that you know who I am?"

"Yeah. It seems like you to run." I don't like the idea of her leaving without a goodbye—a probability.

She laughs, maybe at my audacity. "Running is an interesting word. I call it survival."

"Same thing."

Her smile is tight. The shutters fall and her expression blanks. "I have to go."

She stands and tosses the cloth napkin onto her plate. I wondered how hard I could push before she left. Now I know.

"Dinner was lovely," she says. "I appreciate your discretion."

She walks to the living room and I follow, catching her as she pulls her car keys from her purse. Rather than saying goodbye and fleeing, or "fuck you" and fleeing, she stares at me for a beat. Then two.

"I'm trying, you know." Her jaw stiffens but her voice shakes. "I've fought for years to become strong. It's harder than it looks. I wasn't looking for anything, for anyone. I was fine on my own. Then you gave me those damn shoes and I was reminded of my mom. You treated me like I mattered."

My brow bends in sympathy. Of course she matters. And there should have been a line of people around the block telling her every day for the last six years how much she matters.

"My past is attacking. Walt is back. He seems okay and that's even harder to trust. I'm so goddamn worried I can't..." An exhale stutters from her lips and she finishes on a whispered, "I can't hold everything together indefinitely."

"I know." My simple agreement causes her facade to crack. It's a slow deterioration.

First her arm drops, then her shoulder. Her purse strap slips. She makes a grab for it and misses. By the time it hits the floor upside down, her face has crumbled with it. She lowers to her knees and I'm right there with her.

A quiet, but heart-wrenching sob ekes from her throat. I want her to know she doesn't have to be strong all the time. It's impossible to be strong all the time. As a tough kid with a thrice broken nose and an eyebrow full of stitches, I learned anger only masks pain. Everyone has their breaking point.

Instead of giving that speech, I reach for her. She comes with only a little encouragement. Her arms tighten around my neck. Her sobs are loud in my ears. I hold her, gripping her tightly as we stand together.

"I have you," I tell her. Once upon a time I needed someone to count on desperately. The Owens were there for me.

Vivian needs someone to count on now. It's me. And I just as desperately need her to count on me.

Chapter Fifteen

Vivian

The last guy I dated who I considered a serious boyfriend was Charlie Barnett.

Charlie was a lawyer. Slick, well-bred, good-looking. He'd made partner at his firm and we were both up-and-comers. When the news broke of my father's lies, he told me I'd hang for my father's crimes.

He turned his back on me so fast I was surprised he didn't have whiplash. We were together a year and a half. We shared a lot of hopes and dreams and dinners and sex. We'd talked about marriage and moving in together at one point.

Even when things were good, Charlie never handled me as carefully as Nate handles me now.

When he scooped me off the floor I gave him the weight of my body and my grief. Instinctively, I knew he could take it. Honestly? I'm glad he knows the truth.

Usually I'd die before I let anyone see me cry—how weak. With Nate there was never another option. Like it was inevitable we'd have sex the night I came home with him, so was the breakdown after he learned from whose loins I'd sprung.

We're on the couch, me on his lap, my nose against his neck. I like being here and not only because he smells like the ocean. I like his wide hands, hands that have fought and pummeled lesser men. On me they're gentle. Careful.

I'm being held like I might break. To be fair, I just did.

I'm not crying now. I'm *luxuriating* in him. With my fingers in his hair. My lips resting against the strong pulse beating in his neck.

He turned on music while we were sitting here and the song playing has a soft, soothing beat. I don't recognize the artist, but I like his voice. I like Nate's voice too. He's humming low in his throat and my lips tingle from the vibrations.

My plan was to move to Clear Ridge, find a job, find an apartment, and keep my head down. I wasn't supposed to make friends or find a man who consumed my every other thought. I wasn't supposed to connect with anyone. I did a good job for months, but now...

Now.

Pressing my lips against his pulse, I kiss and then suckle the skin of his neck.

His arms tighten around my body. His hum fades into a low growl. I open my mouth and taste him again, scraping my teeth along his neck. His hand slides beneath my dress to cup the back of my thigh.

We stay in that position for several minutes. Me kissing his throat, his palm on my leg. By the time his hand slides higher, I move to straddle his lap and press my lips to his.

His mouth.

So much better than any I've ever had on mine. So much headier. So much more powerful. *Irresistible.* Not that resistance was an option. Either I'm not that strong or he's that good.

There are good guys.

His words echo through my mind as I tangle my tongue with his. Is he a good rich guy? An exception to the rule?

His fingers unknot the tie holding my wrap dress closed. He

flattens his hand on my stomach and lays me on my back. Then I lose his mouth. I'd complain, but he roughly moves the cup of my bra and takes my nipple on his tongue—so much better. When his hand slips into my panties, I'm wet and ready for him.

I arch my back and shut my eyes.

Whatever happens, this makes everything worth it.

He knows who I am. And he wants me. *Still.* It's a superpower I haven't possessed before.

"We never make it to the bedroom," I mumble as he kisses a trail down my belly. He yanks my panties down my legs.

"Next time," he promises, dragging his teeth along the sensitive skin of my stomach.

I smile. I like the sound of next time.

His tongue delves into my folds, seeking and finding the perfect spot. He remembered. I widen my legs to accommodate his shoulders, giving myself over to him. He knows what he's doing. He's talented at making me come, at making me feel on a deeper level than I've allowed for a long, long time.

I'm naked with him, even when I'm mostly dressed. I'm slightly skeptical about trusting him implicitly, but I shelve those worries in favor of momentary bliss.

He takes me there in record time. The shimmer of my orgasm washes over me like summer rain, leaving me damp and panting.

"I like those yeses." His voice is low and reverent as he makes his way to my breasts again.

I didn't realize I spoke. I laugh, and that feels as decadent as the orgasm.

Nate is over me, hooking my leg over his hip. His lips first kiss one of my eyelids, then the other. Then my nose. He smells like musk. Like sex. Like me. How strangely erotic.

"Open your eyes." His tone is commanding. When I do, I am assaulted by his.

"Your eyes are so blue." Dumb, right? But that's what I say.

"Don't look away." He rolls a condom on without breaking

eye contact. I do as he asks and keep my gaze on him. Not a hardship. He's nice to look at.

"Watch me."

I nod and nearly break my promise when he slides into me. I accept him inch by inch, reveling in the way he fills me—to the brim, just like last time. Unlike last time, his pace is slower. More intentional. His expression is pained like he's struggling to keep his own eyes open.

We could shut each other out and blindly take what we need. This degree of intimacy isn't what either of us bargained for.

He squeezes my hip, sucks in a breath. His release is on the precipice. I clench my inner muscles around his glorious cock and watch a struggle erupt on his face.

Power. I have it.

After he shuts his eyes briefly, they land on me again. There's a resolve that wasn't there before. Slowly, he draws out of me and then plunges in slower.

"Vivian," he warns when my world goes black. "Eyes on mine."

I wrench my eyes open and hold his in challenge. Rising to meet him. He's all I see. He's all I hear. The beats of the music blend in with his labored breaths and my quickened huffs of excitement. I barely hear the lyrics beyond the sound of my own heartbeat sloshing in my ears.

His control slips. I place my hand on his cheek. He's moving frantically, his teeth bared, the tendons in his neck tight. He's a beautiful sight.

"Give it to me," I breathe.

He takes one of my wrists and then the other, trapping them over my head.

"You first." He ducks his head and suckles my nipple while stroking into me. Harder. Faster. He holds me down and I feel powerless and safe at the same time.

I like it.

A few more deep strokes is all it takes for him to wring

another orgasm from me. It flows like warm honey, spilling out and leaving me drained yet full. He's not far behind. A low groan works its way up his throat. He's coated in my pleasure, and I squeeze him again, milking his release from him easily. The hand around my wrists releases.

Spent, he sags on the couch, his arm shaking as he holds his weight on one elbow to keep from crushing me.

I skim my fingernails down his back and he gives me a little more of his weight. The pounding of our pulses slam our chests and where we're still connected. He drops a slightly sweaty kiss on my neck and I wrap him in my arms.

"Thank you," I whisper. For knowing me. Believing me. For sticking with me. For making sure he gave me what I needed when I needed it. Emotional after that soul-crushing act, a tear trickles down my cheek and into my hair.

He presses a firm kiss to my mouth, stroking my cheek with his thumb. "Anytime."

I smile as another tear falls.

We lie there for a long, long while, neither of us in a hurry to pull apart. Or maybe, not capable of it.

Chapter Sixteen

Vivian

Once again I wake in darkness in Nate's bed.

Like last time, he's not next to me. He was, though. I have memories of rolling over and bumping into his big body. He took up a good portion of the king-sized bed we slept in, and nudging a thigh or an arm every so often was nice.

After our interlude on the couch, I sent a text to Walt letting him know I keep the coffee in the freezer and wouldn't be coming home. He texted back, *Got it.*

Walt is safe. I am safe. What a strange synchronicity.

Maybe we're due some good luck.

I sit up and my foot kicks something at the bottom of the bed. I fumble on the nightstand for the remote and press a button to raise the black window coverings. The room fills with light and my eyes slowly adjust to focus on the item at the end of the bed.

A box.

Large, cream-colored, and tied with a black ribbon.

I smile. The hope balloon I thought was inflated to capacity inflates a tiny bit more. My mind warns that hope is dangerous and I should protect myself. I tell it to fuck off as I untie the satin ribbon.

Inside the box beneath the tissue paper is a pair of sneakers, shorts and a T-shirt. Name brand. High end. The card resting on top of the shirt matches the box, cream-colored stock with black piping. The note reads: *Nate asked me to pick out some casual clothes for you. I hope you enjoy this short set. More to come! Brandy.*

That man. I shake my head. I am guessing any arguments to pay him back or refuse will be met with resistance. I stroke the soft cotton of the T-shirt and smile, deciding to accept the gift at face value.

I take a quick shower and brush my hair into a ponytail. Then I dress in my new duds and practically skip downstairs. I pause when I hear voices. Male voices. Nate's and one—no, two —others.

I slow my descent as I catch a glimpse of the men in the living room. One of them is suited with dark brown hair and a neatly trimmed beard. His scowl seems permanent. The other man is wearing a checked shirt and trousers and shiny shoes that cost about fifteen hundred bucks a pair. He notices me first and grins. He has a full, gracious smile. The other man doesn't smile. I wonder if he's capable.

"There she is." Nate's smile is easy. Not as bright as the other man's, but ten times more welcoming.

"I slept in." I step into the living room. "Your bedroom's a cave."

"And he's the bear," the smiling man says.

"Vivian Vandemark," Nate says, "Meet my brothers. Archer." He gestures to the scowling man. "And this happy son of a bitch is Benji."

I remember him mentioning Archer, the biological Owen, which might explain his air of superiority. Benji looks as grateful as a rescue dog with a home and I warm to him instantly.

"Nice to meet you," I say.

Nate tugs me against his wall of a body and I rest my hand on his chest. Archer watches this with an unreadable expression. Benji is still grinning. Both of them are stunningly attractive, albeit in incredibly different ways.

"We should head out," Archer says. And then, belying his standoffish expression, offers a polite, "Will you be joining us, Vivian?"

I look up at Nate who's looking down at me, eyebrows raised.

"Up to you," he tells me. "Brunch at LaVera's."

"That sounds fancy. And I look—"

"Stunning," Benji tells me. "Come with us."

ON LAVERA'S BACK PATIO, at a white-clothed table covered in white plates and several glasses per place setting, I'm introduced to Nate's adoptive parents.

Will and Lainey have dark hair and olive-toned skin. Italian, I'd bet. Benji's darker golden coloring and black hair hints at Middle Eastern heritage. Archer, with his father's green eyes and his mother's cheekbones, definitely skews Owen.

"So lovely to meet you, Vivian," Lainey says. William stands while I take my seat and I amend that the width of his shoulders resembles Nate's. If you weren't looking closely, you might assume the boys were Owens, born and bred. Even Benji, whose build is slighter than Will's, resembles Lainey in a way.

I look like my mom. Walt looks more like Dad. We were a real family and as flawed as they come. To see a patchwork family like the Owens and feel none of the tension present at my own family's breakfast table is…strange.

Maybe Nate was right, and the Owens are good people.

"Nate tells us you're an inspector," Will says conversationally as he spreads his napkin in his lap.

"Not yet," I answer.

"But she tried to shut you down," Archer interjects.

Enter: turmoil. I bristle in expectation.

"She did," Nate replies easily. The shouting I anticipated doesn't come. "The day I took down the drywall with a sledgehammer."

"Well, no wonder you fell for him," Lainey says as light as you please.

I jerk my head at Nate, who takes his gaze from the menu to offer me a wink. "She didn't flinch. Which is why I asked her to dinner."

A waiter silently delivers a round of mimosas before leaving.

"He was looking for a friend at the bureau. Little did he know he was wooing the one with the least amount of power," I say, joining the banter.

"I was wooing you?" Nate turns his head and my cheeks grow warm.

"An eight-course chef's menu," I mutter under my breath, but his mother hears me.

"We taught you well, son."

"Yes," Nate says, giving her a look of unfiltered gratitude. "You did."

"I'm looking at Miami next," Archer interrupts, evidently tired of the drippy sentimentalism. From there the conversation shifts to business, despite Lainey's request of "no business talk during meals." Will and Benji rationalize they're in public, not at home, and LaVera's is a neutral space.

Contrarily, every meal at the Steele household revolved around business. We might as well have eaten at a boardroom table. The private plans of Walter Steele never came up, but everything else was fair game. My mother usually stared at her plate forlornly, shut off from the family and halfway into a bottle of wine. I wasn't sympathetic of her plight then. I regret that now. When I was very young, eight or nine, she was present. A year or so later, she developed a habit of foisting her children off on the house staff. By the time I reached my twenties, I decided she was the most selfish person alive. That was before we found out about Dad.

In the quiet darkness of my heart I wonder if she was incapable of reaching out. If the grief that ultimately consumed her left no room for my brother or me. In that case, her having us cared for was admirable. She couldn't be there for us so she found people who could.

Even with my grievances, I had an easier childhood than Nate.

He's talking animatedly with his hands about Grand Marin. He's proud. One glance around the table and I can tell the Owens are proud of him. He's so alive in this moment. I envy him, and the passion he has for his work. I used to be passionate about my father's company too. Look what I ended up being a part of.

I'm halfway through my eggs Benedict when Benji turns to me. "Are you coming to the grand opening of Club Nine, Vivian?"

"Um..."

"I haven't invited her yet, Benji, but thanks," Nate grumbles.

"I can tell by her hesitation and your deer-in-the-headlights reaction. No pressure," Benji tells me, and he seems sincere.

"Every time we finish a project there's a party," Nate informs me.

"We celebrate often," Will says. "More work is always around the corner. It's tempting to move on to the next project without first paying homage to the one you finished."

"It's a bad habit," Lainey says. "You have to be grateful for what you've accomplished. Don't you agree, Vivian?"

I don't like lying. I rarely do, save fudging my identity for the sake of not becoming the town pariah. I *don't* agree. I'm not grateful for the role I played in my former life. How can I be when it led to so many others losing their livelihoods, their savings, their homes? It led to me losing my boyfriend and half my family. The house staff that helped raise me turned on me as easily as they did my father.

Karma, as they say, is a bitch.

"I don't like to look back." Hopefully my response is vague enough to be acceptable. Lainey waits for me to expound. I don't. She doesn't call me on it, which I appreciate.

"Now that my brother has stolen my thunder," Nate says, turning in his chair to face me, "you're invited."

"Grand opening for VIPs and family only," Archer supplies.

"Sounds fancy. I have just the shoes for it." I don't have to turn my head to feel Nate's approving smile.

An hour later, we're in his Tesla when he turns from the restaurant's parking lot. "You did well in there."

"No thanks to you. You not only surprised me with your brothers, but you sprang parents on me too."

"The Owens are—"

"Good guys. I know, I know." I consider the easy conversation and the way Will listened when his sons spoke. "They're supportive of you. All of you."

"They are."

"They don't seem to favor Archer, even though he's their biological son. It must bother him." It'd have to, wouldn't it? I was overlooked by my parents for years, for reasons other than adopted siblings, but it'd have to feel similar.

"I'm not going to say Arch didn't have his share of teenage angst, and God knows I came to that house resisting stability. But, we adjusted. We've had a lot of years to learn who we are—all of us. It's not wrinkle-free, no matter how well-adjusted we seem, but Ben and Arch, and the Owens, have my back."

"And you have theirs."

"Yes."

"I smell white knight syndrome," I tease.

"I like to think of it as a savior complex. But if you find a dragon you want me to slay, baby, say the word." His murmured "baby" coils around my heart and squeezes. He takes my hand, resting our linked hands on my leg. Our interwoven fingers are an attractive sight, his thick digits and my narrow, slender ones. His blunt, wide nails and my painted pink ones.

"What are your plans for the rest of the day?" he asks.

"Go home. Check on Walt. House chores. The usual weekend things."

He's already shaking his head. "That's no good."

"Why not?" I ask through a laugh.

"I want you to come home with me. Which is fucked-up, Vivian." He slants me a look hinting he's only half kidding. "I *like* living alone. I like to work. I usually go to a job site on weekends and stay up too late agonizing over details to ensure we're done on time or early. Then came you."

He's too much. I'm flattered. I can't help it. I'm only human. "And I'm ruining your work ethic?"

"You're ruining me."

It's a touch too honest for the interior of the car. There's nowhere to escape. The air conditioning blows on my face, chilling the sweat on my brow.

"I'm sorry." I don't know what else to say.

He stops at a red light and leans toward me. "Look at me."

With little choice in the confines of the small car, I turn my head.

"It wasn't a complaint. Kiss me."

I hesitate. The light turns green. The car behind us honks. He doesn't move. "Vivian."

I set my lips to his for a brief kiss, but he cups my jaw and holds me there. The other car swerves around us, the driver yelling as he drives by. Nate lingers another second before taking the wheel.

"Thank you."

"Welcome," I say, touching my fingers to my lips to hide my smile. He wears his shamelessly. He really is too much.

Chapter Seventeen

Vivian

It's been just over two weeks since Walt came to town and I'm feeling the tininess of my apartment big time. I attended two AA meetings with him until he begged me to stop shadowing him. His exact words were, "V. I've got this."

He does seem to have it under control. I used to worry about him incessantly. Since he's lived in Atlanta, I've toned it down some, but now I'm regressing.

In other developments, he's been job hunting but hasn't had any luck. I asked Daniel if he could use anyone at the bureau. He wasn't keen. Walt's work record is sketchy and rehab doesn't look good on a resumé.

"I was checking into this nonprofit yesterday," I call to my brother who's sacked out on the couch watching TV. I'm watching my toaster oven slowly brown three slices of bread. "They help recovering addicts find work. It might be worth looking into."

When he doesn't answer, I peek around the corner. He's in shorts and a T-shirt, looking tired and worse, bored. Boredom isn't good for an addict.

"Walt?"

"Yeah, sounds good."

I sigh. I've been splitting my time between Nate's house and here, but this weekend Nate is traveling to Miami with Archer to check out that potential job site. I know it's juvenile to say I miss him, but...I miss him.

Sigh.

"Breakfast," I call. "Do you want butter and jam or peanut butter?"

"Butter and jam."

"Well come and get it." I force a smile that isn't completely genuine. I love him, but he's wearing on me. I never wanted a grown man who behaves like a sulky teenager underfoot. He needs to remember he's an adult. I'm not his mother—or his maid. The next step in his sobriety should be him taking care of himself.

He slouches into the kitchen and sullenly paints his bread. I slather mine with peanut butter.

"How are things?" I ask. "Are you feeling the temptation to fill your many hours with something other than television?"

He scrapes too much butter onto the second slice of toast. "Do you mean do I feel like using?"

"Of course that's what I mean." I slant him a tender glance. I want so badly for him to be okay. For good.

"I think of using sometimes, but then I remember Robbie and think better of it." Before I can ask, he explains. "She was one of my roommates in Atlanta. She OD'd and Brewster found her the next morning. It was scary and sad. And gross."

My stomach turns.

"I'm sorry. How are they, your roommates?" He lived with three other people in a cramped apartment. They were each in and out of rehab.

"Brewster texted me yesterday to check in, so he's good. I haven't heard from Dee in a while. I'll call her later. It's scary to call. You don't know who's going to pick up."

"I know what you mean." I've called Walt's phone plenty of

times wondering if the number had been changed or if a police officer or worse, a coroner, might answer. "I hope she's okay."

"Me too. She means a lot to me. She started drinking a few months ago and moved out. Then I came here. I don't know. Sometimes I worry I left her to the wolves, but broken people can't help other broken people."

"You're not broken." I console him with a hand to his shoulder before screwing the lid onto the peanut butter jar and stashing it in the cabinet. "You should call her. She might surprise you. You surprised me."

The more connections Walt has, the more meaning his life has, the less likely he is to harm himself. Being alone is hard when you're *not* an addict.

Before I take my first bite, my cell phone rings. My brother and I exchange glances. The timing is a little creepy after our discussion. I peek at the screen, one eye closed.

"Nate," I say.

Walt rolls his eyes. I stick out my tongue at him. Some things never change.

"Hey," I answer, carrying my toast and cell phone to my bedroom for some privacy.

"Hi, beautiful. Wanted to hear your voice. Are you lost without me?"

"Mm-hm." I chew a bite which takes me longer than anticipated because: peanut butter. Once I swallow, I say, "I haven't had anyone to feed me ridiculously expensive meals or drag me off to boring rich-person affairs in *days*."

"That's more your wheelhouse."

"My wheelhouse consists of being roomie to my younger brother these days."

He allows me this bit of petulance. "How about escaping for the weekend?"

"Tempting." Everything about Nate is tempting. I struggle daily to keep from becoming used to his lifestyle and his attention. Some days I win the fight and other days I lose.

"I'm taking a trip to Chicago next Friday. I'd like you to join me. We'll fly out that afternoon, be back by Sunday night. If Daniel can give you a few hours off on Friday, we're set."

Jettisoning off to anywhere—even Chicago—sounds decadent, and like a bad idea. Walt would be left to his own devices. Don't get me wrong, I'd love to run away, but I also feel obligated to watch over him and make sure he doesn't find trouble. Walt often finds trouble.

"I don't know." I eat another bite of toast.

"Vivian." The low rumble of Nate's voice wanders at a leisurely pace down my body. My eyes slide shut as I enjoy the sensation. "He's been good without you so far."

"I'll think about it." Maybe Walt can find gainful employment by then and I can rest knowing someone is expecting him to show up somewhere. He has his AA meetings. A job would gobble up more of his excess free time. I want to trust him, but I worry.

"Okay. I'll call you later." Nate says goodbye and I press the End button on my phone's screen, staring at it for a while. It's comforting and disturbing to have him in my life regularly.

Explain that.

In the living room, my brother has resumed his position on the sofa, his eyes glazing over as an action movie blows up the screen.

"Let's check out that nonprofit." I kick his foot.

"I have to shower."

"Then you'd better start moving." I smile sweetly.

He frowns but acquiesces, shutting off the TV and heading toward the bathroom. Success.

Once he's employed he can find a place of his own and I can breathe easy. But as I consider the plethora of issues that come with Walt taking care of himself, I wonder if I'll ever breathe easy again.

FRIDAY ARRIVES. I was able to take a few hours off. Daniel wasn't pleased with my request until I told him I would be with Nathaniel Owen on a job site.

"Think of how much valuable intel I'll bring back."

He didn't exactly jump for joy, but he did offer a surly, "You can stay late on Monday to make up for your time off."

Works for me.

I gather my packed bags and set them by the door. Nate's picking me up. He's never been to my apartment, and I'm weirdly nervous. I'm also nervous about going back to Chicago for obvious reasons.

"Are you sure about this, Viv?" Walt asks. He's standing, hands in his basketball shorts pockets, his too-long wavy hair a mess. His color's better than when he first arrived, I hope because he's eating and sleeping better.

"Am I sure about leaving you to your own devices?" I know that's not what he meant. He knows I know, and gives me a slow blink.

"Are you sure about going home with Nate?"

"Nate's home is in Clear Ridge. And so's mine." I gesture around the living room where Walt's dropped not one but two pairs of shoes and left them there. "Clean up while I'm away, will you? We could also use some groceries. There's a list on the fridge."

"Viv."

"*Yes*. I'm sure about going to Chicago with Nate. Why wouldn't I be?"

"Why would you?" he challenges.

A question I've been avoiding asking myself. I sigh and sit on the couch, patting the cushion next to me. My brother sits and leans his elbows on his knees. No matter how many carbs I stuff him with, his lanky form remains.

"You left that life behind for a reason, V. I'm afraid you'll be sucked back in." His concern is palpable.

"Sucked back into running a company for my father only to

learn he's stealing from his trusting staff and clients? Impossible. Our father is on the kitchen counter."

He twists his lips at my morbid joke. We both look at the urn, standing sentinel next to the coffee pot.

"I didn't know what to do with him," he says.

"I don't either. Throwing him out with next week's trash seems harsh, but sprinkling him around a park is too good for him."

"We should bury him next to Mom. Maybe you can look into that on your trip."

"He's the reason Mom's dead, or have you forgotten?"

"I haven't forgotten," he snaps.

"I know. I'm sorry." I put my hand on my forehead and take a deep breath. Tears heat the backs of my eyes, but I don't want to do this now, so I won't. "I will if I have time, okay?"

"Thanks."

"Hey, did you reach Dee?" I elbow him. His shy smile tells me he did.

"She's back on the wagon. Living with her sister. The irony, right? We're both living with our sisters. She said she'd like to come visit. Atlanta can be…Atlanta. I thought if she came here I could take her horseback riding."

"That's sweet." I mean it. But… "Is that a good idea since she's so new in her sobriety?"

"People can disappoint you at any time. New or not."

Sage wisdom from my brother. You heard it here first.

A knock at the door draws my attention. Nate at my screen door fills me with all sorts of muddy emotions. I'm drawn to him and afraid to be drawn to anyone. I want to run into his arms, but don't want my brother to know how nuts I am about Nate this soon.

I wave him in.

"Viv. Walt," he greets. "Nice place you have here."

"It's usually cleaner." I stand and swipe my palms down my skirt, uneasy about him seeing my house. I don't know why. Nate hasn't always lived in a decadent house filled with modern furnishings. I'm not ashamed of my place. Then it occurs to me I'm uneasy because he and Walt are in the same room. They've each expressed concern about the other. The last thing I need is a Popeye/Bluto-style confrontation.

"Viv and I were talking about burying Dad," Walt says. "If you find the time during your trip to stop by Fein Village."

I send a murderous glare to my brother. Nate's reaction is calmer than mine.

"I'm sure we can fit that in. Do you need to bring him?" Nate nods to the urn on the kitchen counter. Look who's Mister Observant.

"I wouldn't want to make the flight weird," I hedge. I'm not sure I'm ready to travel with my father. Or visit my mother's final resting spot for the first time in years.

"It's a private jet. We can fit one more." Nate lifts my bags. "I can come back in for it, unless…"

"I'll take him." I march to the kitchen, steel myself with a deep breath, and lift the urn holding my father's ashes. Then I'm out the door, embarking on a very different trip than the one I anticipated.

Chapter Eighteen

Vivian

I haven't been on a private jet in ages," I tell Nate after takeoff.

"Beats flying commercial." He's stunningly suited, a tie at his neck. He looks good. All that roughhewn masculinity settled into a plush chair. He's waiting on the flight attendant to deliver his whiskey, neat. I ordered a ginger ale. I never was able to drink on a plane without being airsick. Best to avoid vomiting on my suitor's rented airliner if possible.

"Sorry about that." I nod at my father's urn. It's like carrying a genie in a bottle around but instead of granting wishes he gifts bad memories. *Bonus! There are more than three.*

"Don't be. Might help with closure."

I shake my head. "Closure is selfish. People lost a lot of money because of him. Where is their closure?"

He smiles, which I find mildly perturbing.

"What?"

"It's interesting how, after years of having plenty of money at your disposal, you believe it's a finite resource."

"It *is* a finite resource."

"It's not. There's more than enough to go around. If I can turn a million into a billion in a relatively short time, you can out-earn your father. *Without* stealing. You were the source of the income you had, not him. Your talents, your gifts, your sassy mouth." He tilts his head. "Unless you believe you don't deserve it. That's another matter altogether."

"You don't talk like a kid from juvie with junkie parents," I murmur.

A flight attendant steps into the cabin and serves my ginger ale and Nate's whiskey. After she learns there's nothing more she can do for us, she disappears behind a door.

"I didn't mean to mention that so crassly," I mutter to Nate. "I didn't think about being overheard."

He presses an intercom button and the flight attendant appears a few seconds later. "Ms. Vandemark and I will need privacy for the remainder of the flight. No need to check in on us until we land."

"Of course, Mr. Owen. I'll grant you plenty of privacy. Ring if you need anything." She vanishes again, shutting the door behind her.

"Being overheard is no longer an issue." He unbuckles when the seat belt light goes off and I do the same. Then he swivels his seat to face mine. Holding his whiskey, he says, "I had to come to terms with what I deserved. It took a lot of therapy and business classes and numerous sit-downs with William Owen. He left room for no other option."

"A good father. The mind boggles."

"Beneath the privilege is a man who wanted better for his family. He taught me to want better too. Do you, Vivian? Want better?"

"Something wrong with my income bracket, Owen?" I snap.

He raises his eyebrows like he knows he's being baited. "You know that's not what I meant. You were once a high-powered executive. Do you miss it?"

"The power or the income?"

His eyes narrow, assessing. "Neither. The fact that you were where you belonged."

"I failed spectacularly. So, no, not really."

"Failed? The company you were dedicated to collapsed. I'd hardly call that failing."

"My failure to notice what was under my nose is my biggest regret," I admit. "I didn't change my name and career because I wanted to. I was forced to." I think of the press shadowing me at the courthouse. The shouted questions. *Did you suspect your father was stealing from the company? How could you have missed the signs? Will you live in Chicago after the trial?* I clear my throat to keep from curling my shoulders in shame. "I have a lot of critics, Nate."

"I'll bet you a thousand dollars you don't have half as many as you think."

"I wouldn't know. I haven't Googled myself in years."

"I liked your sass from the moment I met you, but I know what it's masking."

I cross my arms, not enjoying this interrogation as much as he is. Still, I'm curious. "And what's that?"

"*Fear,*" he answers and dammit, that feels true. I was never fear*less,* but I used to be brave. Before I knew how bad things could get. "As they say, you can't bullshit a bullshitter, and I used to be brimming with it."

"Don't be so hard on yourself. You still are." I smile sweetly.

His lips curl into a wicked smile, sending shivers down my arms. "You think I won't strip you down and take you on that couch, you're wrong."

"You have a flight crew," I remind him as those shivers shift to heat. I'm flushed, tingly. The idea of us having sex on this plane sounds more appealing than I'd like.

"She's giving us privacy," he reminds me. "I can do whatever I want to you."

"You can." I study my nails and pretend to be bored. "If I allow it."

He's poised to spring, his grip firm on his glass. I'm holding him there with my silence. We both know it. The power is mine, but I'm aware he's the one who gave it to me.

"You have me figured out." He sips his whiskey and turns his chair to face front again. Pretending boredom like me.

Evidently he has me figured out too. What he said about me being afraid rings loudly in my head. I started therapy but quit. I ran from my hometown to hide out. I've been treating my father's ashes as if they were a canister of flour rather than the remains of a man who was harder to love in life than he is in death.

Being with Nate is giving up my anonymity. Am I okay with that?

"I lack resilience," I admit, maybe for the first time. "My easy upbringing didn't teach me fortitude. My mother faded like a flame on a candle that's out of wick. My brother numbed himself into oblivion. If I were raised the way you were, maybe I'd have come out swinging."

"Now who's full of shit?" He arches one eyebrow before turning his seat toward mine again. He sets down his glass. "Your mother and your brother share a sickness. The same sickness that killed my father and is ravaging my mother."

"Is?" He told me he hadn't talked to her in three years.

"I checked in on her." His mouth pulls into a tight line. "She's living in the same unsafe neighborhood where I was born. It's not a nice place. If I thought for a moment she'd move into a penthouse, I'd buy her one."

"She wouldn't move?"

"Living in a rundown apartment on the wrong side of town is comforting to her. I've tried to move her into a new place before. The result was a lot of wasted time and money." He sighs. "I may have come out of the birth canal swinging but that doesn't mean the transition was easier, Vivian. I had no idea what was possible before I met Will and Lainey Owen."

"I did. I'd give it up all over again if it brought me peace."

"Has it?"

We both know it hasn't. I press my lips together.

"What happened is in the past. Your father was accused and sentenced for his crimes and died in prison. It's over for him. It should be for you. If you're happy, then great. I can't escape the feeling you want more. That you want to blaze a trail. " He holds out a hand and I slide mine against his palm. Instantly I am less defensive. "You are a fighter, Vivian. *Not* like me, and that's not a bad thing. I took down a wall with a sledgehammer and then had to replace it at my cost. I can be stupid. Reckless."

"I thought it was sexy," I disagree. "A buff guy in a fancy suit with a sledgehammer. Drywall dust dotting your hair."

"Don't forget I caught you in my arms after that. I saved your life."

"My *life*?" I tilt my head in disbelief.

"I at least saved you from a concussion."

I'll give him that. I smile.

He strokes my hand with his thumb. "You won't be happy until you accept that it's okay to go after your heart's desires. And you"—he tugs my hand and pulls me onto his lap—"are a woman who gets exactly what she desires the moment she allows herself to desire it."

Present party included, I think smugly. I wanted him the night at the museum, and here we are.

"Including sex on that couch over there?" I whisper against his lips.

"Or right here on this chair." He kisses me hard, deep. Not holding back.

I don't either. It feels good to be brave again.

WE HAD to move to the airplane's couch after attempting sex on the seat. It might have worked if Nate was shorter. Or if I was a contortionist.

After the flight we made a quick stop at the hotel to change and then we visited the job site. A posh live-work new-build halfway done. The style is more industrial, less homey than Grand Marin, which suits the area. Nate is specific about architecture and aesthetics. He has a gift.

"No wonder you've grown your wealth in this sector of Owen Construction," I tell him after dinner. We ate at a sandwich shop downtown that served an amazing mushroom Reuben. I'm going to have dreams about that sandwich, mark my words.

"I'll take that as a compliment." He hails a cab and gives the driver an address that is not our hotel's location.

"Where are we going?" I ask as Nate settles in next to me. He smells good, as usual. And in this stinky cab, that's impressive. He leans his back on the seat and turns his head and smiles. I nearly melt into the overly warm vinyl.

"Pint Haus. It's…rustic."

"Rustic." I make a face. That doesn't sound good.

"Not the kind of place you'd frequent, but I like it. I want to show it to you."

When the cab arrives at Pint Haus, I blink. He was right. I'd never step foot five blocks from a place like this. The wall is crumbling, the facade has seen better days—say, the mid '80s—and the thumping of drums leaking from the inside hints that the band is long-haired and tattooed.

"This is what you wanted to show me?"

Nate grins. "Best dive bar in town. A city kid like me is more comfortable here than in one of Archer's posh clubs."

"I like posh clubs." I push out my bottom lip and he kisses it.

"You can take the girl out of the snooty neighborhood…" he teases before helping me out of the cab.

I bristle at the noise coming from the bar. I feel safe with him, though. He'd never bring me into a situation where I was in danger. And if I was, he'd protect me.

Inside, we smash in with the crowd at the bar. Nate orders two beers.

"No dirty martini?" I call out over the noise.

"You want to be laughed out of this place?" He's so damn

appealing in this environment. When he changed at the hotel, he opted for casual trousers and a button-down. His sleeves are cuffed and rolled. I run my hand along the coarse hair covering one ropey forearm. He's so masculine. Painfully sexy.

Beer bottles in hand, we press toward to the band. After a song and a half, the lead singer lets us know they'll be back for a second set after he grabs "tequila and a blow job."

"Charming," I tell Nate as the band files off stage. Long hair and ripped jeans and tattoos galore. I'm a psychic. "You don't have any tattoos."

"Not a big fan of needles after Dad died with one in his arm."

I wince. He bends and kisses my cheek, then says into my ear, "You're cute when you're worrying about me."

"I'm not worried about you."

"Uh-huh." He checks out the crowd and I do the same. "What do you think?"

There are people of all ages and creeds in here. It's a dive bar, but one with a hell of a lot of personality. I don't feel unsafe after all.

"It suits you. I like being in the mix with the commoners." I sip my beer and smile to let him know I'm being purposely obtuse. "I'll never fit in here. If half of them had any clue who I was, I'd be dragged out and tossed into the gutter."

He doesn't smile. "Let's test that theory."

With his free hand, he takes mine and walks me to the first couple we see. They're twentysomething, college kids, I'd guess, given their trendy clothes.

"Excuse me," Nate says to them.

I jerk his arm in protest. What is he doing?

He ignores me. The couple regards us curiously.

"This is my girlfriend, Vivian Steele."

The guy blinks at me. "Nice to meet you. Rocco. This is my girlfriend, Bev."

After a pair of awkward handshakes and a "nice to meet you" from all parties, Nate whisks me away.

"What was that about?" I ask him. "And did you call me your girlfriend?" That detail hits me a little late.

"They didn't hate you."

"They're babies. They don't know who Walter Steele was."

His mouth tips in consideration. He walks us over to a pair of guys. The same intro follows. "Hi. This is my girlfriend, Vivian Steele. She's the daughter of Walter Steele, the rich asshole who robbed a lot of innocent people of their life savings."

"Shit," one guy says, thick eyebrows rising over the rim of his black glasses. "Seriously?"

I give him a sickly smile. I feel like dying.

"Jamal." He offers a hand and I stare at it in shock. He wants to shake my hand? He grips my fingers and holds them for a beat. "That sucks, Vivian. Least you know what not to do with your life."

His friend introduces himself next. Pablo. We part with well wishes.

Not done yet, Nate approaches a pair of forty-something ladies next. They are leaning over the bar, their raucous laughter suggesting the martinis aren't their first. I shoot daggers at Nate as I nod to the drinks. Guess they *do* serve martinis.

He ignores my silent complaint and recites his introduction, but this time when he mentions my father he says, "Do you think Vivian can escape Walter Steele's shadow?"

"Aw, of course, hon." The blond woman squeezes my arm. "We're not our parents. You can make better decisions. You already have judging by your boyfriend." She sizes up Nate a tad lecherously. "A good man is hard to find."

"I thought a *hard* man was *good* to find," crows her friend with a hooting laugh. She then winks at me. "Take it from me, girl. You walk away from your sketchy father and become your own woman. His weakness is your power."

"Thank you." That was unexpected. And strangely poignant.

Nate thanks them too, and starts off toward another couple. I stop walking, my hand in his. He comes back to me when I give his arm a tug.

"I get it," I say. "Not everyone knows who I am, and once they do, they don't care."

"Hate to break it to you, kid. You are not the center of the universe. Also, you owe me a thousand dollars."

I punch him in the arm. He deserves it. He chuckles, but sobers quickly.

"No one is after you." He wraps his arms around my waist. "Not anymore. Walter Steele is dead and his story died with him. It's up to you, and Walt, to be better than him. Mission accomplished. By both of you."

The emotion hits me out of nowhere, similar to the evening I crumpled to the floor at Nate's house and he scooped me up. Luckily, it's not grief or despair gripping my heart. It's gratitude. So much of it, I can hardly stand under its weight.

I cup his neck and pull his mouth to mine. I taste beer on his tongue. Never the shy one, he deepens our kiss and we receive wolf-whistles for our PDA.

The band returns to take the stage, making it far too loud to converse any longer. I finish my beer. I dance. I order another.

I bask in the glow of being anonymous. Ordinary. Overlooked.

Chapter Nineteen

Vivian

It's official. Nate has turned me into a hibernating bear.

I wake to an empty bed in the hotel and stretch my arms overhead. The white bedding is muted given the room-darkening curtains. Thankfully he left them open a crack. If not for the wedge of sun streaming in I might have slept even later. I quickly search the room, but Nate, as per his usual, has already risen *and* shined. Who knows where he's gallivanted off to. I imagine he'll return with a gift, or better, breakfast.

I shower and wash my hair, shaking off the fatigue from our travels and that "one more" beer I indulged in at Pint Haus. That last one is never a good idea. When will I learn?

I'm in the middle of drying my hair, naked, thanks to my towel falling off mid-blowout, when I hear the door open and close. Nate strides by.

"Hey, you." I grab my towel and loop it around my body, intending to flash him when he turns around. What stops me is his expression. Murderous isn't the right word, but close. There's a palpable hurt beneath the rage that makes what he's feeling hard to classify.

He sets down the white bakery bag and offers me a paper coffee cup. "Cappuccino. Croissants."

"How very French of you," I say carefully, gripping my towel. His eyes go to my hand but they don't glaze over with lust. Something is very, very wrong.

He presses his fingers to his forehead as he strolls across the room. I pull on some clothes while he looks out the window, his jeans and T-shirt silhouetted in the sunlight streaming through the now-open curtains. His shoulders are tight. His back muscles twitch.

I approach on cat's paws and touch his arm. "Nate, are you—"

"I saw her."

My heart sinks to my stomach. Not at his words, but his tone. He faces me. The hurt triples as some of the rage fades.

"My mother," he explains. "I found out where she lives and I paid her a visit."

I want to ask how she is but I'm not sure how he found her, so I keep my question to myself. He saves me the trouble.

"She wasn't high."

"That's good."

"She asked me for money so she could *get* high. I told her no. She yelled. She screamed. She told me I was abusing her by not giving her the 'medicine' she needs." He speaks through clenched teeth. I have no idea what to do. Touch him or don't?

"I'm sorry."

"I begged her to go to rehab. I offered to take her right then. Told her I'd pay for her stay and visit twice a month." His hurt-filled eyes hit me like a sock to the stomach. "Know what she said?"

I shake my head. I don't think I want to know what she said. Unfortunately he's going to tell me.

"She told me her son abandoned her. That I was dead as far as she was concerned. Then she attacked me. I think she was going for my wallet." He holds his arm out. In the sunlight, I make out shallow scratch marks.

"Oh my God. Nate." I reach for him but he shakes me off.

"I envisioned reconciling some of the guilt I still feel for leaving her. I thought I could help. I can't help her if she doesn't want it."

"You're right. You can't."

"It's my job to help others."

"No. Your job is to provide homes and workplaces for people who want to be part of a community," I correct. "Not drag people to a conclusion they have to reach on their own."

"What about last night?" he asks, a frown carving his brow. "You didn't need *dragged* to a conclusion that Walter Steele isn't running your life?"

He's angry and I have to be very careful not to snap back at him, which is so, so tempting. I've never seen him like this—not in control. Is this what he looks like when he's out of it? I throw the words he said to me on the plane back at him.

"I know what this anger is masking. And so do you."

A muscle in his cheek jumps when he welds his jaw together at the hinges.

"It's okay to be afraid for her, Nate. You love her."

"Yeah, well, she hates me."

"She doesn't. She's sick. You said so yourself." Unable to keep from it, I lay a hand on his chest. His big, strong heart thuds against my palm. "You're not failing her because she won't listen. Addicts have to hit rock bottom before they ask for help."

"And what if they never ask?" His voice cracks.

I consider his father. My mother. They didn't ask for help and their addictions cost them their lives. I don't have any encouraging words to say so I don't say anything.

"I have to visit the site today," he says. "Do you need anything else before I go?"

"I'll come with you."

"No."

I bristle. I was invited yesterday, but not today. I don't know if he's embarrassed for showing his vulnerability or if he needs to process without me around. I respect his need to be alone, even if I am disappointed.

"Will you be okay here?" Concern leaks into his expression. He's always caring for everyone else, which doesn't leave much room for caring for himself. He's done so much for me. I can't help but want to return the favor.

"I'll be good here." I force a smile. To alleviate his concern, I say, "I can always go shopping."

He reaches for his wallet and I shove his arm. "Don't you *dare*."

"Your addiction, Vivian"—he pulls out cash and leaves it on the desk—"I'm happy to feed."

He drops a fast kiss onto my lips. I hold on as long as he allows. He tastes good. He *feels* good. I want to heal his hurts, and I know what he likes. We spent last night twisting up the sheets and burying mine.

"Call you later," he promises. And then he's gone.

With a sigh, I look at the hundred dollar bills on the desk and consider how unfairly his mother treated him. Hasn't she broken his heart enough for one lifetime? He deserves better. He deserves to be lavished.

A slow smile curls the corners of my mouth.

I tuck the bills into my pocket. Looks like I'm going shopping after all.

Nate

Seeing my mother was a mistake.

All the work I've done over the years to become whole, or as close to whole as I'll ever be, was washed away like a mudslide this morning. Similar to the mud puddling under my feet at the construction site from an earlier light summer rain.

Light.

That's how I felt when I arrived in Chicago with Vivian. So much for my preaching about how I know she's afraid to claim what she wants. And that stunt I pulled in the bar to prove no one is out to get her… Who do I think I am?

This morning I rode those good feelings and the high from the sex last night to what I thought was a brilliant idea. I'd visit my mother. What could possibly go wrong?

Stupid, stupid. *Stupid.*

What possessed me to do it?

Concern, sure, but a part of me was acting selfishly. I was trying to force the final puzzle piece to slide into place. To finally be *whole*. Not so I can reach a state of enlightenment, which, face it, I'm not sure is attainable, but for Vivian.

For the first time, I have a strong connection with a woman. I don't want to be less than she deserves, and she's a woman who deserves far better than me.

I was happier without these thoughts.

"Sign here, Mr. Owen." The inspector, Bill, hands over a clipboard. I jot my name on the line. "I'll email a copy to your foreman."

"Actually, I need you to email it to me before you leave."

He's taken aback by my request but recovers quickly. "I can do that."

I give him my private email and check my phone to ensure it arrives before he leaves. I don't want to deal with lost paperwork. I can't take the stress, or afford the time setback if I have to destroy another wall. Though I doubt a smart-mouthed, dark-haired woman in high heels is going to strut onto my site to set me straight again. Lightning usually only strikes once.

An hour later I'm in a filthy cab, stuck in traffic, my good mood from yesterday a far-off memory. I'm looking forward to two things. Dinner, since I skipped lunch, and a glass of whiskey. Okay, three things. I want to see Vivian, bury my nose in her hair and breathe in her vanilla scent.

I owe her an apology. I should've treated her better this morning.

I'm used to control. Having it. Wielding it. When it's taken from me, it fucking pisses me off. Lack of control makes me feel unstable. Like I'm free-falling. My parents favored that feeling, but I never did. I only wanted to hold everything together.

Viv was right. I was afraid. When my mother wouldn't accept my help, I feared for her life. For her future. I don't know which I hate more, being unable to help my mom or Vivian witnessing me at my weakest.

When I enter our hotel room, I'm momentarily disoriented. Candles flicker from practically every surface in the room. Low flames wink from votive holders on the dresser, the nightstands and the desk. A trail of rose petals leads from the door, to the bed, and off the comforter to the bathroom. I follow the sound of running water to the massive soaking tub in the center of the room. Steam rises, choking the air with mist.

Vivian is perched on the ledge of the tub, her hand testing the temperature of the water.

"Finally," she says, exasperated. "Do you know how hard it is to keep the water warm when I have no idea when or if you're coming back?"

"If?" Surely she doesn't think I'd leave and never come back. "Listen, about this morning—"

"Shh-shh," she hushes me and then stands and drops the hotel robe.

Beneath it, she's wearing a black, lacy garment that sends every thought out of my head. Her long hair spills over her shoulders and her breasts are tucked into two cups creating a hell of a lot of cleavage.

"I spent your money," she informs me with a grin. Her warm caramel-colored eyes sparkle in the candlelight, which also highlights the freckles on the bridge of her nose.

"You spent it well."

"You deserve to be treated too, Nathaniel Owen. You take care of everyone. Who takes care of you?"

"Odessa," I answer automatically.

"Wrong. You only let her do so much. You send her home and serve your own dinner."

"I'm very independent," I argue as she sashays across the room. I'm given a peek of her ass beneath the short skirt of the slip she's wearing. A strip of black material separates her ass cheeks and I grind my back teeth together. "A thong."

She peeks over her shoulder, black lashes fluttering coyly, and then she lifts the back of her nightie to show me the thong in all its glory. "Do you like it?"

"No." My hands clench and release the air as I cross the room. "I *love* it."

"Good. You bought it." She lifts the phone on the vanity and presses a button. "Well, I bought it for you. But you paid for it."

"You spoil me." I can't wait any longer. I must touch her. Anywhere. *Everywhere*. I can't get enough of this woman.

"What do you want for dinner?"

"You," I answer without hesitating.

She covers the receiver of the hotel phone. "I'm trying to place an order."

"You," I move her hand and repeat loud enough to be overheard.

She orders two steaks and potatoes, something else and something after that. I'm not listening anymore, having buried my face in her cleavage. By the time my hand slides past the barrier of her panties, she gasps and finishes her order with, "And champagne."

"Champagne," I say against her parted lips, while I part her other lips with my fingers and give her a tender stroke. She's already wet and the smooth creaminess of her threatens to buckle my knees.

"Twenty to thirty minutes," she breathes as she drops the phone.

"I can work with that."

Her eyes flash with lust and heat. This is my favorite look on Vivian Vandemark, hands down.

"I'm supposed to be taking care of you," she gasps as I stroke into her again.

"Plenty of time for that," I promise. But of course, she doesn't listen. She grabs my cock and tugs. Then we make good use of those twenty to thirty minutes.

WE'RE STILL naked when our food arrives. I wrap a towel around my waist and answer the door, palming the guy a one hundred dollar bill. He nods his appreciation and leaves as quickly as he arrives.

As I wheel the cart into the bathroom, Vivian is slipping into the tub. She added bubble bath and more hot water and now those bubbles are teetering at the edge.

"Dinner in the tub." She slicks bubbles up her arms. "It's been too long since I indulged."

I drop my towel and climb in after her. "This'll be a first for me."

Her face lights up. "You poor sheltered boy."

"Deprived," I joke, but after I say it, it doesn't feel like a joke. I have a lot, but there's always been something missing.

"You look like you're thinking hard about something. What is it?"

She must've caught me at a good moment because I tell her. Sex always limbers up my body. I didn't know my tongue was as susceptible.

"I was thinking…about this morning. How I felt walking into this room. How I was the same but different."

She cocks her head, listening. Wanting to understand.

"I tried to take care of my parents. When I couldn't, I focused on taking care of myself. And when I was adopted by the Owens, and realized theirs was my permanent home, I decided to take care of them." I let out a heavy sigh, understanding what made me feel light tonight after such a heavy morning. It was more than sex. "You… This." I gesture to the cart. It's choked with dishes, condiments, and silverware, a bucket holding a bottle of champagne, and look at that, a whiskey neat. "I'm not used to being taken care of."

"You should try it more often." She hands me the short glass. "It's actually quite nice."

"You didn't have to do this. After the way I treated you, I half expected you to be pissed off when I came back."

"You had a tough morning, Nate. That doesn't erase everything that happened before it."

Fuck, she's sweet. It's nice to be understood. To be seen. To be taken care of, my needs anticipated.

I set my glass aside and wrap my arms around her waist. She turns and I pull her back against my front. She's soft and warm and beautiful. I cop a feel because I can't help myself, but I'm sincere when I rumble the words, "Thank you."

"You're welcome." She squeezes her arms over mine.

"Tomorrow we'll scout a few options for your father's remains." I kiss the edge of her ear to soften the blow. Instead of stiffening against me, she tilts her head and looks up at me. I'm lost in her brown eyes. Even more lost when she smiles softly.

"Sounds good."

I ease into the warmth of her embrace, a good glass of whiskey, and, after, we eat steaks in the bathtub and talk about our day. I could get used to this.

Hell. I already am.

Vivian

We're standing over my mother's grave. The day is windy, cloudy, and warm. The marker reads "daughter, sister, wife, mother" and makes me remember that somewhere I have an uncle. Dad took him for all he was worth. Last I heard he was living in Colorado, but who knows where Stephen escaped to. He didn't have anything to do with us after Mom died. He held Walt and me as accountable as he did our father for destroying her. It was unfair.

Or maybe, I think with a hefty dose of perspective, it hurt too much to be around us after she was gone.

Nate is standing off to the side. Not hovering, an effort to give me privacy. A patch of grass is next to Mom's tombstone. That spot was designated for Dad, but putting him to rest here seems wrong. For a lot of reasons.

"I don't want to bury him here." The moment it's out of my mouth I know it's the right call.

"Okay." Nate comes closer.

I haven't taken my eyes off the flowers we brought. A huge bouquet of daisies. They were her favorite.

"I don't want people to see his name and then look over at my mom and think 'that poor woman.' I want her to have dignity. They weren't in love for years, you know," I say, half talking to him and half talking to myself. "They were more like business partners. There was a chill in the air whenever he came home from work. We all noticed. The jumpy house staff. Walt, when he was there, would climb into himself and disappear. That's how Mom did it too."

"And you dealt with it by being angry."

I nod. Mostly, that's true. "It hurt to feel hurt."

"Yeah. It does."

I turn and look up at him. His hair blows in the breeze. His hands are deep in his suit pants pockets, and his tie kicks from a particularly forceful gust of wind. He knows what it's like to hurt. His own mother disowned him—after being paid off by the Owens to take custody of him.

"Do you hate him? Your biological father?" I ask.

He pulls in a chest-expanding inhalation and looks around the cemetery. "I used to hate him. Now I feel sorry for him."

"What about your mom?"

He pulls one hand from his pocket and pushes the sleeve up. Plucking one of the fat beads on the bracelet between finger and thumb, he says, "She gave me this. One of the only gifts I remember her giving to me. I keep it because it reminds me that, at least once, she cared." My heart aches for him. He frowns. "I don't hate her. I feel betrayed. On some level. On another, healthier level, I understand she can't help it."

"It's exhausting, isn't it? To keep making excuses for their behavior when it affects you so much?"

I turn back to my mom's grave and a tidal wave of emotion slams into me. I'd like to think it came out of nowhere, but I know better. It's been lodged in my ribcage for most of my life.

"She loved expensive shoes." It's such a dumb thing to say. "We had that in common."

An audible sob wrenches from my throat and I'm in Nate's arms a second later. I hang on tight in case the storm inside me, like the wind whipping through this graveyard, blows me away.

His lips pressed into my hair, he keeps me steady.

I let him, painting his shirt with a fresh batch of tears.

Chapter Twenty

Vivian

I wear the red-bottomed Louboutins from Nate and pair them with a new dress I argued and insisted on paying for. He refused.

The dress reminds me of the lingerie I wore when we were in Chicago. It laces up, the bodice is satin trimmed. It's very, *very* short. It's gorgeous, and for good reason. The retail ticket on a Dolce & Gabanna dress hovers around three thousand dollars. Which is why I argued with Nate that I should be allowed to pay for at least half of it. Then he said he was insulted, and I told him I used to have a closet stocked with D&G and it gave me flash-backs. I didn't win that argument either. He pulled me close, the dress still on its hanger trapped between our bodies, and said, "Time to make new memories."

He was very convincing.

He works hard for the money he makes and he deserves every penny. I'm trying not to take advantage of him. When I told him that, he chuckled, the sound low and gruff. Then he kissed me and shook his head and told me to get dressed.

There's nothing slimy or self-serving about the way he gives gifts. He just...*gives*. I can't say any man in my life has treated me well without an ulterior motive.

Since our awkward morning in Chicago, Nate and I are closer than before. Him revealing his emotions and me tending to his needs set us in a different zone than before we left. In short, I dropped my guard even more, which doesn't feel dangerous so much as decadent. Nate is back to his comfortable, confident self. I can tell he appreciated me being there for him. He isn't accustomed to leaning on someone.

He's probably always been a tough guy who tried to have everything under control. It's the role he gave himself, and yes, he's amazing at it, but he's also human. Every human wants to curl up and stop worrying for two minutes. I've been trying to be the person he can lean on, who sweeps away his worries.

Everyone needs someone to lean on.

While I check my lipstick in the vanity mirror of his Tesla, he pulls up to the valet. Club Nine is a splashy big-city-like club, but in Clear Ridge. Tonight's the big grand opening.

"I see the Miami influence," I say. Archer should be proud. It's a gorgeous building, sleek and modern. Neon lights glow from inside and the façade. A lot of well-dressed guests loiter outside waiting to come in.

"He done good," Nate agrees.

He complemented my black dress by wearing all black himself. His black satin shirt is adorned with crystal embellishments lining the button panel and the collar. It'd look ridiculous on anyone but him.

"You look great." I touch his collar.

"Versace." He cranes an eyebrow.

"You wear it well."

I might not be able to purchase him expensive clothes, but I can come with him to this event. I can remind him he's worthy. And that his strength and stoicism are far less important than his willingness to be himself with me.

After the valet takes the car we bypass the line wrapping

around the building. They don't open the doors for another fifteen minutes. Apparently, they are keeping these finely dressed guests in a state of mouthwatering anticipation by making them wait until the clock strikes ten on the nose.

Inside, Benji spots us first. At his heels is a petite blond woman with soft curls surrounding a cherubic face.

"There you are. Archer's at the bar." He tips his head. Their brother is wiping down a bottle of liquor with a white cloth. I'm not joking. He inspects another, wipes that one and I overhear him tell the bartender to "keep 'em shined."

"Committed as usual," Nate says.

"I'm Cristin, Benji's assistant." The blonde offers her hand. "You can call me Cris."

"Life assistant *coach*," Benji corrects as I take my palm from Nate's arm to shake her hand.

She rolls her eyes. "He made that up."

"She's humble," Benji says, his eyes on her. The look he gives her is friendly and flirty—the same way I've seen him look at practically everyone. The look Cris gives him is more than that. Longing and admiration mixed into a cocktail that will one day spill from its shaker.

Another woman enters via the front door. She waves at Benji as she approaches. She's tall, leggy, blond. Her wide mouth is coated in a pink sparkly lipstick matching her dress.

"Hey, Bennie!" She presses her slim body against his and his arm wraps around her small waist.

"Benji," Cris corrects from his side.

"I know." The blonde's smile doesn't waver.

Cris looks like she is about to throw up. I feel for her. I'm tempted to hiss at the blonde in Cris's defense, but I resist.

It's a good thing I didn't. Turns out the blonde is really nice. Along with those Barbie-doll good looks, she's also smart. Halfway through my first martini, she and I are chatting about business integration. Cris chimes in—she's no slouch, and knows what she's talking about. I like her more than I like Barbie, whose actual name is Patricia. She doesn't look like a Patricia, which I told her. She laughed and said she goes by Trish. That makes more sense.

By then the club is full of guests and thumping with bass. Archer and Nate are in a deep conversation in a VIP lounge upstairs. I stayed downstairs in the fog and lights for one reason. My protective streak kicked in when Trish showed up. It kicked into high gear when Trish dragged Benji to the dance floor.

"She's nice," Cris announces miserably.

"She is nice," I agree, not sure what else to say.

She shakes off her malaise and brightens in a blink. "How long have you and Nate been seeing each other?"

I do a quick calculation. "Two months."

Wow, can that be right? It's already August. After each day sluggishly rolled into the next and the one after that, these past few months have flown. It seems like eons since I stumbled onto the Grand Marin job site and threatened to shut it down. And even longer since my brother—who remains jobless, by the way—moved into my apartment.

Grr.

"Nate is cut from a different cloth." She reaches for her drink.

"How do you mean?" I have my own opinions but I'm curious to hear hers.

"On the outside he's this gruff bearlike creature and then he grins and you realize he's marshmallowy in his core."

"His core is quite firm, actually," I argue with a smile. She laughs.

"You know what I mean." She props her chin in her hand. "Is he super gooey with you? I'm a romantic. Indulge me."

Unaccustomed to gossiping with a girlfriend—which reminds me how much I miss Marnie—I hesitate before answering carefully. "He takes care of me, which I'm not used to. I'm more of a fend-for-myself kind of girl."

"Well. He loves a challenge, so I'm sure he's eating that up."

I don't take it as an insult. I *am* a challenge. When I first met him I had trouble letting down my guard. It's still tough for me. My spine is stiffer than I'd like tonight. I can't escape feeling like I'm lying about who I am to a bunch of very kind people—Cris, especially.

"You two look good together. You fit." She turns her head to check on Benji, though I'm not sure she meant to. She consistently clocks his whereabouts. He's dancing close to Trish, his lips grazing her bare shoulder. Cris reroutes her gaze to the upstairs lounge where Archer and Nate lean on the railing, drink glasses in hand.

"I've never seen Nate this gaga for anyone," she says, but it sounds like a cover-up for her actual thoughts after observing Benji.

I pull my attention away from my gorgeous date and his brooding brother. When I don't respond, she winces.

"Did I say too much?"

Sort of, but I'd die before telling her that. "Not yet."

She laughs. "Told you. I'm a romantic."

Which might explain why she's holding out hope for a clueless Benji. If we were friends, I'd give her some hard-knocks advice, but it doesn't feel like my place. I glance up at Nate. He must feel me staring. He turns from his brother and gives me a wink. Archer follows Nate's gaze and gives me a bland blink that might be his version of a smile.

"Is Archer always so morose?" I ask Cris. "His new club is open and packed to the walls. Shouldn't he be happy?"

"I think this *is* him happy."

"And Benji is always happy," I say, unable to resist my curiosity about Cris and her wayward boss.

"Not always. Generally, he's upbeat. His teen years were rough."

I imagine any kid who had to be adopted because his parents were no longer alive would categorize their teen years as "rough." He evidently dealt with it differently than Nate. Benji is as upbeat as a motivational speaker.

"So, you know him well," I pry. I can't help it. The look she's been giving him since Trish arrived is more than a crush an assistant develops for her boss.

"We've known each other going on ten years."

"Wow. Long time."

"I started interning for William Owen when I was fresh out of college. Mostly at the office, but the entire family would pop in from time to time. Benji hired me to manage his personal schedule about eight months ago, but he's always been in my periphery. I mean, not just him. They all have," she amends. "It's hard not to notice the Owens. They're each so…unique."

They are. Nate's gruff good looks mask a tender heart, Archer's scowl seems to be hiding more turmoil, and Benji's joy and happiness are absolutely contagious.

I suppress a smile and sip my martini. Benji hired Cris eight months ago. He's oblivious, unlike his super-observant brother, Nate.

"Have Benji and Trish been together long?" Not to rub salt into a wound, but I need more details. I don't tend to hold back, in case you haven't noticed.

"I met her one other time. She had a meeting with Benji the other night that ran late." She rolls her eyes. "He's a player and a half. Any woman would be crazy to become involved with him."

"You should warn Trish, being his life coach and all."

"Life *assistant* coach," she corrects, holding up a finger.

I laugh. I like her. Way more than I like Trish. "What does that even mean?"

"It means he can pay me more than William paid me. I demanded a raise." Her tone suggests she believes she deserves it. Interesting. Maybe the "thing" she has for her boss is nothing more than inconvenient attraction brought on by proximity.

Inconvenient attractions can fool you into wanting more. Trust me.

I crane my head to look for Nate, but he's gone. He appears beside me a second later and runs his finger along the back of my arm. I jump and spin around, startled. He fills the space around me. I always imagined those open cracks would let the monsters in, but look who's guarding the door.

"Dance with me." He sets his empty glass on the bar and takes my hand. I check on Cris, hesitant to leave her alone.

Archer is next to her offering her his hand. "Shall we?"

She smiles up at him and Archer slants me a knowing glance.

"Who knew Archer had a heart," I remark as Nate leads me to the dance floor.

"We hide our hearts in whatever way is convenient," he says. "Benji with his women." Nate settles his hands on my waist, claiming me. "Archer with his warm, fuzzy personality."

I laugh at his sarcasm. "And you?"

My arms around his neck, I sway to the slow beat of the song. We move well together. Just as good as when we're wrapped around each other on the couch. Or a hotel bed. Or in the bathtub…

"I hide behind giving luxurious gifts." He gives up his secret easily. "What about you? Where do you hide your broken heart, Vivian?"

"Up my skirt," I answer cheekily. "Want to check?"

"Behind that sass," he answers for me. Then he lets me off the hook with a, "And yes, I'll have a look for it later."

Chapter Twenty-One

Vivian

There is a strange woman in my house.

I don't know her but Walt does, and he's fond of her, given his wide, goofy smile. He excitedly introduces her as Dee. I recognize the name. This is one of the "friends" he lived with while he was in Atlanta. Oddly enough she resembles him. She's thin with dark hair, though she's a good foot shorter than him, and covered in tattoos. Just on her arms and legs from what I can tell, but there could be more.

Beneath a pile of black eye makeup are pale blue eyes. She doesn't strike me as a particularly warm person, but she's friendly. She's chattering about how she recently achieved her thirty days of sobriety. Hence the visit to Clear Ridge.

"We're heading out for tacos. You want to come with?" Walt asks.

No way am I going on a date with my brother and this chick. Don't get me wrong. I'm glad he has a friend in town to occupy his time who isn't me, but I'm not hanging out with them after a full day of work. I mentally tack on that Walt hasn't worked a full day in a very, *very* long time. I want to vent, but I don't feel comfortable in front of a guest.

"Can't. Nate and I have plans tonight."

Before Dee walks outside she turns, her hand on the doorframe. "Walt told me about your boyfriend. Said he owns a bunch of properties. I heard he's super rich."

I don't know what to say so I nod. My brother also used to be "super rich." I wonder what he's told her about our family, if anything.

"The car is here," she tells him and then she skips outside to climb into an Uber. Walt tells her "one second." After she scampers outside, he turns to me. "Can I borrow twenty bucks?"

"Is that why you invited me? So that I'd pay for dinner?"

"Don't be a bitch, Viv. I need an allowance or something."

"You need a *job*." But I'm already en route to my purse. I hand him forty dollars and he makes a plea for an additional twenty. I give that to him too. I don't have the energy to argue or teach him a lesson tonight. I have a feeling it wouldn't stick anyway.

After he walks out the door, I call Nate. Before I can launch into my tirade, he says, "Come to Grand Marin. I'll take you to dinner." Then he shouts goodbye over what sounds like large machinery chugging away in the background.

I guess venting can be done in person as easily as over the phone. I drive to the job site and find him in the office, hovering over a laptop. He's dressed down in cargo pants and a T-shirt today. This is probably the most dressed down I've ever seen him.

"The wall looks good." I point over my shoulder and his eyes flare with heat. That was the first time we met. Had we known then what we know now... "Doing some of your own dirty work?"

He doesn't honor my joke with an answer, standing from his desk to kiss me hello. "I hope you're okay with casual dinner or carry out. I didn't bring a change of clothes."

"Nope. Eight course chef's menu or I walk."

I'm teasing, but he nods his head curtly.

"I'll make a reservation."

"You do well with high maintenance, do you know that?"

He grins. Yeah. He knows.

Within half an hour, we are being seated at a very relaxed Mexican restaurant. Of course I didn't let him make reservations. That's ridiculous. He would've though. He's spoiling me and I'm starting to like it. Not because it reminds me of my old life—but because this is a whole new experience. *Nate* is a new experience.

I like the chips and salsa here. La Piñata is a place I've been to more than once. After a quick look around to determine this wasn't the same taco joint where Walt and Dee absconded to, I relax.

"So you were saying…" Nate motions for me to talk while he drags a chip through the dish of salsa. I started to tell him about what was going on with Walt on the drive over, but then he took a phone call. The gap gave me time to reconsider my approach. I no longer feel like fuming, unless it's at Walt, but that will have to wait.

I summarize, explaining how I gave my brother and his "friend" money for dinner. "I don't know where she's staying while she's in town. I bet she's staying with Walt. Also, me."

"Tell her she can't." He shrugs as if it's that easy. Arguably it is. Telling Walt is the hard part.

"I don't want to let him down," I mutter, noting how weak that sounds.

"You're afraid if you upset him he's going to start drinking or using again, aren't you?"

It's times like these I remember Nate has had experience with substance abusers.

I hold up my hands in surrender. "Textbook codependent."

"No, you're not there yet." He reaches for one of my hands and holds it. Just then our margaritas arrive. We place our orders. Quickly, since most of the menu is broken down into numbers. I order the number fourteen and he chooses twenty-eight. We dig in to the basket of chips again.

"If he had a job, he could find his own place," I say as I add salt to a chip. "I don't know how much longer I can stand him living with me. And if she stays too…"

Ugh. I can't even think about it. Three adults, one bathroom?

Horror.

"He can work for me." Nate munches another chip.

"You don't know what you're offering. Walt has no work experience. He's barely sober. I'm not sure he's reliable."

Nate surprises me by laughing. "As his representative, you don't sound very confident in him."

"I'm looking out for you. I don't want you to regret giving him a chance."

"You don't have to look out for me. First of all, I can look out for myself. Second of all, I was like Walt at one point. Unreliable, and worse, mercurial. I needed somebody to give me a chance. Hell, William gave me plenty of chances. I wasn't gracious about it. It's possible this is a nudge from the universe to pay back the kindness shown to me. I'm okay with that."

How does he do that? Admit how he's feeling so casually? I blink at him in wonderment before saying, "I might have to look into going back to therapy."

"Stick with me, kid." He winks. "I'll teach you everything I know."

AFTER DINNER we drive back to Grand Marin. I settle into the passenger seat, stuffed on fish tacos and way too many chips. Why can I never turn down the second basket? Out of the blue, Nate makes a suggestion I don't see coming.

"Why don't you go back to your apartment and pack enough clothes for the next few weeks. You can stay with me. Think of it as a trial run for Walt having his own place."

He parks next to my car and watches me calmly. There's no fanfare involved and he just asked me to move in with him. Sort of. Fear ripples along my spine. I'm already shaking my head, self-preservation kicking into gear.

"You can make this into as big of a deal as you want to," he tells me. "But you sleep at my house enough to justify you packing a bag. Plus, I want you there. I like you there. It's not permanent, but it could be. Maybe staying with me would be a good trial run for you too."

My heart skips a literal beat and I open my mouth to suck in a breath. Definitely he sort of, kind of asked me to move in with him. Not right away, but later. My head is spinning.

"Walt needs me at home."

"Why?"

I choke. I don't know why. I just feel this innate need to protect him.

"Afraid Dee will rob you?"

"No." Not really. My distrust of her is more because she's an addict and has recently relapsed.

"Afraid she'll lead Walt astray?"

"Yes."

He nods. "It's a possibility. But you can't wrap him in bubble wrap. He's an adult and the decisions he makes each and every day impact his sobriety in a negative way or a positive way. You have your own life to think about."

"What about you?" I ask a tad defensively. "You have your own life to think about and here you are offering me refuge in your apartment."

"Refuge?" He chuckles. "I like having you there. Thought you liked it there too."

Rather than admit staying with him officially freaks me out, I hedge. "The commute to work is longer from your house."

"That's true." He nods, patient now.

"It'll add another twenty minutes and I already spend way too much time there." Yes, this argument is sound.

"You can say no," he offers, once again looking out the windshield.

"It's not that I want to say no, it's that I have to drive to my stupid job and sit at my stupid desk and answer to my stupid boss and I'd rather not add insult to injury by tacking on another twenty minutes." Exasperated, and slightly winded from my mini rant, I take a breath.

"You could quit the job."

"Ha! Sure. I'll just quit and earn zero dollars. My landlady will love that idea." I offer a sweet smile I hope is covering for my fraying nerves. I haven't depended on anyone in years. The idea of leaning on Nate might strip me of my very identity.

Arguably, that went away with my name change. I was never this jumpy. I never knew my whole life was held together by a single thread. My father.

"You don't like your job," he points out. "Your boss is an asshole."

He's not wrong. I snort and tack on, "Creating spreadsheets and filing forms is as mind-numbing to me as a frontal lobotomy."

"So find a new job. One that challenges you."

The way he's looking at me is making me nervous. He points to one of the Grand Marin buildings. "See that corner office with all the windows?"

"Yes."

"What do you think?"

"It's gorgeous." The sidewalk is freshly poured and slim-trunked trees stand at even intervals at the corner. Overlooking the street is a second-floor office. Its interior is dimly lit, but I can make out the shape of tall plants by the window and a large desk.

"I had it furnished by a state-of-the-art designer today. It's where my property manager will have his or her office when I hire one. I need someone smart, timely. Someone who won't screw me over."

"Walt is smart, but I'm not sure about the other two," I reply with a laugh. My brother would be a terrible fit for that position.

"I'm not talking about Walt. I mean you. How would you like to run Grand Marin?"

"Run it?"

"In addition to being the contracted builder, my company also oversees the property management. It's my ass if I don't put a superstar in that office."

"I don't know anything about managing a property."

"I'll teach you." He shrugs. As if it's that easy.

I look up at the corner office and picture myself in there. In a smart, black suit and heels, chatting on the phone or flipping through reports. Popping down to the sidewalk to buy a foamy cappuccino and then sitting on a park bench in the common area to drink it.

It's terrifying.

I was once in charge of a lot of employees. I had an entire department reporting to me. I instructed men like Nate on a biweekly basis, all of them earning more money than I was. I don't know if I can trust myself in a high-powered position again, and that's not the only argument for why it's a bad idea.

"What if…something happens?" I ask instead of sharing my worries about bombing spectacularly in a managerial position.

"Something like what?"

Like we break up and hate each other. Or worse, we break up and tolerate each other. But that's presumptuous, isn't it? He asked me to stay with him for the week because he knows my brother and his girlfriend are annoying me. Maybe he was being nice. And maybe this job offer is a simple solution to his problem and mine.

A long-dormant part of my soul surges forward at the idea of once again rising to meet new goals. I miss the feeling of purpose I had when I worked for my father's company. I thought I was fostering a great legacy. Little did I know.

I send another wary gaze to the Grand Marin office and bite my lip.

"Life is short, Viv. Don't waste another minute doing something you don't want to do." He thumbs my chin, his eyes broadcasting sincerity. "Those drab walls and worn carpet don't suit you, anyway. And I won't micromanage you. You'd have full autonomy."

No, I wouldn't miss the drab walls, worn carpet, or Daniel. Amber's nice, but we could have lunch together after I quit CRBI. I imagine telling Daniel I'll no longer be his lackey, and my chest expands with the fullest breath I've taken all day.

"Just a thought," Nate says, as if he didn't radically change my entire life by offering me the key to the prison cell. "Think it over, but I need to find someone soon. It would save me a lot of advertising and headhunting. I'm incredibly picky about who I put in charge."

"No pressure," I joke.

"None whatsoever." He leans in and kisses me soundly. "When you come over tonight, bring a bag. You and I can talk about where Walt would fit working for me, and what it would look like if you work at Grand Marin. And then you can stay with me for a week and try it on for size."

"Funny, this *feels* like pressure."

His grin isn't one of denial.

"Where would Walt work anyway?" I ask, happy to change the subject. "Grand Marin is almost complete. You won't need more construction guys here."

"True. But I have other sites."

"Like the one in Chicago." As much as Walt tends to chap my ass, I'm not ready for him to be far away.

"And elsewhere. He lived in Atlanta without you. What makes you think he can't live somewhere else without you?"

"Maybe I don't want him to go too far."

"Maybe you hovering isn't good for him."

That spikes my blood pressure. "I'm not hovering."

"Family is important. I know better than anyone. But you have to let people make their own choices. We can't watch over them twenty-four/seven. He's not your responsibility, and I don't want you hurt if he does backslide." Nate squeezes my forearm with gentle pressure, comforting me.

"But I worry."

"Of course you do."

"He was in a rehabilitation home most of the time he was in Atlanta. That's a far cry from living on his own," I continue arguing, hearing how resistant I am. Do I not trust him? Or do I need a project? Would Grand Marin be a better use of my micromanaging skills?

"You can't take care of him the rest of your life. You're going to have to trust him to be on his own at some point."

Damn Nate and his valid observations.

"If I stay with you for the week," I start, and his smile spreads his mouth in a slow, tantalizing way, "it doesn't mean I'm not going back to my apartment at all. It's still my place and if I want to make a big pot of mac and cheese for my guests, I will." I thrust up my chin in defiance.

His smile is cocky, but it's also sweet—his signature.

He kisses me one more time. "Fair enough."

Chapter Twenty-Two

Nate

By the end of the week, I'm used to the way Vivian returns home from work.

Through the front door with a greeting to Odessa first, who's here most nights prepping dinner. Then Viv greets me with a kiss when I come downstairs, usually from the direction of my home office.

Today I'm in the living room when she comes home, choosing a vinyl record. Nat King Cole, I decide.

Odessa is busy in the kitchen preparing dinner for this evening. A bigger affair than usual since we're expecting company.

At the mouth of the living room, Viv spots me and smiles. "Well, this is a surprise. I thought I knew your patterns."

"After a few nights? Doubtful."

"Dinner smells good."

"As do you." I place a kiss on her neck and then her mouth. When we part, her eyes flutter closed. "Ready for tonight?"

"As ready as I'll ever be, I suppose." Her eyes are stunning sienna brown with flecks of gold. I've either noticed the more nuanced shade since she's been living here or the overhead lighting makes them look different. "It was nice of you to invite them."

Them is Walt and Dee. I suggested dinner to discuss Walt's job rather than an in-office interview with HR. Given his past, I thought he'd appreciate not being subjected to the formality.

Walt was the only one invited, but when he asked about Dee, who did end up staying in Viv's apartment, by the way, Viv told him to bring her. It doesn't bother me that Dee is joining us, but it bothers Viv. She confessed last night while we were curled up in bed. Her pressed against my chest, my arm around her shoulders. I'm used to her in bed with me, and I'm devising a plan to keep her there longer than a week.

"I'm going to change." She kisses me again and heads upstairs. She looks amazing, but especially in the outfits Brandy selected for her.

"I'll join you." I follow her upstairs and lean against the open double closet doors while she takes off her outfit for the day—a pressed white pair of slacks and a spring-green top. She sweeps aside one hanger then another before holding up a gray dress. When she reaches for a pair of bone-colored high heels, she sends me a derisive look.

It's for show.

I've received few complaints since the first night she entered my closet and found a dozen outfits and as many pairs of shoes lining "her" side. But those complaints were followed by sex in this very closet. I'm fairly sure I'm forgiven.

"Spoiled," she mumbles as she slips the dress over her head.

"I hope so." I zip the back of her dress, kissing a line up her spine as I do.

"I never wanted it back, you know." She turns to confront me. Which makes me want her again. I consider unzipping her and kissing a few more places. "This lifestyle," she specifies. "It's ridiculous. Who lives like this?"

"You. Me. About a million other people." I pull her into the circle of my arms. "Stop worrying how you'll live without it and enjoy it while it's here."

"That's not what I'm afraid of."

I want to ask what she is afraid of, but that's a question for tonight when we're in bed, not twenty minutes before company arrives.

Downstairs, Odessa removes her apron and hangs it on the inside of the pantry door. The table is set in the dining room, the candles lit, a flower arrangement in the center. "Anything else, Mr. Owen?"

"No, thank you."

She tells us goodbye and exits the house.

Viv turns toward me. "You're the only rich guy I know who doesn't want his chef to serve the meal."

"I'm capable of serving myself and a few friends. I just don't want to cook it."

Her smile falls when the doorbell rings. We go to answer it together, a unified front. That's different, but not uncomfortable. Walt is wearing jeans and a button-down shirt. The creases in the sleeves from where it was folded suggest he bought it recently.

"I borrowed your dress," Dee says to Vivian.

I can tell by Viv's tight shoulders she didn't know Dee was borrowing her dress. It'd piss me off if someone rummaged through my closet to borrow my clothes without permission.

"It's really pretty." Dee smooths a hand down the pale blue fabric. The dress is too long on her. She's a few inches shorter than Viv, and she doesn't quite fill out the bustline.

"Yes. It's one of my favorites," Viv replies carefully.

"What can I pour you to drink? I have wine, beer and—" I offer automatically before remembering they're in recovery. "Shit."

"Shit sounds good. I'll have that," Walt says with a laugh.

"I love Pepsi," Dee says.

"I have Coke."

Her nose wrinkles. "Water is fine."

"Still or Perrier?" Vivian offers.

"Rich people, am I right? Viv, you fit right in." Dee laughs. Walt and Viv exchange glances. I wonder if Dee knows she's about to have dinner with the one and only Walter Steele, Junior.

There's warm, crusty bread in a basket in the center of the table. I invite Walt and Dee to help themselves while I grab the main course. Vivian offers to fetch the drinks, following me into the kitchen.

"Water for you as well?" She pulls Perrier bottles from the fridge.

"Bourbon, preferably. But I understand if that's an issue around Walt."

"I have wine in my apartment and it didn't bother him. But Dee..." Vivian lowers her voice.

"You sound unsure."

"I have to look out for my brother. He hasn't been great at looking after himself."

"We'll check for missing silverware after they leave." I kiss her forehead and smile. I don't miss the eye roll she gives me as I bypass her to serve our guests.

Vivian

I don't mind that Dee borrowed my dress. Okay, I *do*, but I wish she would have asked. I would have let her borrow it if she'd asked. She didn't though, just like she didn't ask if she could move into my apartment with Walt and eat the groceries I paid for, and that's the problem. She's as entitled as if she's an extension of Walt, but she's not. She's an interloper.

"How goes the job search?" Nate asks, his eyes shifting from Walt to Dee. She looks at Walt expectantly.

"Not great." Walt tears a piece of bread off and butters it generously. "I used to work in an office and now it's the last place I want to be."

"You did?" Dee asks, which makes me wonder what the hell they talk about all the time.

"Sort of," I answer for Walt. He frowns. "He worked for our family's company part-time."

"I'd rather work outside." My brother gives me the stink-eye.

"I have an opening at Owen Construction if you're interested," Nate says. Walt's eyes go wide with interest. "It's a starting position with a decent salary. Travel is required, but the company will reimburse you. You'd be based outside of Chicago."

"Back home," my brother says, and the longing in his voice breaks my heart. I know he misses our old life. Our family. He has better memories of it, probably because that office job he alluded to was really, *really* part-time. Plus, whenever he returned from a stint in rehab, he was treated like the prodigal son come home.

"You'd be required to have a sponsor and attend AA meetings regularly. I'd need proof. And weekly check-ins with the project manager. Drug screenings too."

Walt's gaze shifts to mine. "What is this?"

"An offer. You haven't found a better one."

"I'm not a criminal, Viv."

"You are," Nate says. "You have been caught with illegal narcotics repeatedly. Why do you think a company won't take a chance on you?"

"And, what, you are because Viv begged?"

I open my mouth to argue, but Nate is faster than me.

"This was my idea. I had junkie parents and a criminal record. I had the opportunity to have a new life, a fresh start."

"By being adopted by billionaires. That's lucky."

"You were born into a billionaire family. That's lucky too," Nate counters.

Dee's mouth drops open. "You were?" She seeks me out next

since Walt and Nate are in the middle of an intense male stare-down.

"We lost everything when our parents passed away." I'm not so much covering for Walt as avoiding having to explain. It's hard to admit who our father was. Hell, Nate had to call me on it or I might never have told him.

"Speaking of, I had a thought about Dad's remains." My brother pushes his plate, and the subject of him working for Nate, aside. I told Walt about visiting Mom's grave, about how wrong it felt to put Dad in the ground next to her. "You're right about keeping them apart. In life they barely got along, why doom them to spend eternity together?"

I quirk my lips. It's a dark subject for dinner.

"How about sprinkling him in the water? He loved the ocean and the lake. Mom never liked either."

Thinking of her again splits me open. I blink back tears. I was so angry with her when she took her own life. I've had moments of grief, but usually it comes with a side of anger. Today is the first moment sadness eclipses the anger.

A burial at sea for Dad is better than he deserves, but he can't sit on my countertop for the rest of my life.

"There won't be any record of him, Viv," my brother says softly. "He'll be gone. Finally."

I nod, knowing it's the right answer.

"Lake Michigan, maybe. Close to home," Walt says. Dee puts her hand on his shoulder and promises to go with him.

"We can rent a boat," Nate offers. "While we're there I can show you the job site. You can look for an apartment nearby."

"That's going to require money." Walt looks at me expectantly. I shake my head.

"That money is earmarked for rehab."

"I'm out of rehab."

"For now." I slide a glance at Dee who's watching me just as expectantly. I'm being overprotective of him, but for now I'm okay with that. "I need a lime wedge for my water," I lie, standing from the table. Halfway to the kitchen, I feel someone follow me. To my surprise it's not Nate.

I grab a lime from a bowl on the counter and make use of the small knife and cutting board next to it. I'm aware of Walt glaring at me, arms folded over his chest.

"I'm done with rehab. That was my last stay. I'm going to attend AA meetings for the rest of my life, but I'm not going to be admitted ever again," he tells me. "Don't you trust me?"

I don't answer, squeezing a lime wedge into my glass. Then I reach for a bowl from a cabinet and pile the remaining fruit into it.

"V."

"I trust *you*." I think I mean it. "But things happen outside of our control. Outside of *your* control. What if you have a bad day at work and you need a release valve? What if you and Dee have a fight? What if she—"

"What is your problem with her anyway?" He keeps his voice low.

I peek into the dining room. Nate has started a conversation about who knows what, and Dee happily obliges him by listening. He's good.

"She's an addict," I whisper.

"So am I."

"You've been clean longer than her."

"She'll get there. And if she doesn't"—he takes a breath, his eyebrows lowering like it pains him to consider it—"I will still be clean. You're doing to her what everyone did to you during Dad's trial."

"What's that supposed to mean?" I mentally remind myself to keep my voice down.

"You haven't given her a chance or the benefit of the doubt. She hasn't done anything wrong and yet you're sure she's going to. You're betting on her to fail, and you don't even know her."

"And you do?" I let out an incredulous laugh.

"Yeah. I do. You need to trust me." He sighs, sounding tired. "I'm taking meditation classes to help with the stress."

He is? "You are?"

"They're online, but yeah."

"Oh. I thought you were listening to music." Or sleeping. Every once in a while I'd notice him with a laptop on his lap, headphones on, eyes closed. I never considered he was meditating. I have been underestimating him. And, possibly, Dee.

"I'm not fifteen any longer, V. You can't hold my money hostage until I reach a summit you've chosen for me."

Then again, maybe I haven't been underestimating him.

"It's not *your money*." I argue with that rather than the summit part. I realize a little guiltily I have been setting peak goals for him. Every day they are farther and farther out. "It was Dad's money. Which means it wasn't technically *his*, either."

"Unlike you, I don't care about its origin. There's no sense in suffering needlessly. Dad's dead. There are no more strips of flesh you can take from him. He's gone."

My lips compress. Why does it suddenly feel like everyone is ganging up on me?

"Can you be nice to her?" He picks up the bowl of lime wedges. "For me?"

I nod. Solemnly.

I follow him to the dining room and do my damnedest not to stomp. I would feel better if he were thanking me, but that's about me too, isn't it? Resigned, I settle into my chair and force a smile.

"Dee, what is it you do in Atlanta?" I ask.

"I used to write code for websites, but before I went back into rehab I started working on a horse farm and I really liked it."

Really? I want to ask but don't.

"That's why Walt wanted to take you horseback riding," I say instead.

"Yeah. I love horses." She smiles.

"When you go back to Atlanta, will you live with your sister again, or are you planning on renting your own place?"

"Um..." She turns to Walt. He cocks his head at me.

I send a silent message to him that *hey, I'm being friendly, here* before I realize he has an announcement.

"She's not going back to Atlanta." He holds Dee's hand on the table and dares me with his eyes to argue. "We're getting married."

I can't breathe. My baby brother, who can barely care for a plant, is going to marry a girl from Atlanta who has been sober for a little over a month and loves horses? When I am forced to take a breath, lest I lose consciousness, I blow out, "Walt—"

"Congratulations," Nate interrupts me to say. Under the tablecloth he squeezes my knee. "Sounds like you'll both need to agree on an apartment."

"An apartment costs money," Walt points out again, his eyes never leaving mine.

"If you accept my job offer, you'll have money," Nate supplies.

"Your job offer comes with a lot of strings, Owen." I don't like this power trip Walt is on. He's being reckless. I narrow my eyes across the table. Lovestruck Dee isn't far behind.

"I'm not parting with your salary for any less than a guarantee you won't shoot it up your arm." Nate's voice is low and hard, and I'm momentarily shocked. Guess he's not as mellow about this as he seems. Walt has always been able to recognize authority. He recognizes it now and sits up straighter. "My offer isn't charity, Walter. It's a hand up, not a handout. You want to work for me? You'll have to work hard. You'll have to prove yourself. Eventually, you could be running one of my job sites in Dubai if you want, but we have to build trust from the start."

"You're in Dubai?" Walt asks, flabbergasted and impressed. So am I.

Nate only smiles, liking that he caught us off guard. "Not yet."

I EXCUSE myself to the backyard after dinner. I need another opinion. A woman's opinion. Preferably a woman who knew both my brother and me well and will agree that no, Walt doesn't need money for a place and yes, marrying a woman who's fresh out of rehab is a horrible plan.

I position myself under the porch lights, which frame me in an unattractive yellowish glow, but Marnie will forgive me. If she's available. Fingers crossed.

I text her and ask if she has "a moment to video chat before I lose my mind" and then I check the windows and find Nate fiddling with the knobs on a speaker. I can't make out what song he's playing, but the bass vibrates the glass. He's granting me privacy. I like that about him. Or maybe my brother drove him as crazy as he drove me and this is his way of coping.

My cell phone rings in my palm and beautiful, flawless Marnie takes up the screen with her perfect face.

"Auntie Em," I say in greeting.

She lets out a throaty laugh. "I'm en route to the fridge," she says as she slides through the kitchen and pulls open the door on a wide, stainless-steel refrigerator. "This sounded like a conversation for wine."

"It's also a conversation I should have had a week ago before I fell into fantasyland." I hold my phone in one hand and a wineglass in the other. I poured a chardonnay the second my brother and his *fiancée* left.

"Ho boy. Let's hear it, sister."

"I feel like I only call you with problems."

"Vivian. I'm here."

She is. No matter how long I go without reaching out, she's happy to take my calls. I love her for that.

I summarize dinner with my brother and Dee and then mention Chicago and where we're going to bury my father. Then I admit I'm living with Nate and how it's borderline suffocating. I breathe out the entire diatribe in one whooshing breath while pacing the yard. My face on the screen goes from half-lit to fully lit to completely dark.

"Okay, okay," Marnie says, her presence calming. Or maybe

admitting all that stuff aloud is what calmed me. "Take a breath. A big one."

I obey. And then take two more like she instructs.

"That always helps me." She's now lounging on a wicker chair by her crystal-clear in-ground pool. She lifts her white wine to her lips for a quick sip. "Let's start with you staying at your billionaire boyfriend's house."

"Ugh." I collapse into a chair and sit much less elegantly than my friend. "Have I leapt from the pan to the fire?"

"Not unless he's embezzling money." She smiles. I smile. It feels good to smile.

"Am I blowing everything out of proportion?"

She shrugs one slim shoulder "If you feel you need to stay close to Walt, honey, you should. He's your family. He's important."

"He told me I'm making a snap judgment about Dee. He said I'm doing the same thing people did to me after Dad's trial."

She seesaws her head in thought. "Sort of but sort of not. See, Dee *is* guilty of what you're accusing her of—using to the point of detriment. You were accused of stealing money and you never did. Not the same thing."

"So, what, I refuse to let Walt leave?"

"You don't want that either. But if he ends up taking a job elsewhere, who says you can't go with?"

I sit up straight. "Yeah, who says?"

"You haven't committed to anything, Viv. You didn't agree to live with Nate forever. You haven't taken the job he offered yet. You can do whatever you want."

"Right. You're right." I'm not trapped. I'm not committed.

"Unless you're having feelings for him..." Marnie raises her eyebrows in question.

I shake my head, both to communicate I haven't developed feelings for him and to keep out any stray thought to the contrary.

We chat a while longer about her wedding plans, and she invites me to the small gathering. It'll be intimate, she tells me, with around twenty-five people in attendance, and it's not until next year. She jokes that I can bring whatever man I like as a plus-one, and I joke that I might show up stag.

But when I look through the windows at Nate, part of me warms at the idea of him being around next year.

I shove the thought away, and remind myself family comes first. Self-preservation, though, is a close second.

Chapter Twenty-Three

Nate

Vivian comes in from the backyard and I turn down the music. She looks different. More relaxed and on edge at the same time. That wall she hides behind had been crumbling, but since she's been staying here "officially" she's been rebuilding. I wonder if she's aware she's doing it.

Dating her keeps me on my toes, that's for damn sure.

The girls I went out with as a punk teenager deserved better. They had the same idea in mind as I did, I guess. Make out. Have sex sometimes. We'd park and sit in the car and listen to the radio and smoke or drink or both. Thank God I wasn't busted for any of it or Will and Lainey would have strangled me.

When I was an adult, and learned how to tie a tie, I connected with women the only way I knew how—although the make-out sessions happened in a much nicer car. When we were bored, we'd shop rather than park, or eat at an expensive restaurant or fundraiser.

Until Deborah. The older woman who pulled me off her ex-husband's job site and paid me to build hers. She and I connected, or at the time I thought we did. I suspect she used me to fill the lonely hours in her day. Meanwhile, I was hacking my way through the overgrowth hiding an unused heart. I wasn't familiar with love until the Owens accepted me as I came. Not that their love had prepared me for romantic love. That's a whole other ballgame—with a dynamic set of rules.

Vivian sits on the couch next to me with a *whump*. I take the wineglass from her hand and set my drink next to it on the coffee table.

She needed a moment after dinner to decompress. I get it. I maintained my cool for her sake. I noticed Walt challenging her at every turn. I saw in his eyes how much he enjoyed dropping the marriage bomb on his big sister. Had one of my brothers used me in that way, I'd have been upset too.

I wrap my arms around her waist and her hands lift automatically to encircle my neck. She tilts her head to the side like she's deciding whether or not she still likes me. She does. She has to. I'm a catch.

"Kiss me," I beg.

She indulges me, tentatively at first but I take that kiss to the brink. After a deep, long, wet meeting of the mouths, she pulls away and swipes her bottom lip with her index finger.

"I'm addicted to your flavor." I spike my fingers through her shiny, thick hair. I haven't nearly had enough of her tonight.

She hums, her mind elsewhere. Maybe on how to further fortify the fortress she's rebuilding around herself.

Evidently she needs *another* moment. I release her and sit back on the couch, taking my drink with me. "When you came to my job site, you were a hot ball of fire in a hardhat. You challenged my authority, which I did not like."

"Yeah, the sledgehammer move sort of gave away your emotions."

I ignore her sarcasm and keep talking. "Soon after, you challenged a belief I'd held for a long, long time."

Her eyes hit mine. I have her attention.

"Which was?"

"I believed I didn't need a relationship with a woman lasting more than a few casual nights." I shrug. "My life is busy. I'm committed to excellence. I have a family I can't let down. Women are too much work."

She nods, accepting what I said at face value. "And I'm proving your theory right."

"You're sure as hell trying to."

Her throat bobs as she swallows, but some of her guard drops. It's no longer a steel wall. It's a sheer veil.

"The jig is up, Viv."

Her eyebrows lower in confusion. She doesn't know what I mean, which is exactly what I intended.

"We connected in Chicago," I tell her, realizing this conversation might send her running for the hills. But I refuse to live life walking on eggshells. We're two incredibly strong people and that means we fight it out in the arena, not from the stands. "And at your mother's gravesite."

She reaches for her wineglass.

I set my glass aside and fold my hands, remembering that afternoon. "I felt a camaraderie there, standing over her tombstone. You understand what it's like to lose someone you love. And you felt it too. That bond between two orphaned kids." Even though she's living, I can't count my birth mother as a parent, which Vivian now understands. "We've lost a lot. But we have a lot to gain."

She grunts.

"Say it," I tell her.

"*You've* arrived, Nate. I'm dead weight. What do you want from me, anyway?"

"Are you shitting me?" Her snarky comment cut deeper than I wanted it to. "I don't want anything from you. *I just want you.* Is that so hard to believe?"

She opened up to me in Chicago. She was tender and understanding. She didn't come out, sword swinging, like she's been doing since Walt reentered her life. If he has a hangnail she drops everything to take care of him. He's starting to piss me off. "I thought you were settling in here."

"This isn't real life, Nate." She shakes her head pitiably like I'm the dolt who doesn't see what's right in front of him.

"I don't like when you use my name as a swearword," I tell her. "And I disagree. This *is* real life. This is *my* life. You're here and you're real. I'm real. This is a life we're making together. Don't you recognize it when it's in front of you?

"Walt and his issues have taken center stage since we came home from Chicago," I continue. "I think focusing on his problems is your way of masking your own needs."

Her eyes flame with anger. She stands and slams down her glass. "And what do I *need,* Nate? Eight-course meals? A selection of designer clothes? Expensive shoes? Sex?"

"Aside from the great sex, that's all stuff." I stand too, plunging my hands in my pockets to broadcast that no matter how much her dander goes up I'm maintaining a level head. "I'm offering you more than stuff. I want you here. I'm in no hurry for you to leave."

She blinks at me but stays silent.

"Have you thought about managing Grand Marin and quitting the bureau?"

"No," she huffs.

"No, you haven't thought about it, or no, you don't want the job?"

"I'm trying *not* to think about it."

Exactly my point. She's ignoring her own life to hyper-focus on her brother's. I lean close. "Why not?"

"The other shoe always drops. Always." Her voice is small. I hate when her voice is small. She's stronger than this.

"It *dropped,* Vivian. Both of them. You threw them at me on my job site and then I put the broken one in the dumpster along with its mate. Remember?"

I didn't plan on admitting this so soon, but here goes nothing.

"I'm falling for you."

Her mouth opens softly. I cup her jaw. I need what I'm saying to penetrate her stubborn mind.

"I didn't expect to fall for you. I knew you were a challenge and great in bed. I didn't put expectations on what we had. I'm busy. I have a ton of my own baggage to sort through. You don't want a guy like me in your life. You've proven that time and again. You're cagey and jumpy and uncertain."

"A-and you're *falling* for me?" She lets out an exasperated laugh and I fall more.

"Guess so."

"That's not very smart." Her smile is shaky, but it's there. I scared her. Understandable. I scared myself.

"I'm not always smart. Case in point."

She bites her bottom lip.

"Who did you call out there?"

After a beat, she tells me. "Marnie."

I wait for her to explain.

"She's a friend who knew me back when."

"Back when you were Vivian Steele."

"Yeah." She pulls in a deep breath. "I called her to vent. I needed someone to agree with me."

"And did she?"

"Yes. She did." Vivian elevates her chin in a regal tilt. That's my girl.

"Good. We all need friends who take our sides."

I sit and pat the sofa in invitation for her to join me. She literally looks over her shoulder like she's gauging the distance from couch to front door, before sitting primly on the edge of a cushion.

"So, now what do we do?" she asks her hands.

"Finish our drinks. Go to bed. Talk about when we're introducing your father to Lake Michigan."

Her laugh seems to surprise her. "You're crazy."

"Like a fox," I mutter.

She looks tired, but not like she's beat. Like she's finally able to relax. Like she's trying on the idea of my falling for her and it's a more comfortable fit than she expected.

"I have nothing to lose," I tell her. As lies go, it's a whopper. My heart is thundering, and it's suddenly hard for me to breathe.

"Everyone has something to lose."

She called me on it. We're not as different as she'd like to believe. My real family was as neglectful as hers, but in a different way. I had too little, she had too much. She believes wealth saved me, but that's not entirely true. I was saved by hope. William and Lainey Owen gave me hope and purpose, and that was why I left the familiar walls of the juvenile delinquent center.

It's hope that made Viv's brother, Walt, accept the job I offered him tonight. It's hope, and a hefty dash of Steele family stubbornness, that made him announce his plans to marry Dee. His grumbling about the hard lines I drew was a deflection. He wanted to say yes to me so badly he couldn't sit still. Like his sister, Walt fears hope too.

"You're right to be wary. Life isn't without risks." I slide her hair from her cheek. She's watching me with wide eyes and yeah, there's a glimmer of hope bursting through.

"And I'm a risk?" she asks.

"The biggest one I've ever taken."

Her smile quirks to one side and a second later she's on top of me. I wasn't ready for her, so she succeeds at knocking me to my back. The wind is stolen from my lungs when she closes her lips over mine. I slip my tongue into her mouth and she accepts it greedily. For long minutes, she's kissing the life out of me, writhing over top of me. I don't mind her changing the subject to a language we both understand. Sex is our primary form of communication, after all.

My hands roam over her back, her ass, her legs, and then travel up her skirt. I don't know if she's in a hurry to make me forget my proclamation, or if she feels the same way I do but wants to show instead of tell.

Me? I don't care why she's attacking me, only that she is. It's better than her icing me out.

If you thumb back through my timeline, you'll notice I spent most of my thirty-six years not understanding a hell of a lot about love. My mother's depiction of love was to take what she could for herself. Even her subservience to my father was about her getting rather than giving. She needs to be needed, and in my family that's as dangerous as a loaded gun to the temple.

As Vivian moves her lips over mine, I wonder if I have the same tendency to need to be needed. Do I love her because I need her to love me? Am I as misguided as my mother?

No.

The answer comes swiftly enough that I trust it. Vivian doesn't come with any guarantees, which I've known from the start. She may *never* love me in return. Not the most pleasant realization, but that also feels true.

For right now she's here. With me. Accepting my hands as they pull off her clothing. Accepting my cock as I slide deep and settle into her luscious body. As long as she's here; as long as she wants me, I have nothing to complain about. She doesn't have to make a grand announcement. It's enough to have her in my house, her warm, breathy pants heating my neck while I drive her into the arm of the sofa.

All good things are simple. That's what I'm saying.

Humans tend to complicate life, but life isn't complicated. Maybe, I think as I maneuver my hand between her legs, if she stays around long enough, I can help her understand that.

If. Big if.

But hell, why not try?

Chapter Twenty-Four

Vivian

On a chartered yacht in Lake Michigan, Walt and I are in the process of tossing our father's ashes overboard.

Dee came along for the trip, but for this private moment Nate pulled her to the side to teach her how to drive the yacht. He knew Walt and I needed a moment.

My brother and I watch as a cloud of ashes hits the water, the individual granules settling for a split second before sinking below the surface.

"He must have started out wanting to build a business for the right reasons," he says, his eyes on the water. "Don't you think?"

"I like to think so."

"No man makes a goal to become a criminal and rip off the people who love and trust him. That's insanity. Dad wasn't insane."

"No, he wasn't. He had an ego the size of this planet, though. Earth couldn't hold him, I guess." My attempt at a joke falls flat as tears pool in my eyes. I didn't expect them, though I suppose I should have. My brother wraps an arm around my shoulders and squeezes. More tears come.

"You don't have to be strong, V," he whispers. "A rug was pulled out from under you, and I have been a pain in your ass."

"Ya think?" I ask, my voice watery. I feel him smile as he squeezes me against his side.

"I'm sorry. I've been a selfish dick. I'm taking things seriously now—taking my life seriously. Thanks to you introducing me to Nate, I have a job. That was huge."

I sniffle. His gratitude means a lot to me.

"Strength comes naturally to you. The rest of us have to work at it."

"It doesn't come naturally," I argue. I practiced for years and years, and the habit somehow became part of my new personality.

"It's okay to be emotional. That's where real strength lies." Walt releases me and smiles, his own eyes welling.

I swipe my cheeks. "I told Nate I should look into therapy again, but maybe I'll go to a twelve-step instead."

"Spend the money on therapy. Addiction isn't worth it," my brother says with a self-deprecating wink. We turn and stare down at the water in silence.

Nate and Dee leave the helm and peer over the side of the yacht a few minutes later. They're still standing apart from Walt and me.

We spent the first four hours of the day apartment hunting. Walt and Dee asked if we could come along and offer our opinions. It was a peace offering I accepted. I went through about a million emotions while touring those dwellings with my brother and the woman who might someday be his wife. It was strange. I'm trying not to micromanage him but it's difficult. All I can see when I look at the two of them is the potential mistakes they might make. No matter what Nate said about shoes already having dropped, I know there are always more shoes. Which makes it hard to stay comfortable for long.

Nate navigates Dee to the other side of the boat and points out a building. He starts describing its history, buying me more time with my brother. He always seems to know what I need.

"Things with Owen seem to be progressing," Walt says. "You haven't been home much lately."

"I'm giving you space." Guilt stabs me. "Do you need something? Groceries?"

"I need you to take some of the money you've been saving for me and pay yourself for my loafing on your couch," he says.

"Excuse me?" I wiggle my pinky in my ear for effect. "Did I just hear you offer me money?"

"Don't rub it in." The wind kicks his longish hair around his head. "Dee told me I should have offered."

Wow. One point for Dee.

"Don't look so surprised. She's a good person."

I quirk my mouth in consideration. To be fair, I never believed she *wasn't* a good person. I just worried she could be an anchor around my drowning brother's neck.

"I might've judged her too harshly," I admit.

"Yeah, well, in the back of my mind I thought you were dating Owen because he's rich."

I gasp.

"I don't think that any longer," he continues. "I didn't live in rehab my entire life, sis. I remember when you dated. None of those trust-fund douchebags were like Nate." Walt turns his head to check on Nate and Dee before addressing me again. "Nothing like him."

"I'm nothing like I used to be, so that makes sense."

This brings forth a big laugh from my brother.

"What?"

"You are *exactly* the same as you used to be. Driven. Talented. Playing it safe."

"Excuse me?" I prop my hands on my hips, prepared to defend my former life. "How was being the vice president of marketing and data analysis at Dad's firm 'playing it safe'?"

Walt gives me a bland blink as if it should be obvious.

Should it?

"You should be running your own company. Instead you're at some dinky city bureau working for a guy you don't like."

I huff, mainly because Nate said something similar while we sat at Grand Marin looking up at that beautiful office.

"That's easy to say from the outside—" I start deflecting.

"I wasn't always on the outside. You could be a billionaire on your own. I'm the one who needs corralling."

"Is that what Dee's doing?" I incline my chin in her direction. She might well be his first attempt at caring for someone other than himself.

"I'm in love with her. That's all I know."

God. Is it in the water?

"How do you know? That you love her?" Before he becomes defensive, I add, "I'm not patronizing you. I mean, *really*, how do you know when you're in romantic love with someone?" I whisper the last part to avoid Nate overhearing.

"Well…" Walt squints at the sun, bright overhead thanks to a cloudless sky. I don't know if he's thinking of a way to explain, or if he's unaccustomed to having to explain. Maybe he's trying to find an appropriate way to explain it *to me*.

Finally his dark brown eyes return to mine. "At some point, you have to decide to let yourself feel again. I blocked out the hurt by using, but the problem is you block out the good too." He sighs. "There was so much hurt at home, V. Mom was unhappy. Way before we found out what Dad was doing."

"I know." I worry I'm doomed to repeat her misery.

"You're not like her," he says, reading my mind. "If you open up again, you can have the good."

"There's more hurt than good in the world, little brother."

"That's one way to look at it." He casts Dee a glance. His expression is earnest. Loving. The sickly sheen is gone and he's put on a good ten pounds since he's been in Ohio. Sobriety suits him.

"There's more than one way to look at it?" I ask quietly.

"Many more ways than one," he answers with a soft smile.

Dee must feel him watching her. She blows him a kiss. My heart pinches with what might be envy. Worry is there too, but at least another emotion has joined it.

I look past her to Nate and try to decide if he looks like a man in love. Or a man, as he put it, who is "falling" for me. Seems he built in some safeguards after all. He didn't use the L-word.

Nate struts over, Dee skipping ahead of him. He looks as good in shorts and a sleeveless shirt as he does naked, which makes no sense. He just plain looks *good*. Maybe him looking good in spite of what he's wearing, or that imperfect nose, is a sign I'm in love with him.

Hmm.

"Nate agrees the apartment on Palmetto is perfect." Dee beams. "It's my favorite one."

"I liked that one too," I offer. Her smile turns gracious. Nate's smile is proud.

She bounces on the balls of her feet. "Do you think we should do it?"

"We can definitely consider it," Walt says.

"I'm worried we'll lose it if we don't decide fast. It was the only open unit in the building." She pouts.

"The deposit—" Walt starts.

"Is covered." I wave a hand. "You might be new at this managing-your-own-money thing, but you have enough for deposit and first month's rent, easily. And with your position at Nate's site, you're solid."

Gratitude lights up Walt's face.

"Even without the money you're keeping for yourself?" he asks, taking advantage of our audience to convince me. Oh, but I'm the big sister here. I know what he's doing.

"We'll see."

My brother acquiesces with a slight nod before turning to Nate. "Do you mind taking us back? Evidently we need to hustle over to Palmetto."

"Yes!" Dee bounces some more. "I'm more of a land lover anyway."

Walt hugs her close and corrects with, "Landlubber."

"What?" She wrinkles her nose and he kisses it.

"Nothing."

Okay. That was cute.

AFTER WALT and Dee are on land, Nate takes us out onto the water again. I lose the cover-up and lounge on a bench on the deck of the yacht.

"You done good today, kid," my captain says as he refills my champagne flute. We snacked on a packed cooler of goodies we brought with us. Odessa put it together. Chickpea salad sandwiches and homemade dill dip and cucumbers. Dessert is chia-seed pudding with fresh raspberries, but I'm saving it for later.

"What do you mean?" I sip my champagne.

"With Dee and Walt. Making sure he knew you weren't going to fight him on the money. That's a big step."

"Yeah, well, I'm still going to look in on him."

He hoists an eyebrow.

"Occasionally."

Chuckling, he sits next to me on the cushioned bench. A few other boats are on the water, but far enough away that we have privacy. It's peaceful.

"Why don't you own a boat?" I ask.

"Too much hassle."

"I never owned one either," I tell him. "I worked too much to take the time."

"That's part of the reason I don't have one." He touches the gold embellishment on my bright pink bikini top. It's shaped like a seashell and nestled in between my breasts. "I like this."

"Thanks."

His hand is wrapped around a beer bottle he rests on one wide thigh over his shorts.

"I appreciate you bringing us out here," I tell him. "It's sad. Not an ideal date setup."

"It is sad." His gaze returns to me. "You okay?"

"I think I am okay."

"If not, I'm here."

That should be his motto. Instead of a snarky comeback I take another sip from my champagne flute. The breeze blows off the water and cools the sweat glistening on my skin. I need another layer of sunscreen, but right now I'm enjoying the heat. "Do you think Walt and Dee are good together?"

"For now they seem to be."

I appreciate his honesty.

"Do you?" he asks.

"I worry."

"You wouldn't be you unless you worried." He takes a pull from his beer bottle. "Walt seems stable. I don't know him well, though. What's he like when he's out of rehab?"

"Twitchy," I answer immediately. "He's had one cigarette today which is crazy. Normally he's a chain smoker. I'm not familiar with Dee's patterns. She could do this all the time. Leave rehab, shack up with a guy, claim she's in love with him." I didn't know this tirade was in me until I started talking. I guess being nice to her and looking for her ulterior motives can exist at the same time. "She could be using Walt for money or a place to stay. She could have stayed longer not because she's in love with him but because it's convenient."

"Is that so wrong?"

I frown. Is that what Nate's doing? Is that what *I'm* doing? I'm not brave enough to have that conversation. Today's been hard enough.

"You can't know for sure, Viv. Wait'll the cards play out. They always do. In the meantime..." He gestures to either his golden-brown chest, which is a lickable sight, or the sun-and-water backdrop.

"You're irritatingly well-rounded. Where did you learn healthy boundaries, anyway? Wait"—I hold up a hand—"Let me guess. *The Owens.*"

"A combination of the Owens and my actual parents. They had no boundaries or scruples. That was just as valuable a way to learn how to have them as what the Owens taught me."

I huff a frustrated breath at his pragmatism. He's hard to argue with when he's sensible. "Do you worry about Archer and Benji?"

His face pinches. "Why?"

I can't help laughing. He's such a man. "They seem...stunted. Benji and his girlfriend *du jour*. Archer has adopted scowling as his life partner."

I earn a half smile for my observations.

"Benji is charismatic. You'll learn that as you're around him more."

"And Cris? Does he not notice her watching him like a love-struck hawk?"

"Don't go there," he warns. "Benji's denial isn't just a river in Egypt. Archer and Dad are butting heads at the moment, so he's more frustrated than usual."

"Really?"

"Arch has a lot to learn."

"And you know this from your many additional years of life experience?" I tease.

"*Year.* I'm only a year older than him. And I can tell because Will isn't my blood father. Archer and his dad have the same volatile personality traits: perfectionism with a splash of control."

"I thought Will was a saint."

Nate shakes his head. "Not a saint, but he was very level with me, which was what I needed when I was adopted. With Archer, Will is the heavy—he demands excellence and rarely settles for less. Archer doesn't appreciate anyone demanding anything of him."

"What about Lainey? Is she as saintly as she appears?"

"Angelic. A pure light," he says with so much reverence that I believe him. "She's a great contrast to Will. Archer has her to thank for half his DNA, or else he'd be a complete asshole."

I smile at the brotherly affection. "Who do you have to thank?"

"Lately? You, mostly."

"You have mad game, Nathaniel Owen." I shake my head at his audacity.

He touches the gold metal shell between my breasts again. "A romantic midday funeral yacht is kind of my thing."

"Well, it's definitely the *strangest* thing anyone has ever done for me." I smile at the man who has radically changed my life. I didn't expect today to be one of the best days of my life, but here we are.

He kisses me. I kiss him back.

For the oddest, most unexpected moment, life is so, so good.

Chapter Twenty-Five

Vivian

I'm inexplicably nervous for tonight.

Nate, as per his usual, is not nervous. How does he do it? Maybe I have nerve issues like those tiny, shaking dogs people carry around in shoulder bags. He's more pit bull in nature. Determined, doesn't fight unless forced, and a big belly-baring softie once you get to know him.

While I'm musing about what an unlikely dog couple we'd make, he answers a call on his cell phone. I've been ready to leave for five minutes. I'm dressed in a gorgeous chevron dress with gold threads and gold strappy shoes to match—not the horribly uncomfortable ones from before.

He's in a suit, deep navy in color. No tie. He looks delicious—I use that word a lot, but it's the best descriptor. We're attending a silent auction hosted by his parents, what Nate calls "rich person bullshit."

"Stop pacing," Odessa reprimands with a cluck of her tongue. She finishes loading the dishwasher and starts the cycle. It hums almost silently. My apartment's dishwasher sounds like a train barreling by.

"I don't want to go." I fold my arms and pout. Odessa chuckles. We've become close since I've been staying here. I like how much she loves her job. The house managers at my parents' house were so proper. I found their cardboard outer layer off-putting. Odessa *delights* in what she does and it comes through in both her meals and her smile.

"You are beautiful, Vivian. Have fun showing off with Nate and smile for the cameras."

"Cameras?"

"Lainey packs her Christmas letter with photos from the past year. Wait'll you see it. All done via email so as not to ruin the environment."

"Dammit. I really do like them."

"Yes, it's a shame isn't it?" She smirks. She totally has my number. She unties her apron and hangs it on a hook in the pantry.

"You think I'm ridiculous because I haven't moved in yet."

"No. I think you're stubborn for not moving in yet," she corrects. "I think you're ridiculous for not unpacking your toiletries."

She has me there.

"As if not taking up a drawer in the bathroom will create some sort of magical boundary." She wiggles her fingers.

"Agree," Nate says as he steps into the kitchen.

"No one asked you," I shoot over my shoulder but he only grins. It doesn't bother me, which is telling. I'm already comfortable here. In his house. With him. With Odessa and soon, I imagine, with the Owens.

Hanging out with Nate's family tonight will be intimate. I'm half worried I'll be intruding. Who am I to pretend I'm one of them?

"Ready to leave, beautiful?" He kisses my forehead. Odessa smiles, and I consider stashing my toiletries in a drawer in the bathroom after all. I lean against Nate, so comforting. At least I can find solace in him if tonight overwhelms me.

The event is hosted at William and Lainey Owen's house. I'm floored by the sheer size of it. A pair of columns two stories high flank a large overhang, and a massive chandelier twinkles through a second-story cathedral-style window.

"Wow," I whisper to Nate, my hand in his. The sun is setting and painting the sky a lovely orangey-purple-pink.

We walked by a fountain and a rose garden on our way in. Several guests are seated on the massive seating area on the porch enjoying cocktails. The faint scent of cigar smoke hangs in the air.

"Am I to believe you're impressed by this?" he asks me at the front door.

"This is a far cry from Chicago," I admit. Tall buildings and swanky lobbies and modern furniture is one thing. Clear Ridge's wealth is country chic amidst rolling green hills and lots of trees. The flower gardens aren't limited to a box here or there. They are expansive and fragrant. "Peaceful."

I tighten my hold on his arm as we step into the house. I hope that peaceful theme continues the rest of the night. Even though Odessa warned me about cameras, a photographer surprises me as I give my handbag to the coat checker.

"Look at each other, please," he instructs, "and let's see a smile." The checker—a college-aged student with stunning skin and straight, silken black hair—and I put on our best camera-ready smiles and stare at each other for an awkward beat.

"Third picture he's taken of me doing this," she says between her teeth.

I like her already.

Nate gives me a brief tour of the house. The opulence is staggering. Granite floors in the entryway, real-wood floors, probably walnut given the color, throughout the living and sitting rooms. There are dramatic displays for auction items set up on podiums throughout a wide sitting room, and ballot-like boxes mounted on the sides of the podiums where bidders can insert their bids.

"What should we buy?" he asks, pointing out a stunning photo of a mountainside advertising a wellness retreat for couples. There is also a private dining experience at the very restaurant where Nate and I had our first meal together, which makes me nostalgic.

"We? This is all you, buddy."

"Not if I put in for the retreat." He wraps his arms around my waist. "It's for couples. You're required to attend."

"You're a romantic sap, do you know that?"

"Bullshit," we hear behind us. Nate releases me and we turn to find Benji, cocktail in hand. "Nate is a lot of things, Vivian, but if you believe he's romantic, he has you snowed."

"Benji considers himself the romantic one, but serial dating isn't romantic," Nate says.

"I second that." Cristin appears at Benji's elbow.

"I assume you approve of my date tonight." Benji tells Nate as he cups Cris's elbow. Having just taken a drink of her wine, she sputters into her glass.

"This is not a date." She clears her throat. "You're paying me to be here as your life assistant."

"Life assistant *coach*," he corrects, and she rolls her eyes.

"Whatever. If you're paying me, it's not a date."

Ho boy. These two.

"Archer," Nate greets as the middle brother joins our gaggle. They shake hands, formal as per their usual.

"Vivian," Archer greets.

"Benji's on a date with Cris," Nate supplies.

"It's not a date," Cris growls. "Where's your date?" she asks Archer.

"Right here." He holds up his cell phone. "She's slim, beautiful, and agreeable."

"You mean boring," Nate says. "Agreeable is a good quality for a coworker, not a girlfriend."

Cris and I laugh. Me a little harder since "agreeable" is not one of my crowning qualities.

"Are you bidding on the retreat?" Benji asks, nodding to the photo we're standing in front of.

"No," I say at the same time as Nate says, "Yes."

"Interesting. I wonder if you'll outbid me." A glint of challenge sparks in Benji's eyes.

"It's for a good cause." A familiar stubborn expression takes Nate's gorgeous mug. "Bring it."

Cris shakes her head. "I have a mad case of testosterone exposure. Viv, accompany me to the bar?"

"Gladly. I don't want any part of this." I wave to the three billionaire brothers and take my leave.

TWO HOURS LATER, I'm as bubbly and light as the champagne Cris and I sipped while mingling around the silent auction. I ended up bidding on several items including a spa day, but I doubt my meager offer will take the top spot. This place reeks of money—I'm familiar with the stench. I return my empty glass to the bar at the same time Nate shows up with a full whiskey for himself and more champagne for me.

"Want to go outside?" He hands me the flute.

"Sure." I'd agree to anything right now. My limbs are loose and my mind's a little fuzzy, but not in a bad way. I never understood my brother's and mother's problems with substances. Bottoming out a vodka bottle never appealed to me. An evening sipping bubbly is more my jam.

Outside, Nate and I are walking along the path and admiring Lainey's rose gardens when two deep voices slice the air. We are out of sight, hidden by the lush floral landscape.

"Is that—?" I whisper.

"Archer and William." He takes my hand and we creep closer. We're eavesdropping, but I'm curious and Nate must be too.

"You're a talented designer and builder, Archer. When you were a child I imagined you erecting museums and churches when you grew up. Not clubs and bars. I humored you when you said this was what you wanted to do in the company. I never dreamed it'd be the cornerstone of your legacy."

"The money—"

"Is secondary," William interrupts. "The Owen name is synonymous with greatness. Establishments with spinning lights worshiping overindulgence are—"

"Beneath you. I know." Archer's tone is lethal. William's answering sigh of exasperation suggests this argument is one they've had before, and will have again in the future.

"Enough of this," William says. Soft footfalls on plush grass vanish in the direction of the house. When we make our appearance from the mouth of the garden, Archer is the only one standing in the backyard, his head inclined as he studies the stars.

Nate clears his throat and Archer turns. If not for the flash of surprise on his face, I would've guessed he knew we were there.

"Nate. Vivian." His surprise fades swiftly.

"We were admiring Lainey's roses," I needlessly explain.

He watches me for a beat. "Sorry you had to hear that."

"I didn't hear much. Only that you're ruining the world by building bars." I offer a sympathetic smile.

Archer's lips twitch, almost returning my smile, but not quite. "Dad and I don't agree on the evolution of Owen Construction."

"When my dad was alive, he and I didn't agree on much, either." I feel Nate's eyes on me, approving. "He was…difficult."

"Did your brother think so?" Archer asks, his features stone.

"Um, I don't know. Walt wasn't around as much as me."

"My brothers don't find Will difficult." His challenging gaze shifts to Nate.

"Do you have amnesia?" Nate asks. "Did you forget how hard he was on me when I moved into this house?"

"And you bloomed." Archer drags the word out. He shakes his head, a subtle move. I have the impression he's coiled and ready to strike even though his casual stance hasn't changed. "I don't respond to him as well as you do."

Before they can lunge at each other like rival vampires, I say, "Why don't you two have a cigar?"

Nate turns to me, his eyebrows lifting in surprise. "*Really.*"

"Yes, *really.*" He gave me space to be with my brother, and the least I can do is return the favor. "I'll be inside." I squeeze his arm and turn to leave, but he pulls me close and kisses me before I can.

"Thank you," he mutters, his blue eyes sparkling.

"You're welcome." It's nice to be able to give him what he needs.

I wave to Archer and head inside to find Cris.

Chapter Twenty-Six

Vivian

The bureau received an official invitation to the grand opening of Grand Marin, so Daniel arranged for the three of us—me, him, and Amber—to attend. It's three thirty on a Thursday as the hot sun beats down onto the crowd. An intimate group of sixty or seventy of us sits outside on folding chairs facing a stage.

The temps reached eighty-eight degrees at noon, and the breeze isn't helping cool me down. I hope the mayor's speech won't take long. I send a longing gaze at one of the shops, coveting its air-conditioned interior.

Amber and I are in the front row. She's fanning herself with the program and Daniel is acting as if he's on the verge of spontaneously combusting. He keeps murmuring under his breath about how he's uncomfortable, and then shifting in his seat. I'm doing my best to ignore him.

"Nate Owen is a staple in Clear Ridge, and I don't know what we'd do without him," Mayor Dolans is saying.

"We'd have a lot less headaches," Daniel mumbles. Nate is trying to zone a residential area to include retail. Daniel's been complaining about it for a week. It's making my job less pleasant and that's saying something. I've stolen a few glances at Grand Marin's corner office since we arrived, that's for damn sure.

Daniel seems to remember I'm sitting next to him and offers a pained, and possibly sheepish, smile before adding, "Sorry. I forgot you two are..." He gestures with his hand rather than finishing his sentence.

We are.

That's as good a description as any. I've rarely slept in my own bed for nearly a month. I sleep next to Nate.

"How are things with the billionaire?" Amber whispers to me. Amber has become a close friend. We've had lunch together a lot over the last month or so. She's heard my stories about Walt and my suspicions of Dee. She knows about Nate and me, though I kept his proclamation to myself.

"The same. I mean, I drive an extra twenty minutes to work every day now. And Odessa plies me with food the second I come home. She's on a nutrition kick lately so I've eaten a lot of salads and drunk a lot of juices."

"I've always wanted a juicer."

"You can have Walt's. He left it when he moved to Chicago."

"Really?"

"Sure." I think of the juicer on my countertop Walt bought with my money and wish I had insisted he take it with him when he moved. I've watched him spend fifteen minutes scrubbing it clean. No thanks.

"No, I don't mean the juicer. I didn't know Walt moved to Chicago."

"This past weekend." I feel her eyes on the side of my head and turn. "What?"

"Are you okay?"

"I think so. I can't run his life for him." Nate is teaching me that.

Amber looks like she has more to say, but applause erupts around us, signaling the end of the mayor's speech. As he steps aside, Nate, dressed in lightweight gray trousers and a tight pale-blue polo shirt, grins at the crowd from in front of the microphone. I all but purr. His chest is testing the confines of his shirt, the sleeves tight around thick biceps. Even after months together, the sight of him makes me gooey.

"He's pretty," Amber whispers, pausing her fanning to slap me with the program. "Lucky."

Not a word I've attributed to myself in a long while, but I can't argue. He is pretty and I am lucky. Since the start of this whole new-identity thing, I haven't thought too far into the future. Honestly, I half expected Daniel to figure out who I was and fire me. I guess that doesn't make a lot of sense now that I think about it. I slide a glance over at my surly boss and consider while he's not the friendliest person on the planet, I doubt he'd can me because I was Walter Steele's daughter. Until that night at the bar when Nate outed me to random strangers, I believed the world hated me.

"God, it's hot today." Amber fans her program faster and I lift mine and do the same. I allow my eyes to rake over the handsome speaker, sweat glistening on his upper lip, and remember last night in bed and how he was working up a sweat for a different reason entirely.

Mmm.

"Thank you for coming out today. You have vouchers in your programs for food and discounts at the shops," Nate announces. "Take advantage of it, it won't be a regular occurrence." His voice is a low, teasing warning that makes women in the crowd giggle and sends goosebumps skittering over my skin, even in this heat.

He steps off the stage as people begin to disperse. Daniel grumbles something about taking off, and for us to enjoy ourselves as Nate approaches. They exchange dismissive male glances and then Nate is at my side.

"Hi, Amber."

"Hi." She beams. Seriously, she could give the sun a run for its money today. "I'm…thank you. For the…things." She waves her program awkwardly. "Coupons. Whatever. I'm going shopping." She leans a tad closer to me to mutter, "You kids have fun." Then she wanders off.

"She okay?" he asks, looking genuinely confused.

"Don't tell me you have no idea how women react to you." I roll my eyes.

"If you're the one I'm gauging by, I don't," he quips. He doesn't wait for me to argue that I find him hot beyond belief, which I respect. "How about lunch?"

"Sounds good to me."

We choose a martini bar called Coax, which might be the newest, most sparkling restaurant I've ever set foot in. The bar gleams, the tables *shine*. You know the saying the floor is so clean you could eat off it? You could.

There aren't a lot of people in here yet, but I have a feeling they'll flock to Grand Marin after five o'clock. Once we've enjoyed our drinks—Nate, a beer and for me, my usual dirty martini, we snack on an ahi tuna plate and a dish called "sticky chicken bites." The food is delicious, and I'm pleasantly buzzed from my martini. The manager visits the table and strong-arms Nate into allowing him to comp the food. I can tell this isn't their first meeting, and again admire Nate and his business skill. Everyone seems to like and respect him, which is impressive. It challenges the idea I had about how wealthy folk are self-serving. Especially when Nate leaves an impressively large tip on the table for our hardworking server.

Outside, the sidewalks are teeming with people and in the parking lots beyond, cars are pouring in from the road.

"You know how to draw them in," I say, impressed.

His hand clasps mine as we dodge an incoming gaggle of men who look like they just came from the office. They're aiming for a sports bar on the corner.

"I want to show you something," Nate tells me. We cut across the street and pass several retail establishments. A store selling jewelry and handbags, a *boujie* shop outfitted with top-of-the-line dog accessories like diamond collars and sweaters and memory foam beds. So taken with the sights around me, I nearly plow into him when he stops abruptly at an unmarked wooden door with potted plants on either side. He pulls out a key and unlocks the knob and then locks it behind us. The stairwell is cool and dim, but windows here and there looking down on the street let some light in. At the top of the stairs is a glass door with the words PROPERTY MANAGER stamped on them in white.

I know where we are. The office he pointed out and asked me if I wanted to work in, the one sitting above the street and overlooking the property.

He slides a keycard and the door whispers open. You know how there is a "new car" smell? Well, if there's a "new office" smell, this one has it.

The entry is outfitted with a tall white counter. Potted plants adorn the surface, their greenery spilling over the edges. I run my fingers along the spidery leaves of one as Nate says, "This is reception or an assistant's desk. If you—or whomever—takes this position needs some help."

I smirk as he slides me a smug glance.

Behind reception is the office. It looks larger from the inside than from the outside looking in. There are two glass walls, given this is the corner of the building, overlooking the street.

"This is the side you saw," he says. "You can see out. They can see in."

The floor-to-ceiling windows offer a gorgeous view. I could swear there are even more people milling about than a few minutes ago.

"Over here"—he walks us past the desk, bookshelves, and another plant—"is the conference room."

"This is a very nice office." I run my hand along the metal chairs flanking the long, black table.

"It better be. Cost a mint to design."

A wall separates the conference room from the corner office, glass, but there is a half-wall on the bottom, its top ledge draped with a long box of overflowing plants. I touch one of the leaves.

"They're fake," he says. "No sunlight required."

Next, he points at the shoppers below. "They can't see us over here. There's a coating on the windows on this side." Then he turns his back to the window, where people wander to and fro. He reaches for his belt. "Want me to moon them to prove it to you?"

I cup a hand over my mouth to stifle a laugh.

"Caught you off-guard and you *actually* gave me a big grin."

"Did not." I affect a serious expression. He walks over to me and rests his wide palms on my hips.

"What do you think? Would you like to run Grand Marin?"

My heart races at his proposition. At the idea of being in charge of this entire place. Of being in charge, period. It's scary, and my track record is terrible. But the gorgeous office, the stunning view, the opportunity for challenge and excitement…

It's tempting. And frightening at the same time.

"I have no idea how to be a property manager, Nate."

"And yet you're absolutely breathless at the prospect of learning. You're excited. Admit it."

"How do you know what excites me?"

He dips his head and sweeps his tongue into my mouth. Bending me back over his forearm, my ass hits the boardroom table and he runs a firm hand from my hip to my stomach and then up to my breast. He toys with my nipple over the fabric and then stops as fast as he started. In one swift move, I'm on my feet again, hot and bothered, and he's peering down at me with that same smug expression he's been wearing since we arrived.

I can't let him get away with that.

I grip the fabric of my light summer dress and begin hiking up the skirt. Slowly, I reveal my legs and then my thighs. His smile fades. His eyes are fastened to my body and I walk over to the glass, skirt hiked high.

"You swear no one can see?" I peek over my shoulder and a

strand of my long hair sticks to my damp cheek. Given the empty office isn't air-conditioned at the moment, it's stuffy in here.

"That's what the window guys tell me." His eyes go dark with want, and I long to see them go darker.

"Only one way to find out," I say, and then I pull the dress over my head.

Chapter Twenty-Seven

Nate

This isn't why I brought her up here, but I'm not complaining.

Vivian stands in front of the windows in naught but a buttercup yellow bra-and-panty set. There are little bows at the side of each hip and one in the center of her cleavage.

"If you're trying to get the job, you already have it." I love this side of her. She seems free. A hell of a lot freer than she did even a few days ago. "Not that I'm arguing with your tactic."

"Don't waste time arguing." She reaches behind her and unclasps her bra, dropping it to the floor. Her nipples are round and full and perched in the center of her round and full breasts. A little trickle of sweat slides between those breasts as she wiggles out of her panties.

It's fast approaching boiling point in this room but I'm not going anywhere. I tug off my shirt and make quick work of my pants. Then I lift her and deposit her onto the table meant to discuss quarterly reports, occupancy, and other stale topics.

She peeks over my shoulder. "No one seems to be gaping up at the window, do they?"

I pretend to check. "Nope."

"You must be right about the glass."

"Maybe they're being polite." I kiss a trail along her salty skin. She tips her head back to give me better access.

"Let them watch. It's been a while since I had a scandal in my life."

I pull my head up and blink, dazed.

She giggles. "Sorry. I'm no good at this seduction stuff."

"Disagree." I lower my head and suckle a nipple into my mouth. She gasps, drawing her knees up, her sandals stuttering along the table's surface. I continue licking and suckling until I reach the apex of her thighs. Then I have a seat and pull her ass to the edge of the table and lower my face to taste her.

Her hips arch and she thrusts her pussy into my face. I continue my attentive assault, enjoying her taste and the scent of her vanilla perfume and lotion—she has both, I know that now. She calls it "scent layering." I call it her driving me out of my mind with need.

A few more delicate licks and nipple plucks later, she's moaning and coming. I waste no time standing and spreading her thighs. I grip my cock and stroke, admiring her damp folds, the glistening tips of her breasts, and the sated, satisfied look in her eyes. I can't get enough of her.

"Condom," she whispers. I blink to reset my brain. Right. Condom. That would be important. "Tell me you were a good Boy Scout and brought one with you?"

"I was never a Boy Scout," I mutter, pretending to be insulted. I bend down and fish a condom from the wallet in my pants pocket. Rolling it on, I send her a smile. "Street smarts."

I scoop her into my arms. I consider pressing her ass against the glass and finishing us both off, but I'm not sure if the one-way glass works with body parts smashed and gyrating against it. Better not risk it, for her sake. She's had enough publicity for a lifetime.

Instead, I wheel her around to an empty wall and settle her

against it. Her hair slides up the wall as I bring her body over mine. I enter her in inch by precious inch and watch as her face melts in ecstasy. She mutters "so good, so good," over and over.

I put my biceps to work lifting and dropping her onto me, and fit in a calf workout by holding her suspended. Soon we're both panting, grunting, and God help me, she's *begging*. A high, breathy "please, Nate, please" and I can't resist those words from this woman. I weld my back teeth together to keep from blowing too soon as I work her into a generous lather.

She goes over again and it's not a moment too soon. I follow, half-growling, half dying given the cramp in my thigh. By the time I finish with a colorful swear word, we slide down the wall in a sweaty heap, her on my lap, my hand gripping my hamstring.

"Fuck me!" I grumble, stuck between immense sexual satisfaction and the most intense yet stupid muscle pain known to man.

And what does my girl do? She laughs at me and follows it with a smart-assed comment.

"I thought I just did."

AFTER CHECKING in with my foreman in Chicago, and determining the site is well on its way to completion, I can rest a little easier. I'm looking at a live-work near Cincinnati next, a ritzy older neighborhood needing a boost. I'm toying with the idea of keeping the original buildings and zoning for retail and residential in the same area.

Of course that means a re-zoning fight, like the one I'm embroiled in with Daniel for another Clear Ridge property. And, those older buildings will need updated wiring, plumbing, structural repairs. A smile curves my mouth at the prospect. I do love a challenge.

After Viv and I left Grand Marin, she let me know she was staying at her place for a few days to do a deep clean. She's been meaning to since Walt moved to Chicago to work on my nearly completed site. I probably could have used him elsewhere, but I wanted to pitch him an underhanded softball. Most of the problems have been ironed out at the site. All we have to do is hustle it to completion. If he can show up and do grunt work, he's in good shape.

I'm planning a party for the completion of the job. At a pub downtown named O'Leary's. Like Lainey says, we have to celebrate our accomplishments, and this site reflects a year's worth of hard work. There is always the chance of something going sideways at the end, but I have smart women and men working on that site. And I'm never more than a private plane ride away if I need to step in and help.

Anyway, as a result of Vivian's nesting in her own apartment I've been without her in my bed for three days. I'm aware she needs a breather, and her brother moving a few states away wasn't easy for her, so I've let her be. I fell into my old routine of working night and day, and honestly? I've been enjoying it.

Yesterday I found another site in Clear Ridge that would make an excellent spot for business professionals. Lawyers, massage therapists—one-man-or-woman shows in need of sophisticated, mature workspaces. The buildings are dated, and not in the sexy way the older buildings in Cincy are, so I'm probably looking at a raze and rebuild.

Flowers in hand—a spur-of-the-moment purchase from a guy at a red light on the way here—I cross the street toward CRBI to surprise Vivian under the guise of telling her about my idea and wooing her away from her desk to come take a look at the site with me. The last time I heard from her was yesterday afternoon. Just a quick text about how she and Amber just ate the best sushi in town. I'm glad she has a close friend at work. Her guard seems to drop a little more every day.

I convinced her to take the Grand Marin job, by the way. I don't know if the sex put her over, or if her being in the office helped her envision her future, but I'm damn excited about it.

Owen Construction's home office is handling the particulars for the time being. She insisted on giving Daniel notice and I insisted on giving her time to get used to the new normal. Walt in Chicago. Her at Grand Marin. And soon, her in my house full-time.

I smile to myself. I have to be careful with her, but I'm okay with that. She comes around eventually, I've learned.

Stepping into the bureau, I nod as I walk past reception. Elizabeth knows me by now. The grandmotherly woman continues speaking into the phone while waving me through. I stroll past a copy machine and a few tall file cabinets and arrive at Vivian's cube wall.

"Delivery for Ms. Vandemark," I utter, thrusting the flowers through the opening while the rest of me stays hidden. When I don't hear an answer, I step around to reveal myself and find her cubicle empty.

A squeak of a chair turns my head. Amber leans out of her own cubicle. "She didn't come in today."

My brow furrows. Amber matches my expression.

"She didn't call you?" she asks.

"No. Did she call you?"

She shakes her head, and concern causes my stomach to do a barrel roll. My phone is to my ear a second later. While I listen for the ringer, I hand the bouquet to Amber. "For you."

She probably thinks that's weird, but I don't wait around to find out. I'm walking at a fast clip past the copier and past Elizabeth and out the front door. No answer. The ringing gives way to a message and I leave a voicemail.

"Vivian, it's Nate. Call me as soon as you can."

I peck in a text message communicating the same and then cross the street to my Tesla and drive to her house.

The first of Vivian's neighbor's doors I bang on answers. An elderly woman in a pair of pale green polyester pants and a loudly patterned floral shirt listens as I calmly explain I haven't heard from Vivian today and I want to make sure she's all right. I already knocked on Viv's door and rang the doorbell. I also tried the windows, which were locked tight. I stopped short of breaking and entering.

"That nice man who was living there gave me a key," the woman tells me. "Her brother, I think it was," she's calling out as she rummages through a drawer in her kitchen. I'm nervous and worried. I check my texts. Nothing.

"I can't give it to you, though," Viv's neighbor tells me with earnest concern. "I was entrusted with a key and I can't let just anyone inside."

I force a smile even though my patience has dwindled. "That's fine."

She toddles across the stoop to Vivian's door and opens it. She turns around, probably to tell me she'll go inside and check without me, but I'm already in the living room.

"Vivian!" I shout, calm but loud. The kitchen is clean, dishes in the rack. They're dry. Not a drop of water on them. The oven is cool. The coffee pot empty and sparkling.

Back in the living room, I notice a basket of laundry in mid-fold I missed when I blew past it. Almost like she was interrupted. A stack of folded clothes sits on the coffee table. The TV is on, a big bold MUTE in the corner.

I jog down the hallway and quickly search the two bedrooms and the bathroom.

When I return, the neighbor lady is wringing her hands from the doorway. "Should I call the police?"

Fuck. Is that where we are? Mind spinning, I nearly leap out of my skin when the phone rings from my back pocket.

"Vivian," I answer.

"Nate, hi. Sorry, I was asleep."

A whoosh of air leaves my lungs and I put my hand to my chest to calm my racing heart. Seems ridiculous to spout out that she is to *never do this to me again, young lady!* but the urge is there all the same.

Instead I manage, "Are you okay?"

There's a pause long enough to put my heart through its paces again, but then she says, "I'm in Chicago with Walt."

I nod at her neighbor and tell her quietly, "It's Vivian. She's fine. I'll lock up."

No longer concerned to leave me in the apartment, her neighbor nods and asks me to tell Vivian hello before heading across the stoop back to her place.

Too wired to sit, I pace the short distance between front door and kitchen. "Is he okay?"

"He's fine. Physically, anyway. Dee overdosed. He called me last night around ten o'clock. I was sitting on the couch watching TV."

I pick up the remote and flick off the television. "While folding laundry."

It takes her a second. "You're at my apartment."

"I went to CRBI to surprise you. Amber didn't know where you were. You scared the life out of me, Vivian." Now that I know she's alive and well, anger creeps in.

"Well, excuse me for not calling. I was trying to comfort my brother so he didn't have to go through this alone."

"How is Dee?" I rein in my anger enough to ask.

"Stable," Vivian says, sounding groggy. "Finally. They think she took antidepressants in addition to drinking a lot of wine. Walt and I spent the entire night in the waiting room of the ICU. Finally, the nurse convinced him to go home and get some sleep, that Dee was going to be okay for a few hours while he rested. When we arrived at his apartment, he was pacing and half-crazed. I sat with him until"—there's a pause while she presumably checks the time—"God. An hour and a half ago. I feel like someone kicked my head in. I've never been so tired in my life."

"Walt didn't use?"

"He's sober. Thank goodness. I wasn't sure until I arrived at the hospital, but he's all right. I'm not going to be coming home any time soon, though."

I blink at this announcement. I don't know if she means for a day or two or a week or two. Or longer.

"I'll come to you." The next best logical thing. "I can charter a jet. Let me know what you need from home. I'll pack you a bag."

"I packed one," she tells me.

"Okay, then give me Walt's address. Did he rent the place on Palmetto?" I rummage through a kitchen drawer in search of pen and paper. "Better give me the hospital name too."

"No."

The word freezes me into a solid block of irritation. "What do you mean, *no*?"

"I have it under control, Nate."

"Doesn't change the fact I can help if you let me."

"We don't need help. There's nothing to do. I'll come home when things are settled."

Hearing she doesn't need my help is akin to her saying she doesn't give a shit about me. Old childhood wounds wriggle out of my subconscious. I've been rejected before.

"You should have called me," I bark, which is probably the wrong thing to say to someone who's slept for ninety minutes in the last thirty or so hours. "I would have flown out with you. I could be there for you."

"That's not your job," she replies coolly.

"Speaking of, I won't hold the Grand Marin position open indefinitely." It's petty, but I'm angry, so that's what I say.

"Fine. Don't. My brother is my number one responsibility." She's calmer than I like. Meanwhile, I'm like an overheated Hot Pocket, a steamy mess inside, roughly the temperature of lava, and beginning to ooze from the cracks. "I'm going back to sleep. Lock my front door on your way out."

"Vivian," I say, my tone gruff. When she doesn't respond, I think she's hung up until I hear her draw a breath. Rather than argue, I mutter, "Call me when you wake up."

Chapter Twenty-Eight

Vivian

It's evening on the same day Nate called, and I'm walking back to the waiting room with a cup of steaming coffee in hand. It's not for me. I don't want to be jumpier than I have been for the last twenty-some hours.

Walt and I spent the day grabbing catnaps here and there before coming back to the hospital to visit Dee. She's out of ICU. They're keeping her for observation through tonight.

I encounter her sister, Shannon, who flew in this afternoon. She looks as tired and bedraggled as I feel. I managed to put on makeup and pull my hair into a ponytail, but that's as good as it's going to get.

"One cream, two sugars." I hand the cup to Shannon who offers me a weak smile.

"Thanks."

"You're welcome. Where's Walt? With Dee?"

She nods as she sips from the paper cup. "He's worried."

"Well, he can join the club." We lower ourselves into the seats we've been warming for most of the day.

"I'm going to convince her to come back to Atlanta," Shannon announces, and my stomach sinks. I know that's what she needs to do, and I know Dee needs to go with her. "They can't get married."

She says the word "married" and my stomach tightens. For a moment, I was sucked into a fantasy with Nate that could have ended up there. But, like I said, the other shoe always drops. His assertion that the shoe already dropped was premature. Life had a bigger shoe waiting.

"They say they're in love." Shannon snorts. "Like they have any clue. Dee jumped from one addiction to another. She thinks your brother is going to solve her problems? She's delusional." She slants me an apologetic look. "No offense. I don't mean anything bad about your brother."

I hold up a hand to let her know no offense was taken. I should have expected this scenario the moment he showed up on my doorstep. If there's one thing Walt and I can count on, it's that love hurts. Losing our parents, his multiple visits to rehab, and now this. What more proof do we need?

"I'm a bitter divorcée, can you tell?" Shannon's smile is wry. She's pretty in a rough way. Taller and squarer than her younger sister. "I wasn't ready for marriage, and I was stable. What about you?" Her eyes snap to my naked left hand to check for a ring.

"I'm not the relationship type." I don't like how that sounds, and worse, I don't like how it feels. Like it's true. Time and again I've watched love tear people apart. And then I tiptoe though the tulips with Nathaniel freaking Owen believing I'm going to come out the other side intact.

I'm the delusional one.

Over the last few days I spent alone, I came to the conclusion that what Nate and I have is too big to hold on to. Like a deflated hot-air balloon wadded up in my arms slowly, slowly filling.

Last night Walt called panic-stricken over Dee. He hadn't been able to get ahold of his sponsor and didn't know who else to call. I didn't think, I acted. Threw together a suitcase and climbed in the car. I stayed on the phone with him for the first leg of the drive, stopped and picked up coffee, and then called him during the last hour to see how he was. Better, for sure, but not great. The phone call I didn't make was one to Nate.

I thought about his mom using. I thought of the way she treated him, trying to take his money and breaking his heart all over again. I thought of my mom and her teaching me to walk in high-heeled shoes. The way I cried in her closet after she died, both hating her and loving her with equal intensity. I thought of Nate's dad, who begged, borrowed, and stole for his next hit. I thought of Walt, and then Dee.

Addicts have a way of swirling the environment around them into a funnel cloud and sucking in everyone nearby. Nate has worked hard to separate himself from the addicts in his life. He stayed away from his mother for his own self-preservation. When he went back to her, she hurt him all over again. The pain never goes away. There's no avoiding it.

Staying with Nate subjects him to Walt's addictions, which are an ongoing battle. I can't abandon my brother, but I can choose not to subject Nate to any more pain. He's been giving and caring and putting himself on the line for me since we met. He'd have dropped everything to come here, and if I truly loved him, I'd never ask him to do that.

Do you love him?

"She's asking for you." Walt steps into the waiting room and gestures to Shannon. Dee's sister takes her leave as my brother sits next to me and lets out a gusty breath.

"Shit, V. Addicts, am I right?" He pulls his palm over his face. "I'm sorry I dragged you here. I was freaking out."

"I understand." And I do. If Nate was in the ICU, I'd lose my marbles alone in a waiting room. *Because* I love him, I realize miserably.

Love hurts.

If it doesn't hurt in the moment, wait around long enough and it will.

"Nate called me earlier today." Walt, elbows on his knees,

scrubs his palms together. "He wanted to make sure I was all right, and he asked if I needed anything. He's a good guy."

"He's the best." My voice is hollow.

"Look, you have a job and a life to return to. You don't have to stay here and babysit. I freaked out, but I'm okay. Dee's okay. I just…it was such a flashback to the friends I've lost."

"I don't mind showing up for you, Walt. We're all we have. Our parents bailed, but I never will."

"Thanks, sis." His smile is weak.

"I was thinking I'd stay a while. Just until you're on your feet."

He's already shaking his head.

"No arguments."

"You have a life in Ohio." He sounds annoyed. "Don't blow it up on account of me."

"I'd do anything for you, you know that."

"That's what I'm afraid of." His sigh comes from the depths of his soul. "I'm going to grab a bite to eat. Want anything?"

I shake my head. He takes off down the corridor and vanishes around a corner. I stare in his wake for a minute before blinking when a different man appears walking toward me.

Nate.

He came.

Of course he came.

I watch his sure and strong gait, relief filling me to the brim. Definitely, I love him. Which makes him being here harder. I realize now I have to choose. Between Walt and Nate. My brother, whose life is chaos, and Nate, who believes his calling is to keep everything—and everyone—around him stable.

He deserves better.

I stand, the sight of him so welcome, I want to throw my arms around his neck and bury my nose in his ocean-scented neck. I want to be held and comforted. He'd do it, no questions asked. No one cares about me as much as he does.

But.

In my efforts to live unselfishly, I've been a very selfish girl.

Nate has done nothing but give me gifts, treat me well, grant me space. Even now he doesn't look angry that he's left his home, his work, and God knows what other obligations to come to my aid.

If I loved him, I'd let him off the hook. Let him find someone whole—someone who's already stable. Someone who won't break his heart repeatedly. Hasn't he been through enough?

Tears prick my eyes. He looks tired, his shirt rumpled probably from sleeping during the short flight here.

"Hey." His smile is crooked. Like his nose. God, I love his nose.

"Walt told you where we were."

"Well, you wouldn't." He cups my nape and presses his lips to my forehead.

I close my eyes and draw in a deep breath. Pushing him away will be the hardest thing I ever do.

Nate

Not that I expected a parade when I showed up, but hell, would that have been too much to ask? Once again, I remind myself that addicts are not easy people to deal with, not by a long shot.

I was mollified by the fact that Walt seems even-keeled. I called him again when the jet landed and he told me he was in Dee's hospital room watching her sleep. He also told me where to find Viv, and then apologized for being an asshole. All I could think was *we've all been there, kid.*

He's going to be okay. I feel it in my gut. Vivian needs to give him space to be okay, but that is a muscle she has to exercise. I'm uniquely suited for her given I've been dealing with this sort of relationship since birth. I came out the other side. So will she. So will *we.*

The brief press of my lips to her forehead reminds me how much I miss her. I never should have let her go home, but then, what was I supposed to do? Tie her to the radiator? Lock her in a tower like Rapunzel?

Tempting.

"I passed Walt on the way in. He said he was grabbing a bite. Want to join him?"

She averts her eyes, sliding her hands into her back pockets. She has to be exhausted. She drove from Ohio to Illinois. I'm still pissed she didn't call me, but now's not the time for that conversation. She's struggling to deal and on very little sleep.

"Somewhere else, maybe?" She frowns.

"I know just the place."

The deep-dish-pizza joint is open twenty-four hours. It's between a pawn shop and a salon in not the best part of town, but fairly close to the hospital. I have a hunch she doesn't want to venture too far away.

Our pie arrives, packed with meat and cheese, and on Viv's half, per her request, "lots of olives." I remember the olive I ate from her martini the night I showed her the rose garden. The night she changed my life by agreeing to come home with me.

We eat in silence. I wolf down two slices by the time she's eaten half of one. Today's been hectic. I had three meetings to cancel and one I had to show up for before I could fly out.

"Here you are again," she mumbles to her plate. "My knight in shining armor."

"Flattery. My ego loves that." I make a gesture indicating for her to compliment me more, but her smile is brittle.

"Hey." Serious now, I bend my head and try to meet her downturned gaze. She looks up, pain in the depths of her eyes. "He's all right. I talked to him. He's going to be okay."

Her voice is watery when she asks, "For how long this time?"

I want to tell her for good. I want to reassure her and make promises. But the life of an addict is a slippery slope. Recovery is a day-to-day consideration. At any moment anything could happen. So I tell her the truest thing I know.

"I don't know, but whatever happens we'll deal with it." I

reach over the table and take her hand in mine. She starts to cry. "What can I do?"

"That's just it." She uses the scratchy-as-cardboard napkins to swipe tears from her beautiful face. Even with a red nose and puffy eyes and tangles in her normally bouncy hair she's beautiful. "You do everything for me. For us. You can't be stopped."

I can't be. I let out a chuckle. "I care about you. What do you expect?"

I love her. I don't say that. Her misery seems less about Walt and tiredness and more about something else. When she tugs her hand into her lap and sits back in her chair, the alarm siren in my head wails. My mind goes berserk imagining one bad-news scenario after another.

"I can't do this anymore, Nate." She sniffs, straightens her back. Shoring up. "I've been fooling myself believing you and I were building a life together."

"We *are* building a life together." My heart throbs. Aches. She can't do this.

"Not any longer."

I think of the painting of the dragon at the art institute and for the first time picture myself as the beast and not the knight. It's me who's being stabbed to death. Me who's losing the battle. And by battle, I mean *her*.

"You know as well as I do Walt's fight isn't over," she says. "If I don't push you away, you'll go down alongside us."

"I'm a big boy. That's my choice," I say, as firmly as I can.

"No. It's not." Her head shakes and more tears run down her cheeks. "I don't *want* you to stay. It's not worth it."

"I'm in love with you. It's worth it." I hadn't imagined making that proclamation as a Hail Mary, but here we are. She doesn't respond the way I hope. Her face falls and her eyes broadcast a combination of hurt and sympathy. Committed to my foolishness, I prompt, "And you love me."

I didn't mean for it to sound like a question, but it came out like one. And then, right there in a twenty-four-hour pizza place, she plunges the sword into my chest to the hilt.

"I don't know how to be in love. That's not your fault. I never meant to hurt you."

"Bullshit," I growl, growing angrier by the millisecond. "You're scared. You're not thinking clearly."

"I'm not scared. I'm *terrified,*" she admits, with another angry swipe of the napkin across her face. "I'm thinking plenty clear. I've seen what romantic love does to a couple. You believe it saves the world. The Owens have been your shining example. You are able to believe, and that's a miracle." Her smile is faint before her expression hardens once again. "I live in a different world. One where love hurts and bad things happen, regardless of what you do to safeguard against them."

"Dammit, Vivian," I say, pissed off and every bit as terrified as she is. I'm losing her. In real time. "Don't do this."

"Look around." She throws her arms wide. "It's done! Why do you think I didn't call to ask for your help? You've cashed in your last get out of jail free card for me. I don't want your help. And I don't want *you.*"

"Oh." That's a different story, I think numbly. That numbness chills my face, then slides down my arms and over my chest. I can't feel a fucking thing from the neck down.

Her bottom lip quivers, but her voice is steady. "Go home. It was only ever a fantasy, anyway."

She stands to leave and I push myself to my feet unsteadily. My voice is reedy but I try one last time. "Viv."

"Goodbye, Nate." She pauses at the door briefly before she walks out of it. And out of my life.

I have my suspicions it's for good this time.

Vivian

I dash outside, aware of my surroundings as I run for the parking lot lights shining outside the hospital entrance. I sneak a look over my shoulder to see if Nate followed. He didn't, and my heart suffers a fissure down the center. I know what's best for him but a deep, dark, hopeful part of me wanted him to come for me.

Apparently I'm an addict too.

I thought I was so independent and so strong, pushing him away in the beginning. But the real strength comes by pushing him away when I want nothing more than to hide inside him. To be taken care of. To let him chase away the monsters…

Outside the hospital entrance, air burning my lungs, heart slamming into my ribcage, I bend in half. Grief eats my insides like acid. Hand over my mouth, I attempt to stifle a sob, but it escapes anyway, and brings with it another. My cries shake my shoulders and weaken my legs. Tears pour from my eyes in steady streams.

I blink as a cigarette butt hits the ground at my feet. Strong hands wrap around my shoulders. It's Walt, gaunt and tired. My only refuge.

He's asking what happened, but I can't speak yet. So he holds me close while I cry instead. Here for me, like I'm here for him.

I automatically check the parking lot floodlights for signs of Nate. But there is no tall, broad figure coming our way. No knightly billionaire swooping in to save me.

He left. He actually left.

I hope, for his sake, he chooses to save himself this time.

Chapter Twenty-Nine

Nate

I wake up in my brother Benji's guest bedroom with a headache the size of a jumbo jet. My stomach tosses as the blinds are pulled, letting in copious amounts of Ohio sunshine—a rarity for the Midwest. Which Benji points out before setting a steaming mug on the nightstand.

It's been close to a week since Vivian dumped me on my ass. I tried calling her, she didn't pick up. Texts have gone unanswered. Walt hasn't ignored my calls but he let me know she needs space. The last time we talked he told me he'd find another job if he had to, whatever would make this "transition" easier for me.

I should have appreciated the selflessness of his offer, but I couldn't since it seemed like the final nail in the Nate-and-Viv coffin. I, rather miserably, told Walt he always had a job at Owen Construction as long as he kept his nose clean. Then I climbed into my car and drove to Benji's to get hammered. I'd been holding it together until then.

Or so I thought.

When my brother answered the door last night, he gave me a bland blink and said, "About time. Tequila or whiskey?"

"Hot ginger tea," he tells me now. "Cris assures me this will fix you."

Does it fix broken hearts, because if it doesn't, I don't have high hopes. I give him a look to communicate that, and he holds his hands up in don't-shoot-the-messenger fashion.

He's dressed for the day. He's no doubt been busily crunching numbers in his home office since five a.m.

"Brought you this too." He chucks a newspaper at my chest. I fumble it once before holding it up. My vision is blurry, but I make out the bold headline.

"Owen Masterpiece Opens to Exuberant Public."

It's an article about Grand Marin and its many amenities. I should feel pride and validation. Accomplishment. I scan the article and find nothing but praise. Words like "decadent" and phrases like "perfect gathering place" and "five-star cuisine" litter the article. But I don't feel proud or validated. I am empty. I had Vivian in my life, sharing my passion, sharing my bed. Now I have nothing.

"My head hurts." I toss the paper aside.

"Drink the tea." My brother leaves, but not before instructing, "Get your ass dressed."

I cradle my throbbing head as I stand and stumble to the shower. I've spent the last several days working my ass off—aka, pouting over Vivian. Nothing helps you forget your troubles like sixteen-hour workdays. Except I didn't forget her. Which is why I came to Benji's to drink and drown my sorrows.

He let me moan and wail about the unfairness of it all. Listened to my indignant claims that she didn't appreciate me and how I did everything for her. I climbed up on a pedestal of my own making and told the tale of how I, Sir Nathaniel Owen, singlehandedly swooped in and saved Vivian from her own life.

He, of course, called me on my shit. I railed at him for that, even though somewhere in my tequila-pickled brain, I knew he was right. Like a good brother, he sat with me and drank. Clearly not as much as I did given his chipper state this morning. He must've switched to water when I wasn't looking.

When Vivian stalked away from me and into one of Chicago's not-so-safe neighborhoods, I followed. You didn't think I'd let her run off alone to be mugged or God knows what else, did you? I didn't stop caring about her just because she dumped me, although it'd be easier if it would've worked out that way.

I followed as she made the five-block trek to the hospital where she doubled over and cried. I was at the edge of the lit parking lot, intending to run to her, pull her into my arms and say whatever I had to in order to win her back. Then I planned on taking us to a hotel and stripping her beneath me so I could remind her how good we were together. I'd hold her in my arms through the night and we'd wake up good as new.

That's not what happened.

Instead, Walt pushed away from the wall he was leaning on and crushed a cigarette under his shoe. He became the man she wouldn't have wanted me to be right then. I slunk back into the shadows and let him.

I have a thick skull. It's taken me the better part of a week to accept what she said in that pizza place.

She doesn't love me. That's the bottom line.

If I could find two remaining brain cells to rub together, I'd realize a smart man would take that news as a win. She's difficult and challenging and combative. She doesn't want me. That should be the end of our story. I can move on with my life.

But I never claimed I was smart.

Benji said I did the right thing leaving Walt to tend to her. That I can't expect to come between family. He pointed out Viv and I are the same. That I'd do anything for my own family too. He's right. I would. I didn't mention Viv had already become like family to me. I couldn't bear seeing the pity in his eyes; the head-shake communicating I'm a bigger moron than he originally thought.

I shower and suck down Cris's godawful tea, and then make

my way to the open-plan kitchen/living room. She's standing at the counter, tapping a tablet, her brow furrowed in thought. She looks up when I walk in.

"Good morning." As usual, her smile is bright.

"There was something wrong with this tea," I grumble, returning the mug.

"Benji warned me you'd be grumpy."

Grumpy is a tame descriptor for my volatile mood. I scowl but she only brightens further.

"It's a family hangover recipe." She rinses the mug in the sink and then fills it with coffee from a brimming pot. When she slides it over the counter to me, I cradle it in both hands.

"You're forgiven," I say and hear a gentle laugh.

I settle onto a barstool at the marble island. She leans both hands on it like a diminutive bartender. "How are you, really?"

"Oh, you know. Ran my girlfriend off." I should have stayed in Ohio. Given Vivian another day to herself. Maybe then this wouldn't have happened. Can you tell I'm in the bargaining stage of grief?

"Walter Steele's daughter? I doubt you have the power to run her off."

I lift my face and my eyebrows at the same time Benji walks into the kitchen, his hand wrapped around his own coffee mug. "Vivian is Walter Steele's daughter? Holy shit."

My attention is on Cris. "How did—"

"I recognized her the moment I saw her." She waves a hand of dismissal. "Didn't you?"

No. I was besotted by long hair and a sassy attitude. Cheap shoes and that entrancing wiggle in her walk.

"I recognized her brother," I say instead. "Then she told me. Or maybe I asked her. I can't remember." God. How many brain cells *did* I annihilate last night? I scrub my forehead. "The point is, we talked about it. Eventually."

"She seemed guarded around everyone but you. She must love you." This from Cris.

"Very funny." But it's not funny. Cris is a woman and as a woman has a very unique take on my situation. Which leads me to ask, "Why would Viv dropping her guard mean she's in love with me?"

"You found her tender underbelly, Nate," Cris answers. "And then she rolled over and showed it to you."

"Uh, yeah, and then she left. People in love don't leave." Plus she told me she was *incapable* of loving me. Not the most wholehearted of assurances.

"You left your mom," Benji tells me. "And you love your mom."

My frown deepens, and Cris shifts on her feet like she's uncomfortable. Benji's allowed to call me on my shit, straight-up. He knows that. Cris does not know that and probably worries we're about to come to blows. He gets a pass because he's adopted too. He understands the pain of losing family, and the challenge of acclimating to a new one.

"She didn't leave you so much as show up for her brother. You made her choose, Nate." He shrugs. "She chose."

"I didn't make her choose." But did I? "I simply warned against micromanaging him. I wanted her to realize her life was her own. I wanted her to depend on me. To trust me."

To love me.

I fiddle with the bracelet on my wrist and listen as it gently scrapes the face of my watch. "I went to visit my mother but she wouldn't accept my help. She told me I was dead to her. I don't want Vivian to feel that sort of pain, especially from a family member she's so close with. I was trying to keep her from being hurt."

"Now who's micromanaging?" Cris asks softly.

This time when I scowl, she steps partially behind Benji and shoots me a nervous smile.

"I just remembered I have a phone call to make." She scampers from the room and my brother folds his arms over his checkered shirt.

"Way to go, now you ran off Cris."

I do not laugh at his lame-ass attempt at a joke.

"We all fuck up, Nate."

"Yeah. Some of us more than others." I stare into my coffee like it might hold the answer, but after I finish that cup, I realize it doesn't. Cris and Benji have disappeared into his office. I hear them chatting quietly. Me? I'm sitting here like a pouting giant who's run out of village people to terrorize.

The adage about loving someone and setting them free trickles through my mind and as loath as I am to admit it, for the first time in my life I wonder if it holds some truth.

Vivian

Dee went back to Atlanta yesterday.

I didn't stay in my brother's apartment. I've been holed up in a decent hotel near his neighborhood. Worried as I am about him, I didn't want to be underfoot. Especially when Dee ended up coming home with Walt immediately after her stay at Chicago Memorial Hospital. Shannon wasn't happy, but she understood there was only so much she could do. When Dee made the decision to call her sister and return home, it was hers. I know it was hard for Walt to let her go.

I feel his pain.

I arrive on my brother's doorstep expecting to find him disheveled and depressed that his fiancée is gone, but instead he's dressed in jeans and a T-shirt, a cup of coffee in his hand.

"Hey." He opens the door wider and I step in. The apartment is clean, and nearly empty.

I give him a once-over. "You seem...okay?"

He nods in a seesaw direction like he's not sure how to answer. "I've been meditating. It helps."

It must. I should try it. My head's been a tangled mess ever since I told Nate I couldn't be with him any longer. I had to block his number so I wouldn't be tempted to answer his calls. Or maybe he stopped calling. It's what I told myself I wanted him to do. Now I'm not sure.

I haven't texted or called him. I've had the urge about a hundred times. But I was the one who ended it. I asked. I received. This is what I deserve.

Move on. Go forward. Push ahead.

I've been doing a combination of those things since the world discovered my father was a criminal. Since I discovered my life was built on a foundation of his lies. Pressing on should come as second nature by now. Why did I believe I could settle down and live a life that wasn't mine? Being Vivian Vandemark was supposed to offer me a reprieve from people knowing who I am. She wasn't supposed to be an identity I lost myself in.

"How's Dee doing?" I ask Walt.

He lets out a heavy sigh. Like me, he's accustomed to hiding how much he hurts. "The last time we talked she said she's clean for good. She said landing in the ICU was a wake-up call."

His tone is flat. I wonder if he believes her. My heart bleeds for him and for the addiction haunting his every step. I want better for him. I'm pissed that the world won't let him have it.

"I should have seen this coming," I say as I pour myself a cup of coffee I don't need. I'm overly alert, despite my lack of sleep the last few nights. "I should have—"

"Stop."

I carry my coffee cup to the built-in bar in the kitchen and sit next to him. He looks exasperated. Confused. Heartbroken.

Relate.

I lay my hand on his arm. "This isn't your fault."

"I mean it, V. *Stop.*" Anger etches lines into his forehead. His sharp cheekbones are dark and shadowed.

"Stop what? Looking out for you? I'm your older sister. It comes with the territory."

"You're *three* years older than me. You don't know a hell of lot more than I do."

My head jerks on my neck. "Thanks a lot."

"I'm a grown man."

"You're an addict."

"So are you." He holds my gaze, daring me to ask him to explain.

"What's that supposed to mean?"

"You deserve better than you accept. Always have. You dated a billionaire who is a hell of a nice guy, Vivian. And then you blew up your life. As per your usual."

"I'm looking out for myself," I defend. "And you're wrong. I accepted lots of things from Nate."

"*Things*, sure. Shoes. Clothes. But not a future, which I suspect is what he wanted. What about Grand Marin? The property manager offer."

"What about it?"

"You blew it off."

"I didn't blow it off! I had to come here. I had to stay—"

"You didn't *have to* do anything! Admit it. You're punishing yourself for the shit that went down while you were one of the head honchos at Dad's company. You watched everything crumble, felt helpless, and decided never to put your ass on the line again."

His shot hits its target—the center of my chest. He's right, which I suspect he knows given the way he watches me.

"You wanted that property-management gig. I could tell when you mentioned it. And you wanted Nate. I could tell when you collapsed in my arms at the hospital and wouldn't listen when I told you to call him and tell him you fucked up."

I purse my lips. "It's too late now."

"Is it?"

Silence hangs in the air as heavy as lead. He sips from his mug and stays silent. I decide to change the subject.

"My future isn't in Ohio. I've been thinking about moving to Chicago."

"No, V." He laughs, which hurts my feelings.

"Why not?" I push my bottom lip out. He has the audacity to laugh again.

"You don't want to live here. *I* don't want you to live here." He pads that blow with a comforting hand to my shoulder. "I've fucked up a lot. I know that. But I'm figuring it out. I'm trying to live my life. You should do the same."

Then again, maybe meditation turns you into a jerk.

"You only get one life. Or in your case, Ms. *Vandemark*, two."

I slug him in the shoulder and he smiles. His smile reminds me of the kid he was before he started drinking. He had a light, easy way about him. He was a hell of a lot of fun. He was my best friend. He still is, I realize. I'd do anything for him.

Including blow up my own life. Twice, as it were.

"I appreciate you showing up the night Dee was in the hospital." He grows serious and it makes him sound mature. Wise. "But I regret asking you to come. If you'd stayed in Clear Ridge you wouldn't have lost Nate."

I drink my coffee too fast. It burns my throat and my eyes water. At least that's why I tell myself my eyes are watering.

"You don't know that."

"You self-sabotage almost as well as I do," he tells me. "There's no rehab for pushing people away."

"What could he possibly love about me?" The question has plagued me each and every sleepless night I've spent in my hotel room.

"If you can't see why..." Walt trails off. He cuffs the back of my neck, lowering his gaze to mine. "You are the most amazing woman I've ever known."

A traitorous tear spills down my cheek. He swipes it away and sits back in his chair. I bite my lip. I'm tired of crying.

"One more thing," he says. I have a feeling he's made a decision and it doesn't involve me. I brace myself.

"I don't want any more of the money you saved for me." Before I can argue, he adds, "I mean it. I don't want a safety net. Not one I didn't install myself. Most of my problem is I've been bailed out my entire life. And most of your problem is you've been taking the blame for everyone around you who fucks up."

I frown.

"I have a good job. I make my own money."

"I know," I whisper. He wasn't fired or penalized in any way. I expected as much. Nate's not petty.

"My plan is to someday run my own site. As soon as I get my shit together." He drains his coffee and sets the empty mug in the sink. "I gotta catch the L if I hope to be on time. Late people aren't handed promotions, or so the foreman keeps reminding me."

"I had no idea you aspired to climb the company ladder."

"I have potential," he says, proudly. "That's what Nate told me."

My heart. Oh, my heart. Picturing Nate mentoring my brother flays me. I've been underestimating Walt for years. I've been swooping in on a wave of self-importance and telling myself I had to take on his problems. Nate knew what I didn't. Walt needs someone to believe in him, not coddle him.

Don't we all?

"At least consider taking some of the money," I say, unable to fully sever the cord. "I don't know what to do with it."

"Whatever you do, don't buy an apartment near mine."

I make a peeved noise in my throat.

"Love you, sis. I don't want you to hover." Walt is ready to be free of the chains of his old life too. My over-involvement was one of them. "Lock up when you leave. Toaster pastries in the cabinet."

"What happened to your juice cleanse?"

"I left my juicer in Ohio." He grabs a packed lunch from the fridge, which is so responsible I don't even know what to think, and then he kisses my cheek. "Go home, V."

"Love you too," I say.

Long after he's shut his front door I linger over my coffee and think about Ohio. About the life I built there. About my job at CRBI, and my friend, Amber. About my apartment and my neighbor and the elm tree out front. But then I think of Nate and Grand Marin and the nights I spent curled around him in his bed and my chest seizes. How can I go back after behaving so poorly?

I finish my coffee and wash the mug and then lock the door behind me. I hail a taxi and take it to my old stomping grounds: the lush, wealthy, manicured lots of Fein Village. There's another home I long to return to.

My childhood home.

The home of Vivian Steele, the woman who is trapped inside me, scratching at the walls. It's time to set her free.

Chapter Thirty

Vivian

Back in my parents' old neighborhood I feel like a time traveler. I used to walk these pristinely manicured streets with my head down. My eyes were usually on my cell phone, checking email or taking a call. Whenever I visited for dinner I'd slip away from the table to work. My father often did the same. He understood the importance of handling issues expediently. Even on a Sunday. Even if it meant leaving your family at the dinner table.

Now, though, I walk along the sidewalk, head up. The trees wave in the wind, wiggling green-leaved fingers. The sky overhead is blue and fathomless. Despite the ache in my heart, today's a good day.

My parents lived in the enormous house on the corner. It's where I lived for nineteen years before I moved out on my own.

Yesterday, I visited my mother's grave again. I laid fresh flowers on her headstone. I cried. I forgave her. I'm working on forgiving myself.

"Vivian?" A woman's voice prompts me to turn around. My mother's friend, Bette, is approaching, her puffy white dog at the end of a fluorescent green leash. I rack my brain trying to remember his name…it's a food, I think.

"Bette. Hi."

"I haven't seen you in ages." She grins. She's my mother's age —or the age my mother would have been if she was still alive. Bette engulfs me in a hug and automatically, I stiffen. My family didn't have many friends left after Dad was arrested. "Goodness, honey, I'm so sorry."

Her blond hair blows over her lip gloss and she peels the strands away. She's in a shorts set and sneakers. Her dog barks hello.

"Hi, Marshmallow," I remember suddenly. I stoop to pet his soft fur. He's an American Eskimo. His features are ladylike and dainty, from a tiny pink tongue and pert black nose to dark, expressive eyes. "I wanted to visit the neighborhood again," I tell Bette as I stand.

"New owners." She pushes the sunglasses to the top of her head and casts an unsavory look toward my parents' former house. "Hope you aren't expecting a tour. They keep to themselves."

I shake my head. "No, there's nothing there for me any longer."

"You've been through it, honey. Your mom was a good woman." Bette was a good friend to her. "I quit drinking."

"Really?"

She nods. I remember her and my mother casually imbibing. No wild parties or anything. I never thought of Bette as having a problem, but she never turned down a screwdriver or mimosa first thing in the morning either.

"I was relying on alcohol too much," she admits. "And after my divorce from Bernie—"

"I'm sorry to hear that." I don't know what kind of relationship they had, but it seemed okay.

"Don't be. It was a long time coming. It's great to see you.

Would you like to stay for dinner? I'm cooking for one"—she points to herself—"but sometimes Alfie swings by to eat."

Her son. He and my brother used to hang out. They're the same age. "Oh, no, thank you. I have plans tonight with Walt."

"How is he?" Her eyebrows bend with concern.

"He's doing well. Back in Chicago." I spare her the details. Who has the time?

"Good. You're both back where you belong."

As tempted as I am to let that platitude go, especially since she's trying to be supportive, I don't. "*Do* I belong in Chicago?"

I face my parents' former house, remembering when I lived there. And after, when I lived in the city. I don't belong here any longer. I am a stranger in this place, and to the woman I used to be.

My new life is a combination of my old one—privilege and money—and my new one—hustle and heart.

"I'm living in Ohio now," I say, even though I haven't been there for a week.

"Oh. How lovely." She's being polite. "What do you do there?"

"I manage a live-work property," I lie. Most likely I'll be begging Daniel for my job back now that Nate and I are through. Even if he would honor his word and employ me at Grand Marin, I wouldn't feel right about accepting the position. I've put him through enough.

"How perfect for you," Bette praises. "You were always such a good leader."

Her compliment means more than she knows. My smile is brittle, my voice watery when I say, "Thank you."

"You take care, okay? And tell Walter Junior I say hello." She gives me another brief squeeze. She smells like menthol, and it reminds me of the mornings she and my mother used to sit on the patio, laughing while they smoked cigarettes and drank mimosas.

It hurts remembering the good times but it also helps to remember there *were* good times. Maybe that's what this trip was about. I've visited where my mother is buried. I've thought through the tragic events leading to her burial. Today was about visiting my past and finding out what power it held.

Almost none. I shield my eyes from the sun and take one final mental snapshot of the house on the corner. My past doesn't hold any power over me.

Not anymore.

WALT TURNS out a piece of chicken onto my plate that has seen better days. It's black on the ends and, I'm assuming, rubber-tough in the middle. He serves himself the remaining charred chicken breast before popping open a can of green beans. He dumps them into a glass dish, the sucking sound incredibly unappetizing. "How long do you microwave vegetables?"

"No idea." I give him a lame smile. "Uh, two minutes?"

He sighs, sends a disheartened gaze at our dinner plates, and picks up his cell phone. "Pizza?"

"I'll buy," I rush to offer.

Thirty glorious minutes later a piping hot pizza is delivered. Walt throws open the lid and we both lean forward to take a whiff of the heavenly scent. Olives cover the entire pie. I think of Nate and his disdain for them. Thinking of Nate hurts.

"I miss this," Walt says after a bite of Papa Leo's pizza. It is the best local franchise in Chicago.

"Me too. I wish Leo would open a restaurant in Clear Ridge."

Walt stops chewing to ask, "You going back?"

I pick off a piece of pepperoni and eat it. "I don't know. Yes."

"I wasn't talking about missing eating pizza, by the way," he says. "I was talking about missing spending time with you."

"Does that mean you don't want me to leave?" He was booting me out of here yesterday.

"It means I want you to visit more. But your life isn't here, V."

"And yours is?"

He takes another bite, chews, and considers. "Yeah," he

decides. "It's more than the job. It's the vibe here. I feel...I don't know, weirdly at home."

I send a slightly judgmental glance around his apartment. "You could stand some better furniture." I kick the coffee table where our pizza box rests, and it wobbles like it might collapse.

"Humble beginnings," he explains. "I don't need more to care for right now. Plant, pet, person."

"Plant, pet, person?"

"If I can care for a plant, then I can care for a pet and then I can consider a relationship." He points at an orchid standing on the ledge of his only window. I hadn't noticed it until now.

"Orchids are tricky. You're starting at the top."

"They need sun. They need love. They need company. Like us." He shrugs as if he didn't say something profound.

"Is your 'person' going to be Dee?" I venture.

"I hope so. I love her."

I sigh.

"You don't give up on someone when their issues become inconvenient."

"Tell me about it." I shoot him a pointed look.

"Yeah, but you're stuck with me. We're blood."

"True." I eat another bite.

"You should be glad there are people out there who don't give up, or else you'd have lost Nate."

My heart skips a beat at the mention of his name. I finish chewing before saying, "I *did* lose Nate."

"Hardly." My brother snorts. He pulls his cell phone out of his back pocket and shows me his text messages. Nate's, in particular. They're time-stamped. There's one a day going back several days. They all say the same thing.

How's Vivian?

"You replied *fine*."

One fine. One okay, one good, and one not sure, to be precise.

"Yeah, but I said more when I spoke to him last night."

My blood chills. "You talked to him?"

"He's my boss." Walt's tone says *duh.* "He's in town."

"He's in town?"

"You a parrot now?" He watches me while he chews. "What do you care? You're not in love with him anyway, right?"

It's not that I'm not, it's that *I can't be.*

"Tomorrow night we're meeting at O'Leary's for dinner to celebrate completing the site. You have to celebrate your accomplishments."

Lainey Owen said that the day I met her. I think of Will and Nate's brothers. My chest is aching.

"You could come. I am allowed a plus-one."

"I can't…what would I say to him?"

"'Sorry for what I said when I was in love with you'?" Walt suggests.

"I'm not—"

"Who do you think you're talking to, here?" He dips into the box for a third slice. I'm still working on number one. Now that I know Nate is close by and has been asking about me, my appetite is gone. Do I have a second chance? Am I brave enough to take one?

"I thought about what you said about the money," Walt says.

"You'll take it?" I chirp.

"You can give me twenty-five percent of it, but it's going to be invested, not spent. You have to keep the rest, though." He holds out a hand. "Deal?"

"I'll keep *half,*" I amend as I grip his hand.

"Seventy percent." He tugs my arm.

"Sixty," I argue. He watches me for a beat, my hand still in his.

"Sixty, and you come with me tomorrow night."

We have a stare down that I know he's going to win. "You're an asshole."

"Then we agree." He grins and pumps my arm once.

"This is blackmail." I forlornly eat another pepperoni.

"I owe you. The money you earmarked for me, that's not

really mine. It's for us to start new lives. I've started mine. You should start yours."

"I *did*. You're the one who crashed into my new life."

"I shouldn't have done that," he admits, sheepish.

"I didn't mean it. I love having you back." I smile. "I'd like you to stay like this." Before the moment turns sappy, I add, "But with better furniture."

"I don't want to be the reason you and Nate aren't together," Walt says, sincere concern in his expression. "You two have a real shot. You deserve a man in your life who won't let you down like Dad and I have."

"You didn't let me down." My lip trembles. "You couldn't let me down."

He drops his pizza slice and wraps me in a firm hug. I hold on to him and lecture my tear ducts not to leak on his shirt.

"I'm here for you too, you know," he says into my ear. "Let me take care of you. Just this once."

I pull away and swipe my eyes, crying anyway. I'm a freaking sprinkler system lately. "You don't have to take care of me. I can—"

"Take care of yourself. I know, I know. You can still take care of yourself and love Nate as much as he loves you, can't you? I don't think those two things are mutually exclusive."

"When'd you get so smart?" I ask, swiping my nose on a napkin.

"Meditation." Walt taps his temple and then picks up his pizza.

Chapter Thirty-One

Nate

The Owens came out to help celebrate the completion of the Chicago site. I'm not entirely sure they wanted to. I suspect Benji rallied everyone for my sake. I've been a sullen son of a bitch lately.

Lainey was adamant about coming when I talked to her earlier this week. She mentioned sightseeing and said she'd like to go for a boat ride and do some shopping while she was here. She asked how I was without prying and I'm guessing Benji told on me like the snitch he is.

I love him for it though. And Lainey. All of them. Even Archer, who called to check on me in his own way, by asking if I was available to visit potential future club sites while he's in town. I appreciated the offer and agreed. Work keeps my mind off Vivian.

Also, my family loves O'Leary's. We came here for dinner after I was adopted. We were visiting Chicago and they asked my favorite place to eat and this was it.

I should beat myself up for finishing a job late rather than celebrate. Yeah, *late*. By two days, but still. We've met, right? I don't finish jobs late. Ever.

I am notoriously on time. The entire reason Vivian chapped my ass the first time I met her was because she wanted to slow down my project and keep me from my due date. Then we became involved and things at work slipped. *I* slipped. It wasn't unwelcome to have more going on in my life than constantly clawing my way up the mountain of success.

Once I had her in my life, I spent more and more time falling in love and less and less time at work demanding perfection. I'd like to say it was worth it, but I'm not sure it was.

Cris and Benji believe Vivian is in love with me, but I've talked to Walt, and I'm not so sure. The last time he and I spoke, though, he didn't give me a lot of intel. He did mention she lost her job at the bureau. He was hinting at the Grand Marin position, and it was on the tip of my tongue to mention that I haven't filled it permanently. I hired a temp service until I don't know when. I have too many vivid memories of making love to her on the conference table and against the wall and the way we smiled like morons in love after we sank to the floor tangled in each other's limbs to even consider interviewing for that position.

Turns out I was the only moron in love.

I'm walking toward O'Leary's, having parked a block away. Bodies pack the tables inside and laughter and chatter can be heard through the windows. They are hopping already, and it's only six o'clock.

Ideally, Vivian would be here celebrating with me. Best-case scenario, because we flew here together and slept in this morning in the hotel bed. And after that maybe we did a little shopping for a second home in Chicago.

I have to let it go. Let *her* go. I can't keep replaying our time together. It's unhealthy.

The last time I saw her she told me she was incapable of loving me. I don't know if I don't believe her, or I just don't want to. It seems she was right about one thing, though. We didn't last long. Maybe we weren't meant to. She was leagues above where I'm stationed in life. Billions and a new suit can only cover so much of the man I truly am.

Just a guy who wants a family so bad he'd bend over backwards to build one.

I straighten my shoulders and stretch my neck side to one side. Game face time. *You're a happy, successful entrepreneur,* I remind myself as I pull on the door handle to the pub. I rented the party room in the back, typically used for wakes or weddings. We're expecting fifty-eight guests, give or take a few plus-ones. I'm looking forward to having a beer and forgetting, even temporarily, the shit I've been through over the last week-plus. Over the last thirty-plus *years*.

Archer and Benji are at the bar, no surprise there. So are the Owens. Lainey and Will look nice. They dressed up for the event, which is their MO. I wore jeans. I'm at a pub. Despite my upbringing, tradition dictates a suit is not appropriate pub attire. I guess you could say I'm feeling more like myself. My old self. Or a combination of the old and new. The man I was trying to be before I met Vivian versus the man I became after. Before I knew what love was, and after I fell so hard I'm still sick over her.

This fucking sucks.

"Darling, how are you?" Lainey asks as I kiss her cheek.

"Late on a project," I answer as I shake Will's hand.

"Perfection is unattainable," he says. Archer gives him a sideways look. He wants to argue, but chooses to keep his mouth shut and not ruin my big night. I appreciate it and convey as much with a silent nod.

"Benji." I shake my other brother's hand. "Cris didn't make the trip?"

"She's holding down the fort."

"Anyone here yet?" I look through the crowd to the rear of the bar. The room is open, but I can't tell if anyone's in there.

"We were waiting for you. I think we've arrived first," Lainey says.

"Let me grab a draft and we'll go back." After my hand is

wrapped around an ice-cold beer, I walk my family to the private party room. They settle in at a table and a waiter rushes over to present the appetizer options. I shrug when Benji asks what I want. The beer is enough. I just need to survive this night, and then tomorrow, and so on and so forth.

That's my goal from now until the day I'm finally over Vivian Vandemark.

I lift my mug to my lips and pause before taking a drink at the vision walking through the double doors. Unless I'm having a vivid hallucination, the woman who won't leave my head is here.

Walt is behind her. He tips his head as if to say *"Well, here she is. Don't blow it again."*

I blew it by telling her how I felt about her. I blew it by showing up in Chicago. Or maybe I blew it at least ten times before then by not reading the obvious signs that she was always on her way out. But she's here now. That has to count for something.

My mother squeezes my forearm in support. Then she joins in the conversation with Archer and Benji, while Will sips his bourbon.

Vivian approaches me cautiously. She's fiddling with her purse strap as her eyes flit around the room. Walt introduces himself to my family.

I hear Will say, "Steele? Your name is Walt Steele?"

Vivian's eyes snap to mine. Those moments when I told her I knew her name, and after when she collapsed in my arms, come back to me in vivid technicolor. My arms ache to hold her and my tongue sticks to the roof of my mouth.

I love her. I probably always will.

"Hi." Her voice is quiet, but I hear strength there. She's nothing if not strong. I expected her to bounce back from our breakup without a problem. I wonder if she's here for closure. I'm not sure if I'm prepared for it, but here we go.

"I didn't expect you to be here," I admit.

"Walt made me come."

I should've known. He's been cagey about her, limiting what I know. I thought he was taking her side and evidently I was right. She is here for closure. I must've misinterpreted the look on Walt's face when he walked in.

"Can I get you a drink?" I offer.

She shakes her head. "Is there somewhere we can talk?"

"This is the most private room in the bar, although it's about to be flooded with fifty or so people. Whatever you have to say, you should probably go on and say it."

And fast. Maybe once my heart is shattered beyond repair, I can let her go. I have a coffee mug with a chip on the edge. I keep it because it's my favorite. If I dropped it and it shattered into a thousand pieces, I'd finally let the damn thing go and buy a new one.

I don't want a new one, I think as I study her face. The freckles dotting her nose. The cautious yet gentle way her brown eyes meet mine. I allow my gaze to slide past her blouse and jeans to her shoes. She's wearing flats. Not Louboutins. Maybe this whole thing was a dream.

"Okay." She licks her lips and adjusts her purse on her shoulder, accepting the gauntlet I've thrown.

I steel myself. I'm ready to hear whatever she's going to say. So then why is my heart beating triple time? Why do I have the urge to grab her up and hug her, beg her to come home?

I manage not to do either. Instead I take long pull of my draft beer.

And wait.

Vivian

Well. This isn't going the way I expected.

Okay, that's not true. This is going *exactly* the way I expected.

I'm nervous. Nate is unavailable. His shoulders are rigid. His stubborn jaw is set. I pushed him away and this time, it was for good.

"Congratulations. On the site," I say, off to a rocky start. "And thank you. For Walt, I mean. For not firing him."

Nate's eyebrows close over his nose.

"Not that you would, but I appreciate that you didn't. I was considering moving to Chicago. For good. Walt doesn't want me to."

I search Nate's face for a sign that he'd welcome me back to Ohio, to him. That there is some way to salvage what I've destroyed. I'm holding on to the barest flicker of hope, but he snuffs it out when he lowers his voice to speak.

"I shouldn't have talked you into the Grand Marin position."

"You didn't."

"I did. I could tell by your hesitation you weren't comfortable accepting the offer."

I was a big fat scaredy-cat. And I left him high and dry in the process. "I should have either started right away or refused. I left you hanging."

His eyebrows bend but I can't figure out why. Is he sad I didn't take it? Or have I left him hanging in another sense?

A few guests walk in and he shakes their hands. He introduces me quickly, mentioning that I work at an inspection bureau in Ohio. He tells them I "did some work for us" on one of his properties. Then he corrals me to a quieter corner of the room. He's careful not to touch me, pointing the way for me to walk ahead of him.

"I guess this was a bad idea." I laugh, uncomfortable. Coming here was an epically *horrible* idea. I'm not sure what I'm doing here. Walt called me out on being in love with Nate, and he was right, but what am I supposed to do about it? What would be the point? Why would Nate believe anything I had to say after I told him I could never love him?

"Whatever you need to say to make this trip worth it for you," he prompts again, sounding impatient, "why don't you go ahead and say it." He gives me an encouraging nod, granting me an opportunity to speak freely.

I can save a hell of a lot of face, and my pride, by telling him I came by to wish him the best for his future before I head back to Ohio.

Or. I can tell him how I feel. I can be honest with him.

I can be honest with *myself.*

Wouldn't that be a revelation?

I peer up at his beautifully imperfect face. A face I've been trying to come to terms with never seeing again. A face I never could have dreamed of missing someday. He was a billionaire with a sledgehammer in an Armani suit trying to pave a path to the bank. I was a former criminal's daughter, hiding out where I didn't belong.

It never would have worked.

So why am I still here?

"Viv?" His blue eyes lock onto mine. There's a hidden emotion behind them I pray is what I think it is.

Go big or go home, isn't that what they say?

Once upon a time I was brave enough to take huge leaps.

Am I still?

Chapter Thirty-Two

Nate

Vivian is twisting her fingers. I can tell this is hard for her. Regret washes over her face with every breath she takes. I've now accepted she's here for closure. There's one last thing she needs to say to me. I won't make this harder for her. I don't want to hurt her any more than she's been hurting herself.

I never planned on falling in love with her. I planned on having her in my bed. And once she was there, I made damn sure she didn't have a reason to leave right away. What grew between us was more than great sex. We had a connection. Maybe as kids who grew up surrounded by addicts. Maybe as people who know what it's like to have a lot and have a little—even if we experienced it in the opposite order.

But our "connection" was one-sided. She wasn't ready. If there's one thing I've learned in life it's that you can't make someone ready just because you are. They have their own timeline. I don't want anyone pressing me to change before I'm ready. Vivian doesn't want that either.

But damn, she's going to take a lifetime to recover from.

"When my father was arrested," she starts, her voice strong

and her eyes on her hands, "and then sentenced, I watched my life rip at the seams. I blamed myself for the demise of the company. For the friends and relationships lost. For standing by while he tore down our family's future brick by brick." She takes a breath and continues. "Mom died. Walt was using. And then Dad died. By then I was clumsily making my way. I couldn't trust myself in a high-powered, intense job, and I couldn't trust myself in a relationship. I knew I'd sacrifice anything to keep Walt and myself afloat, to protect what family I had left."

I give her a sad smile. I completely understand.

"And then I did." She makes a cute face and my heart squeezes. "I became what I needed: bulletproof."

Keep going, beautiful. You're doing great.

"I came here tonight to be honest with you, Nate."

Here we go. I swallow thickly, realize I'm parched, and take a swallow of beer. I need something stronger. After this shindig I'm buying a bottle of whiskey. Archer and Benji won't ask me to explain, but they will help me drink it.

"Love hurts. That's the speech I gave myself." Her gaze wanders as she adds thoughtfully, "Is there anything worse than lying to yourself? If you don't tell yourself the truth, how can you be honest with anyone else?" Her eyes finally meet mine. I suddenly wish *I* were bulletproof.

"But it's not love that hurts. It's losing love that hurts. I know better than anyone, because I lost you." I'm nodding while she talks, hoping to get through this as swiftly and painlessly as possible. So I can buy my whiskey and drown my misery. So caught up in what I thought she was going to say, I have to stop nodding and rewind that last bit.

"What was that?" The room has grown louder as guests have come in. Maybe I misheard her.

"I love you," she says. "And I lost you because I was too stupid to tell you how I felt. To risk *not* being bulletproof. To risk letting you love me." She smiles, but it has a sad quality. "I love you, Nate."

I shake my head in disbelief. "You do?"

"I do." She cups my face with both hands. "I know I don't deserve a second chance. I know you deserve better than what I can offer. You deserve someone whole, not in pieces. You deserve—"

I press my index finger over her lips and shake my head. "You, Vivian Vandemark, don't get to decide what I deserve and don't deserve."

Her smile appears from behind my finger. She tugs my hand away.

"I love you, Nate Owen. I love you and I'm so, so sorry I pushed you away. I didn't know what I had—what *I* deserved. It was you. All along."

Her voice fades into a whisper and her eyes mist over. I'm in shock, and might be having a very vivid dream. Maybe I'm still in Benji's guest bedroom asleep and hungover. But in case I'm not, I should clear something up.

"I have been so heartsick over you I couldn't breathe. I wanted you and I had no idea what to do to win you back. I was too damn afraid of scaring you off again."

"You didn't scare me. I scared myself." Her hands slide down to my neck and come to rest on my chest. I missed her touch. "I can't say for sure this is the last time I'll screw up, but I can promise I'll never stop loving you. I thought I was protecting my heart. That backfired terribly."

"Oh, I don't know." I grip her waist, ignoring the din of the background voices and music. "I think you're doing fine."

I bend and capture her mouth with mine, my eyes slipping closed as I drink her in. Her warm vanilla scent wraps around me as she clings to my neck. She's all I've wanted—all I've needed—for several days, weeks, hell, a lifetime. I'm vaguely aware of background commentary coming from Benji. Someone claps and others join in. Walt yells, "Finally!"

When I open my eyes, there's only Vivian. The cute freckles decorating her nose. Her silken dark hair brushing my arms. Her slim waist trapped between my palms. I itch for more of her. I want to tear off her dress and be skin to skin with her—as close as humanly possible. Me inside her. Us becoming one. It's been too long.

"Does this mean you forgive me?" she asks, and what kills me is that she sounds sincere.

I sweep her hair aside and cradle her jaw. "I love you too much to let a little thing like you leaving me stand in our way."

She laughs.

"Happiness looks good on you."

"*You* look good on me." Her smile fades. "I have one more question."

"Yes is my answer. No matter what."

"You don't know what I was going to ask." Her smile broadens.

"It doesn't matter." I have no idea what she wants. Does she want to move in with me? Want me to move here? Want me to buy a boat and sail the Caribbean? Don a set of pasties and climb on the pub's bar top? "If it keeps a smile on your face, it'll be worth it."

"Can I…" She licks her lips, trying to be brave. She's struggling. Vulnerability is new for her. She's never been safe before. She had the illusion of safety, but money, for the amazing things it provides, never makes you truly safe. That comes from within.

"Can you…" I prompt.

She bites down on her plush bottom lip, losing her nerve. I lean in closer, my lips over the shell of her ear.

"Come home with me?" I guess. "Marry me? Take over Grand Marin, or hell, build your own Grand Marin?" I pull away to find her eyes wide with surprise but brimming with yearning. She wants some or all of those things. She's only now allowed to herself to want them.

"Marry me?" Her voice is a croak of disbelief.

"All right." I nod. "I'll marry you. On one condition."

Shock and joy burst onto her face like the sun emerging from behind the clouds. Who knew joy was lurking behind her sharp-as-a-knife sass? "What condition?"

"You choose where we live. Chicago. Clear Ridge. The moon. I don't care anymore. I can live anywhere, but only if I'm making a life with you."

Her mouth hits mine and she strangles my neck in her attempt to be closer. Someone yells for us to "Get a room." Archer. I'd recognize his pessimistic grumble anywhere.

"That's a good idea," I call back to him. My hand around her waist, I turn to go. "Archer will cover for me."

Arch gives me a "yeah, yeah" eye roll and waves me off. He has my back. He always has.

"Nate, we don't have to leave," Vivian whispers as I guide her to the exit.

"Oh, yes we do. We have a week to make up for. A lot of naked moments were missed."

"Oh," she purrs. She wraps my arms around her waist and leads us outside. "Your hotel or mine?"

"You choose," I tell her. Once outside, she stops and digs in her purse. Slipping off her flats, she replaces them with a pair of shoes I recognize. The Louboutins I bought her. "You brought them."

She stuffs the flats into her purse and takes my hand. "When Prince Charming gives you shoes, you keep them."

"Is that the moral of the story?" I lower my face to hers.

"No," she whispers against my lips. "The moral of the story is no matter where you go, there you are. So you'd damn well better make the best of it."

"I like that." I steal another kiss.

"I love you. I won't ever deny myself again. Not now that I know what lies on the other side of it. Life is better with you. I don't want anything but you for the rest of my life."

My heart unfurls like a banner.

"You're for me, Nathaniel Owen."

"So are you, Vivian Vandemark." And soon, I think with a

wicked curve of my lips, she'll be changing her last name yet again.

This time so she can take mine.

KEEP READING for a peek at Benji's and Cris's story: Charmed by the Billionaire…

Charmed by the Billionaire PREVIEW

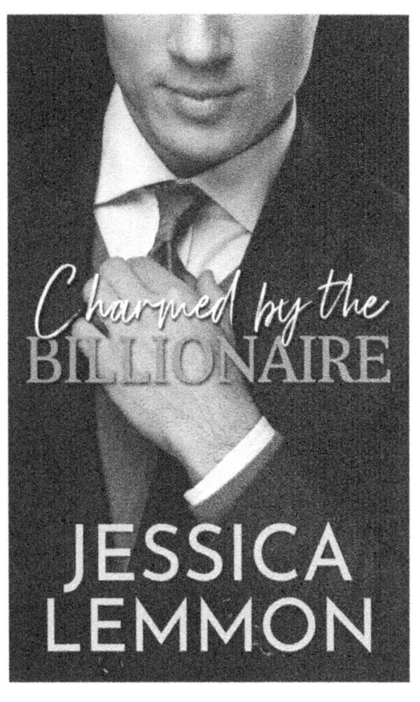

Charmed by the Billionaire

Chapter One

Cris

Working for Benjamin Owen is agony. Pure agony.

Not in the "my boss is an A-hole" sort of way, which would be easier, but in the "my boss is my best friend" way, which is much, much worse. Especially when said boss doesn't acknowledge me beyond his friend and life assistant.

Pardon me, life assistant *coach*.

He's been vocal about the title adjustment, most notably to his brothers, who likely have observed me shadowing Benji's every footfall like a devoted Labradoodle.

"Can I treat you to lunch, coach?" Benji strolls into his kitchen where I'm waiting on the one-cup coffee maker to finish sputtering java into my travel mug.

Coach. I don't like that nickname.

There's nothing alluring or feminine or even personal about it. Not that I expect him to address me as "honey" or "gorgeous." That would be unprofessional. But it would be alluring and feminine and *possibly* personal. If he bothered to notice that I was, in fact, a woman.

Sigh.

"You're looking at my lunch." I elevate my mug of coffee, and his mouth pulls down at the corners. I've yet to give you a full picture of Benjamin "Benji" Owen. Let me do that now.

The basic stats: he's thirty-three years old, having just turned thirty-three on October thirteenth. He's six-feet, one-inch tall if you don't count his hair, which is fantastic. It's thick, ink-black, and tousled into a stylish, want-to-run-your-fingers-through-it mass on top of his head, but short in the back with groomed, neat sideburns that aren't too long or too short. Eyebrows: dark, arched and expressive. Eyes: brown but not just any brown. Caramel brown, almost golden when the sun hits them right. Lashes: enviably long. Nose: straight, narrow but not pointy. Mouth…

Give me a second to pull myself together.

Cue full-body shivers.

Mouth. Straight white teeth thanks to braces when he was a teenager, full lips almost always parked in an appreciative, happy grin, or a smirk hinting that an appreciative, happy grin is about to emerge.

Clothes: *divine.* I've never met a man who dresses as impeccably as Benji. Sure, his brothers dress well, but Archer and Nate do it in a rote way. Benji's outfits are carefully selected. His shoes are Salvatore Ferragamos, which cost between one and two grand *per pair.* His shirts are almost always button-down, usually a checked pattern, and his trousers encase long, strong legs. He's slim, but not "skinny" and boasting a body I've admired when he wears a lot less. Like when he's swimming in his pool or we go jogging together. You could whittle wood with his calf muscles. His torso arrows down to a V marked by delineating lines at his hipbones. And—brace yourself—there's a tattoo on his flank—between his ribs. The words "carpe diem" are etched there in stylish cursive—his own handwriting.

He's damn near perfect from head to toe with but with one glaring flaw.

He grins. "You can't have coffee for lunch, coach."

Other than being able to give a general description of my person (in case of my kidnapping, for example), he doesn't see me. At least not in the way I see him.

"Oh, but I can," I argue, my own smile in place. I've learned how to manage my attraction to my boss-slash-best friend over the years I've known him (ten of them), and over the year-plus I've worked for him. My tactic is simple, and judging by Benji's *blah* reaction to me each time we interact, it must be working. Our friendship is solid, our working relationship steady. We are nailing it.

Even though I'd rather be nailing him. (Insert laugh track here.)

"Anyway, I have to run an errand so I'm on my way out the door."

"Okay, but we're still on for our jog at five today." He sets his mug in the sink and slaps his flat middle. "I don't call you coach for nothing. You keep me in my prime."

"That's my job." I hope sarcasm didn't creep through. His eyes spark, but the glint fades fast. I'm safe for another day. "I'll see you in a few hours."

Purse on my shoulder, I palm my travel mug and head out the door. Twenty minutes later I'm walking around Grand Marin, the open-air-shopping-center Benji's brother recently built and opened here in Clear Ridge, Ohio. It's an absolutely gorgeous April day with plenty of sun, no rain, and mild temps. The shopping behemoth is a live-work facility housing and employing young entrepreneurs who run businesses, restaurants, and rent the offices atop those businesses and restaurants.

I palm the door handle leading up to the property manager's office and then climb the stairs. The office sits at a corner overlooking Grand Marin like a castle in a kingdom. Or should I say queendom? Benji's oldest brother's fiancée oversees this place like the queen she is. She was a government employee when she met Nate. She definitely considers this a step up.

Inside the posh office loaded with live and fake greenery, a receptionist greets me. He's young, twentysomething, and knows me on sight.

"Ms. Cristin Gilbert." Sandy, a name he inherited from his father and refuses to be embarrassed by, stands and smooths his tie. "Vivian just finished with a conference call. Is she expecting you?"

"She is."

"Business or pleasure?" He tips his head and I admire his curious expression. I feel no zings of attraction to him the way I do around my boss and best friend, but Sandy is a cute guy. From his high cheekbones to the way his eyes smile with his mouth, there's plenty to admire. But at five years younger than me, he reminds me too much of my younger brother Manuel for me to find Sandy truly hot. Manuel is more like my kid than my kid brother given I've been raising him and my other two brothers since I was eighteen.

Long story.

"Pleasure. I have a date tonight and I'm in need of duds." I gesture to my basic black dress and flats.

"Say no more. Please." Sandy makes a face to communicate how undesirable it is to discuss shopping or clothes. He then heads to Viv's office door and raps twice. She looks up from her desk through the windows—there's virtually no privacy in this office save for the tinted windows in the conference room—and waves us in. "Your date is here. She's cherubic, cute, and too good for the likes of me. I trust you two will be very happy together."

Viv and I chuckle. Sandy rushes back to his post to pick up the ringing phone.

"Where did you find that guy again?" I joke.

"You found him, remember?"

"Oh, right. I am *really* good at my job." I buff my nails on my dress.

"You *really* are. You ready to do this? I am *so* ready to do this. I've chosen three boutiques to check out. Two of them are here, the other right up the road." Vivian is wearing a plum skirt, fitted, and a silk blouse which is a pale, pale purple. Her long, dark brown hair sits at her shoulders in big, enviable waves. Her eyes are chocolate brown, darker than Benji's caramel irises, and delicate freckles dot her nose and cheeks. She's wearing incredibly tall high-heeled shoes, which never fails to impress me. I wear heels well enough, but she wears them like she learned to walk in them as a toddler.

"I'm as ready as I can be," I tell her as we exit the office, making sure to wave goodbye to Sandy upon my retreat.

"It's not going to hurt to go on a date. A few dates," she amends as she slips sunglasses on her nose. "If anything, maybe Benji will have an opinion about who his life assistant coach is dating. And wouldn't that be fun to experience?"

She means because he'd have to notice me to comment. Which would be new, but I don't know if it'd be fun.

She spares me a grin as sunlight hits her hair. She is gorgeous. You'd never know a few short months ago she was cagey and nervous about being outed as Walter Steele's daughter. Yes, *that* Walter Steele. She's not a criminal like her deceased father but I could understand why she'd be worried about what others think. Who among us isn't?

"Benji wouldn't notice what I was doing if I was doing it on his desk while he was typing up an email." I snort. The truth is always funny.

"We'll see about that," she promises. "Let's not talk about boys today. We'll find you the perfect date ensemble and then grab lunch and maybe a few martinis and have you back to your office by, oh, say six o'clock?"

"No can do." I turn her down with regret in my heart. "I promised Benji we'd jog at five. I am his coach, after all. I have to keep him fit for his myriad girlfriends."

She hums, no longer looking pleased. "Who is she this time?

Blonde? Redhead? Brunette?" She lifts a handful of her own hair to illustrate.

"Honestly, I don't know." I frown as that fact hits me square in the solar plexus. Since I've worked for him Benji has had a revolving door of dates on call. Last year he was in a semi-serious relationship with a tall, leggy blonde named Trish. She was smart and nice which sucked because I really wanted to hate her. Vivian met her and agreed we couldn't hate Trish. She also agreed not being able to hate her was a bummer.

"Well, who cares." Viv waves a hand. "Time to move on. Or at least sideways. Take it from me, Cris, life has a way of working out for you. Especially when you least expect it."

Easy for her to say, I think without animosity. Vivian and Nathaniel are in love and it's adorable and beautiful and enviable. As a closet romantic (though I have come out to Vivian), I watch them together and internally swoon. I want that someday. Not with Nate, obviously, but with someone.

Time to go out into the big, bad world and find him.

Chapter Two

Benji

Each pounding footfall thumps in my ears, my heart keeping time like an orchestra conductor. I hear my own steady, rhythmic breathing over the sound of my steps and heart.

Thump, beat, puff. Thump, beat, puff.

The day is mild, warmish, but a cooler breeze keeps me from sweating too much. The park is moderately occupied, but it's also large, so there's plenty of room on the path for us to run. Cris is ahead of me wearing a pair of hot pink shorts and a white T-shirt with the words "my favorite brother gave me this shirt." It made me smile not because of its outwardly snarky message but because there is zero chance she could pick a favorite brother out of the three her mom saddled her with.

Saddled is a harsh word. I didn't mean it that way. Let me explain.

Cris's mom Selina bailed on Cris and Co., aka, her three bros, when Cris was eighteen years old. Selina, who I'm told goes by Lina, moved to Vegas to marry a guy she's since divorced three husbands ago. I think she's on marriage number seven, but it's been four or five months since Cris mentioned that so who knows if Lina is onto number eight by now.

Anyway, Lina went to Vegas and Cris was stuck with her brothers who at the time ranged from ages seven to twelve. This was while she was grinding out a college education *and* working part-time. Cris told me her mom used to send money regularly, now only occasionally. Money, while damn nice to have, is no substitute for a parent.

When Cris was twenty she started working as an intern for William Owen, better known as "Dad", but he's not my birth father. Sadly, my birth father (and my birth mother) are no longer alive. It's not a circumstance I like to think about.

Anyway. Back to Cris.

I remember the first time I saw her. Spunky, adorable, blonde. I thought she'd come and go, as most interns did at Owen Construction, but she stayed on fulltime, working for my dad, before I hired her for myself. I had taken to working at my home office more often than not. Traveling to headquarters was a drive to the tune of ninety minutes on a light traffic day, which allowed me to get almost nothing done, so I limited my visits there. Plus, I *like* my home office. And my home gym. The in-ground pool in my backyard—heated. Everything I need is at my fingertips. Including my life assistant coach.

It's a title I made up. I needed an assistant, but I also needed a life coach. Her position is bespoke. I was thrilled she was willing to mash together those two separate job descriptions and provide what I needed. The friendship grew out of our spending both work and personal time together. I didn't expect her to turn into my best friend, but she did. Now I don't think I can do anything without her. At least, not well.

But Cris is only *figuratively* at my fingertips. She's not the kind of assistant you hire and then seduce. She's practically family, though family takes on a broader meaning in the Owen family.

William and Lainey Owen had one child of their own who predated me. Archer Owen is three years older than me, but not the eldest of the Owen sons. He's the middle by a technicality. After they adopted me, they went and adopted Nate. Nate is one year Archer's senior, putting him at four years older than me. Ours is a patchwork family. I've heard Archer refer to Cris as our honorary sister, but I can't agree with him there. If I had a sister, I might consider her brilliant or strong, but never *adorable*, which is how I consider Cris.

Not that I consider her.

She's hard not to admire while she's running ahead of me, dappled sunlight streaming through the leaves on the trees lighting her curly blond hair. Her fair skin is what most would consider "tan" but given my brown hue, I don't see anything but "fair." She's a blond-haired, gray-eyed, petite, strong, smart woman…who works for me. As her boss, I overlook her questionable professionalism (she's worn Chuck Taylors and ripped jeans to my office on more than one occasion). As her best friend, I overlook her obvious beauty. In passing, like whenever we stretch side by side after running, I have admired her bare legs, pale against my golden-hued ones, and had a brief vision of what more of her might look like wrapped around me.

I blame that on being a guy. Every guy views every woman through this lens at least once and if they deny it, they're lying. Which is a good thing. Trust me, you don't want to know what goes on in a man's mind most of the time.

"Burst?" Cris asks as she spins around and runs backwards, her curly hair bouncing with her every step.

She's asking if I want to end our jogging session by running as fast as I can to the car, to which I reply, "Race you."

Then I take off.

I reach the parking lot before she does. I spend the moments waiting for her bent in half, sucking air through my ajar mouth and balancing my palms on my knees. Damn. That was hard.

She slows to a walk and pants her way over to me, cheeks pink and eyes dancing. "When will you learn"—pause, more breathing —"that I'm baiting you"—pause, another breath—"when I ask you that?"

"Never." I straighten, grinning. She grins back.

"Good thing I have your back," she gloats. "You got your steps in for the day, I bet."

I check my watch, which tracks a million things, steps included. She's right. I just rolled over my goal. "Nice."

"You're welcome." She winks.

I *am* welcome. She takes care of me. I have a tendency to lose myself in the numbers the way some might get lost in the woods after dark. I go into a deep, trancelike state rendering me unable to tend to my most basic needs. This is where she comes in. She refills my water, makes me the occasional smoothie if I forget to eat, grabs a takeout chicken and spring mix salad and places the container in front of my keyboard, lid off, fork stuck in it like a flag.

She brought me vitamin C the other day because she heard me coughing and worried I might be getting a cold. She does all of this while also managing my calendars (personal and business). She prepares reports on occasion, interviews candidates, spellchecks my work, and travels with me to a variety of affairs. She's even made reservations for dinner with the woman I happen to be seeing (whichever woman it is at the time) or sets up lunch dates so that I can put an end to the "seeing" part, which always happens no matter how great the woman I'm dating is.

It so happens that alongside the nine-to-five gig, Cris fits into my personal life too. She doesn't mind doing extra tasks to better my life, and I don't mind paying her well to do it. Her attentiveness has escalated noticeably since last fall. That was when her youngest brother Timothy went to college. She has empty nest syndrome, and at only thirty years of age. Damn her mother. And damn Cris's father, and each of her brothers' fathers for that matter. They all stuck Cris with their adult responsibilities. My parents would have never left me by choice. Not ever.

Without picking up her feet, Cris shuffles to the car and grabs our water bottles, thermal so the water stays still ice-cold. (She thinks of everything.) As we rehydrate, I make my way to a bench and sit, watching people in the park run along the path and admiring the sway of the trees against a blue sky.

Spring in Ohio. It's my favorite season. There's a whiff of newness in the air, and I love the scent. It reminds me of a Monday, which is truly the best day of the week. Well, if you love what you do. I adore my lot in life. After all, I structured it.

She settles in next to me, her knee bumping mine. Against my own good sense I admire our side-by-side legs. Hers are not long legs, but they are toned and almost sexy if I was allowed to consider Cris "sexy."

"What are you looking at?" she asks, examining her leg. I think fast and poke a purplish splotch on the outside of her thigh. "Ouch! Is that a bruise?"

"Appears to be. How'd you do that? Violent sleeper?"

"It's my new WWE boyfriend." She quirks an eyebrow and pegs me with those gray eyes. Wide, big, expressive. *Innocent.* There is a sweet, generous nature under the naiveté, but the naiveté is there all the same.

"If you have a boyfriend, WWE or otherwise, I hope this isn't how I find out." I suck down more water as a pleat forms between her pale eyebrows. It's followed by a lip-bite and her eyes skitter away before landing on my face again.

"What?" I can't help asking.

"Nothing." She brightens but her suddenly elevated mood a tad disingenuous. I learn why when she confesses, "It's just that"—she seesaws her head back and forth twice before continuing—"I have a date tomorrow night. I didn't tell you because...well."

"Because '...well' what?" Now I'm frowning. I don't like that she didn't tell me. Or maybe I don't like that she has a date. Hell, maybe both.

"Because I worried you'd lecture me. I don't want a lecture. I want to go on a date without anyone offering their opinion. Except for Vivian. Who helped me pick out a dress for tomorrow."

That's where she was today?

"You took her opinion," I say, stung.

She shrugs before resting one heel on the bench and retying the shoelace. I'm still wrapping my head around her not mentioning—even in passing—that she has a date *tomorrow night.*

"You go on lots of dates. I reserve comment all the time." She holds up both hands, communicating her innocence.

"You don't have to comment since I can read your expressions. I know when you don't like who I'm seeing."

A brief look of what might be panic crosses her pretty face.

"Trish," I say in way of explanation.

"I liked Trish!"

"Your voice went high and squeaky, which means you're lying."

"I'm not lying."

"You laughed during the word 'lying' which further indicates that you're *lying.*" I stand and offer a hand. She slaps her palm into mine and again, I admire the way our hands look together. Her small, pale, pink hued skin against my large, long-fingered golden brown.

"Tell me about him—your *date.*" I drop her hand and walk with her to the car, irked and not entirely sure why.

"I don't know. I've only texted him a few times on the app."

"You used an app?" I drop my neck back and regard the sky. "A little help?"

"Who are you talking to?"

I look back down at her. "The Universe. Have you recently consulted your spirit guides?"

"In case you haven't noticed, I do almost nothing but work and hang out with you."

Yowch. I make a face.

"You know what I mean. Timothy's gone and I—" Her voice cracks the slightest bit, revealing the emotion she tries to hide from me.

"You're lonely." I sigh. That's fair. I wrap my hand around the back of her neck. It's damp with sweat, but not in a gross way.

She licks her lips and nods. "A little."

And like that I can't fault her for going on a date. I know what it's like to be lonely. I've felt that way since I was ten years old and heard the news that my parents were in a car accident and wouldn't be coming home for Christmas.

Ever.

I was even lonely surrounded by my giving, loving, adoring adoptive family during that very next Christmas and every one since. Loneliness, I understand. And dating, I *really* understand.

Which is probably why I tell my best friend, "Let me know if you need any pointers."

To buy a copy of Charmed by the Billionaire, go to www.jessicalemmon.com/all-books

Acknowledgments

For John, who puts up with my author brain. I love being married to you!

Thank you to Kristi Yanta for your editorial mastermind (you'll note that I heeded nearly all of your advice!), and to Jennifer Miller who stepped in to further add editorial beautification to what was once quite a clunky manuscript.

To Mary Ruth for making my cover idea sing—you're a true artist.

For author friends Jules Bennett, Mira Lyn Kelly, Lauren Layne and Shannon Richard, who are never more than a text/phone call/FaceTime away.

For Nicole, who championed this project from the start. You always believe in my abilities and make sure to point out my strengths. For a girl who's not great at receiving praise, that means the world to me!

xo, Jessica

About the Author

A former job-hopper, Jessica Lemmon resides in Ohio with her husband and rescue dog. She holds a degree in graphic design currently gathering dust in an impressive frame. When she's not writing super-sexy heroes, she can be found cooking, drawing, drinking coffee (okay, wine), or eating potato chips. She firmly believes God gifts us with talents for a purpose, and with His help, you can create a life you love.

Jessica Lemmon's romance novels have been praised as "purely delicious fun" and "lavish, indulgence-fueled romance" by Publisher's Weekly, as well as "wonderfully entertaining" and "a whole lot of fun!" by RT Book Reviews. She is the bestselling author of over thirty books that have been translated into a dozen languages and sold in over 30 different countries worldwide, with her debut novel releasing in January of 2013.

Her work has been honored with awards such as a Library Journal starred review, an RT Top Pick!, iBooks Best Book of the Month, and Amazon Best Book of the Month. She has been recommended by USA Today and NPR.com, and has achieved the rank of #1 bestseller on Nook as well as earned a seal of excellence nomination from RT Book Reviews.

Through witty banter and fun, realistic situations and characters you'll want to "sit down and have a drink with," Jessica tackles tough relationship issues and complicated human emotions while delivering a deep, satisfying experience for readers.

Her motto is "read for fun" and she believes we should all do more of what makes us happy.

Also by Jessica Lemmon

Blue Collar Billionaires series

Once Upon a Billionaire

Charmed by the Billionaire

Billionaire Ever After

Billionaire Bad Boys series

The Billionaire Bachelor

The Billionaire Next Door

The Bastard Billionaire

A Crane Family Christmas

Real Love series

Eye Candy

Arm Candy

Man Candy

Rumor Has It

America's Sweetheart

Visit jessicalemmon.com for a complete book list.

Made in the USA
Coppell, TX
10 January 2024